IMM⬤RAL
Symphony

a novel by
Bonner DuLong

1   06/10/11

Immoral Symphony
Copyright © 2003 by Bonner DuLong

Fiction

ISBN trade paperback: 0-9744938-5-6
Libray Of Congress Control Number: 2003112753

This book was printed in the United States.

For inquiries or to order additional copies of this book, contact:

Gardenia Press
P. O. Box 18601
Milwaukee, WI 53218-0601 USA
1-866-861-9443 www.gardeniapress.com
orders@gardeniapress.com

FOR THE HOMELESS WHO CALL THE STREETS HOME.

ACKNOWLEDGEMENTS

When I was ending my second career to begin writing, a friend, associate, and author, Chuck Caes, gave me the encouragement and advice that guided me toward my novels. His singular help is deeply appreciated.

Friends at Grumman Data Systems (now Logicon) and the Internal Revenue Service bid me farewell with a virtual mini-library of books about writing. Thanks to them, and especially Lynn Hyland, I was able to begin my learning experience on solid ground.

The Dominican Sisters at St. Mary Grammar and High Schools, in Paterson New Jersey, taught me to read, write, and speak with confidence. These gifts, even more precious as I see the vista of possible educational outcomes, changed my life and empowered me. Special thanks to Sister Joan Roberta and Sister Francis Rita. I could never be sufficiently appreciative.

My writing partner and friend, Terri DuLong, is the perfect associate. Her talent, perception, and patience allowed me to grow as a writer. Her reading and critiquing of my work has been unselfish, instructive, and enduring. I am honored to have a writer of her brilliance as my partner and extremely grateful for all she has done to make me a better writer. Writing, editing, planning, and marketing, we are a forever team.

My wife, Pam, deserves special thanks for supporting me, reading my work, and enduring the throes of yet another of my careers. Even though I resist retirement, Pam encourages me to success. I am grateful.

To my friends, especially those who shared the nucleus of experiences in New Jersey that made me the person I am, thank you. To my readers and supporters, thank you for your faith in me.

All of you have given me the will to say, "Dare to dream."

— *Bill Bonner*

I WOULD LIKE TO THANK THE FOLLOWING PEOPLE:

Ruth Gibbs, for your loyal friendship, continuing assistance and gift for caring . . . all of which I deeply appreciate.

My cousins, Debra (Letourneau) Parenteau and Maria (Letourneau) Rainford for your endless enthusiasm and staunch support.

Bill Bonner, my friend and writing partner for our debut novel. Thank you for the pleasure of creating our characters and story with professionalism, dedication and lots of laughter. I respect you as an author and value you as a friend.

My husband, Ray DuLong, a special thank you for your support and often times difficult task as spouse to an author.

As always, to you the reader, thank you for granting us a space on your bookshelf.

—*Terri DuLong*

We owe a great deal to Laura Vadney, our editor, for her insight, taking care of our story, and for never treading on our voices. She is an accomplished professional to whom we are very grateful.

To Elizabeth and Bob Collins and Gardenia Press for the faith they have in new authors and new ideas in writing. They recognized that Immoral Symphony was truly unique as a two-author, two-voice novel that had never been done before. We are grateful for their publication expertise and understanding and wish them ever expanding success and good health.

To Erich Kocher, thank you for your terrific cover design. You have enhanced our words with your imagination.

—*Bonner DuLong*

CHAPTER 1

Breath surged from my mouth and nostrils forming small clouds around my head while cold air relieved me from the burden of my own odor. Wooden benches in Lafayette Park failed to filter or contain the cold air circulating around me as the wind whipped by. A block away, the grating was much warmer as the heated air gushed up through the grill, but passersby stared at those who lay on the sidewalk. Besides, the air coming from below was damp, and in minutes wetness would invade every part of my dirty clothes. I preferred to sit on the bench and be cold, offering my shivers up for penance as some church would have wished.

Worst of all, I hadn't spoken to an intelligent person for weeks. That included street people with high IQs who were dispatched far from their bodies by booze or drugs, and the ones belonging on a funny farm. After a heavy warm coat, I longed most for eloquent words and classical music. Words written to challenge, persuade, inform or comfort, escorted by inspired notes that eased my eardrums.

I didn't know how I got there, not the whole story anyway. My hand enclosed the stethoscope in my jacket pocket, keeping it warm.

"Move along, Buddy," a cop said, bouncing his nightstick on the bench.

I stared at him, wordless.

"Move your ass."

A groan reached cold bones that resisted rising from the bench. He started to give me another order, but I put my hand in the air.

Okay, I'm moving, my gesture said. This wasn't a missed conversation with an intellectual; the cop was an idiot.

Walking around the small park situated on the edge of the security barrier near the White House, many coppers watched me. The stroll took four minutes to complete the loop around the park. The cop had moved on.

A well-dressed woman, far too wrinkled for her age, came along the path. Her leathery skin told me she was a smoker. "Lady, could you spare a fag?" I asked. "Just one."

She looked worried at first, as if I'd pounce on her in broad daylight and unzip my pants. Jesus, she smiled at me.

"Here, there aren't many left in the pack, keep them and the matches. I've got a lighter at my desk."

"Thank you, ma'am. You're kind," I said, inching closer to her.

"Luckier than you, that's all," she said, with a hint of moisture in her bright green eyes. She walked on as quickly as she had approached.

Lighting up, I stood tall and let the smoke invade my lungs. Smoke was better than sex; although I couldn't remember for sure. Luxuriating in vice, my eyes scanned the dark-blue winter sky before turning to notice the woman about to sit on *my* bench. "What do you want?"

"Nothing from you."

"You like that bench, though. That's where I always sit, making it my territory, lady."

"So charge me rent," she replied. "Who the hell are you anyway? Your image certainly doesn't fit that of a landlord. Where're your belongings?"

I sat down. Pointing to my right and moving a bit, the large plastic travel bag came into her view.

"Yeah, so big deal. Planning a trip with that bag, Mr. Big Shot? Hey, there's plenty of other benches in this park," she said, standing up with some effort.

"It's all right. Besides I need someone to talk to," I said, enjoying the Boston accent coming through her tired words.

She coughed a raspy sound, making me want to help get the muck out of her lungs.

"Oh yeah? Well, maybe I don't feel like talking to you." While running her hand through a tangle of brunette curls that were long overdue for a shampoo, she hesitated before glancing over at me again. "I'll make you a deal. A little conversation for a cigarette?" she asked, sitting back down.

"Sure." I flashed my pack, then lit her cigarette.

"Oh, a gentlemen, huh?" Her laugh had that same raspy quality.

I didn't answer, but observed her grimy face. A scar ran down her cheek and curled toward her chin, pulling my eyes to the imperfection. Under the street dirt, I saw her blush. Without words her embarrassed expression asked me to look away.

The woman inhaled, then coughed repeatedly, revealing the workings of her lungs. "So, what's your name?" she asked. "Not that you'll tell me the truth."

"Mark Puccini."

The woman smiled. "With a name like that, I guess it's real. I'm Maddie Chapelle."

"French? Or is your husband French?"

"Oh, sure, my husband's French. He lives in a chateau in the south of France. I'm just waiting for him to come and rescue me." She didn't bother to hide her anger at the rotten hand life dealt her way. When I remained silent, she put her head down, saying in a low voice, "I've never been married."

"What kind of a name is Maddie?"

"It's short for Madeline. My father was French, but it's a little high brow for a street person. You're Italian, aren't you?"

"Is the Pope Catholic?"

Maddie laughed at my corny joke. For the first time in weeks, I smiled, too.

"What'd you do before you met the street?" she asked, with a lilt of genuine interest in her voice.

"Worked around."

Undeterred by my unfair answer, she continued, "Yeah? That could mean anything. I was an administrative assistant. Top job.

Top pay." Uncertain whether to go on, she paused, taking a drag off her cigarette. "You might not believe me, but I worked for Senator Bryce Pope."

Amazed, I looked past the White House. "Did you work in the Senate office building with all those intelligent and upcoming politicos?"

"No, in his home office, outside Boston. I ran the office, mostly. It was a good job." She paused. "It was a good life." Maddie's head bowed in an infusion of sadness or penance.

"Why the hell are you here?"

Her sarcasm returned. "Gosh, I wanted to see how the other half lived? Or, no, maybe it's because I'm doing research and writing a book?" Her voice got a bit louder. "For all you know, I could have a posh apartment in Georgetown. Who the hell are you to judge me?"

"Maddie, you're dirtier than me. You smell almost as bad with that cologne you're wearing. I don't mean to be nasty, but that's how I knew you're on the street, too, but you speak well. You've been educated."

"Yeah, well, welcome to the new century. This is where a top education can get you." She flipped the cigarette to the ground, crushing it beneath a loafer that had seen better days. "You speak well, too. Where's the accent from? New York?"

Noticing she had slim legs, I said, "New Jersey."

"So really, what'd you do before you made the streets your home? Don't tell me you worked around," she said, studying my face before beginning a series of harsh coughs.

Her spasms almost hurt me inside. "You'd better see a doctor. That cough doesn't sound very well."

"You have some cash to spare for a doctor?" she asked, not hiding her cynicism.

"No."

"Me neither. I'm afraid I've depleted my trust fund." With a flourish of her dark, curly, unkempt hair, Maddie emphasized her sense of humor.

I wasn't sure I liked this woman. A smart ass doesn't have a lot of friends, but I needed one to talk to about all the subjects lingering in my brain. Before long, whatever I'd learned would be gone.

"There's a clinic not far away where they'll give you an antibiotic and something to soothe the coughing."

"I must annoy you," she said smiling. "Just tell me to leave if I'm getting on your nerves with my noise."

I couldn't keep the smile from stretching across my yellowing teeth. "No, you don't annoy me. It's nice talking to you. You've got some smarts."

"Thanks, you do, too. Are you on anything?" she asked. Her eyes opened wider, a gesture to help pull the answer from my brain as she waited for my reply. She was hooked on something. Could she have hoped I was hooked, too?

"Booze, whenever I can afford some. It doesn't help, so they say, but you don't hurt when you're passed out. Nothing else, but a few puffs of crack, although I stay away from the drug set. Dopers get too damned mean. I'll have a sweet reefer whenever I get the chance, but that's all."

"I'm doing lots of stuff. Booze, too. It's that . . ."

"You don't have to explain. It goes with our territory."

Maddie convulsed in coughing once again. Moving closer, I tried to steady her as she pulled deeper from the bottom of her lungs. "Let's go."

"Where?" she asked, her fear palpable in the question.

"To the clinic. There's time before they close for the day. You're sick, lady."

"I don't . . ." The coughing started anew.

Standing, I pulled her up by an arm. She was taller than I had thought, but seemed so frail. The bag I always carried jerked up to my arm after two tugs. Maddie wasn't able to resist, and I felt she didn't want to. Maybe she thought of me as a friend. Two homeless people may have experienced a little luck. If I had a dollar, I'd have played the lottery.

"I don't need you. Understand that," she said.

Her words attacked me, but perhaps she didn't mean them.

Jesus, no one needs to judge me *or* trust me. That's why I'm here because no one can trust me, for Christ's sake. My hands were shaking, but not from the booze. I wanted to say, *Maddie, I'd love to help you, but you can't trust me. Hell, I can't trust myself.* How could she know I wouldn't intentionally hurt her? The guts to say what I should have weren't there. All that was left were words in my mind. *I'm warning you, Maddie. Tomorrow should worry you. You can count on me now, but maybe not tomorrow. I'm only good for now.*

"Come on, before the place closes." That's all I could say.

Walking along the street with Mark keeping me steady, I knew if he didn't continue to hold me I'd probably collapse on the sidewalk. The weakness in my legs was increasing, my chest ached, and I had a fever. Despite his offer to help me, I was reluctant to get involved with him. Doing so went against all the rules and regulations I had imposed on myself a few years ago when living on the street had become my only option. *Don't allow your emotions to come to the surface.* That had become my mantra, enabling me to survive. Sex with various men to obtain drugs was simply a business deal. Feelings never entered into it. My only stipulation was no condom . . . no sex. Not only did it reduce my chances of contracting AIDS, but it also put a barrier between me and my partner for that night.

"Right here," Mark said, as he led me up the walkway to a clapboard building in desperate need of paint.

The structure looked as if it may have been a private residence at one time. It appeared to be struggling to hold onto whatever sense of decency there may once have been. Now it provided a refuge to the poor and the downtrodden, and I knew I was in this category of humanity.

We stepped into a vestibule that served as the waiting room. Beat up armchairs lined the wall on both sides. Stuffing poked through holes in the fabric while stains covered the cushions, making it impossible to discern the original color. An elderly man occupied one of the chairs. Mark steered me past him to two others at the end of the row. The heat warmed my body, so for this alone, I was grateful.

Another spasm of coughing invaded my lungs as I reached for a tissue on the table. I looked up to see an examining room door open.

"Hey, baby," Rudy said, coming toward me. "Not feeling so well?"

I detested this excuse for a human being, but Rudy was one of my best paying customers.

Forcing a smile, I said, "No. Just a cold," as I prayed he'd leave me alone.

He leaned forward with a sneer on his face as he traced my lips with his fingertips. "Well, you'd better get yourself all better. I probably caught the friggin' cold I have from you and I don't appreciate it. I'll be in touch when you're germ free." He sauntered out of the building with the slamming door ringing in my ears.

I glanced over at Mark, but was saved from any explanation when a nurse opened the examining room door, motioning me to come inside.

Chapter 2

Maddie hadn't returned from the examining room, yet the clinic was empty. A half hour had passed, leaving me walking the dingy floor as a nurse came to lock up.

"Oh, I didn't realize you were still here," she said.

"I'm waiting for . . . my friend."

"She's been gone a long time. Went out the side door."

"I must have forgotten she was in a hurry. She said she had to leave." Trying to act like I hadn't been stood up, my face must have reddened under the grime.

Thoughts streaming through my mind were driven by embarrassment and anger. Rudy was a scumbag. I saw him around the druggies all the time. He was a dealer to be sure, but it sounded as though he and Maddie had some connection, perhaps a sexual one. God damn it. I don't need to get involved with a hooker.

Then, it was clear to me. Somehow she knew I couldn't be trusted. Why would she stick around for a tomorrow with question marks surrounding it? There was enough anxiety in her life; she didn't deserve another loser to complicate her shitty existence further. Where would she sleep tonight? For God's sake, where would *I* sleep?

It was late, maybe too late to find a place in the shelter nearby, but it was worth a try. Swirling wind blew stronger now, cutting through my jacket and my dry skin seemed to be cracking as I walked. There was no line outside the Purley Shelter, but I stuck my head inside the door.

"Sorry, brother," a middle-aged woman said, "we're full. Try tomorrow."

"Oh." I had been turned away before, but tonight was different. "Did a slim woman with sad brown eyes come in, coughing a lot?"

"What's her name?" she asked, opening her daily register.

"Maddie . . . Madeline Chapelle."

"No, sorry. Sir, we're serving the supper meal. You're welcome to stay."

The meal was warm and filling. Meatloaf and potatoes with gravy were always among my favorite meals, even sitting near people who smelled worse than I did. Walking back to the park seemed lonelier than usual. Then I found that the best benches were taken. Only the ones located near the route of the police were available. Christ, it was going to be a long night.

I dug my blanket out of the bag, searching for paper to lay on the bench. There was a piece of cardboard box lying in the bushes that could serve as a mat to block the wind and dampness. Wrapping myself in the blanket, I stretched out in a half-fetal position. The bench was too short.

* * *

The dream came back. Weeks had passed since last suffering through it.

The room edges were dark. The only light filtered through the closed wooden blinds, and bright spots showed under intense lights hanging from the ceiling. Lamps were focused and shaded to contain the light on the tables.

There were three of us. An older man spoke to each of us with anger in his voice. Sit still. What're you doing? No talking. He singled out Robbie, my best friend, for the most anger. The man's face was cruel, or maybe worried. I was too young to tell, but he made me afraid.

My friend was in the reading class with me. The other boy was new. I don't know where he was from or where we were, but the room was old and scary. The shadows were scary. The men were scary. There's crying. I'm crying, too. We're waiting for something or someone, and we're supposed to be reading. Read or be punished.

The light's fading and I'm being picked up. Why don't they let me walk? Because I don't want to. I'm dragging my shoes on the floor. The angry man swings me up to the table, holding my arms. Now, the light is so bright, it hurts my eyes. My arms are at my side, but I want to move them to provide shade. My arms are strapped down. They hurt. Robbie's crying and screaming. My eyes are wet, but closed. The light is so bright I see it through my eyelids. Perhaps it's painful, because there are tears running down my face.

A woman, fat with gray hair and scary eyes, has a mask, a little mask. She's going to hit Robbie with it. My head turns toward him. Robbie's crying when I see him with the mask on his face, over his nose. She drops something into his mask. More drops.

There are other people in the room, now. Tall people with white masks and gloves. A cart is pushed next to Robbie's table. I want to help him, even though he's not crying anymore, but I'm frightened. The woman is shaving Robbie's head. I hear the whirring. God, no, why are they shaving Robbie? Soon my friend is out of sight, hidden by a man in a long white coat. The other boy is crying now. The whirring sound starts again. Long shadows move across the room and I want to wake up, but can't. I'm screaming, but there's no sound.

A man holds my head. The mask is coming. God, the mask is on my face. Everything now is about smell. I smell something strong, too sweet, and rubbery, all at once. The smell is going into my lungs and my eyes aren't seeing like they were. I'm in a tunnel. My vision's closing in on me. Why can't I scream? Help me, someone please help me.

My body slashed upward at the scream. I was in the park; the scream was coming from me. Sweat ran down my face and my mouth was dry. My hand went to my head. I wasn't shaved. My dirty hair was still there. Tears rolled down my cold face. In the freezing night air, my sweat and tears flowed unimpeded. There would be no more sleep for me. I found the bottle of Muscatel in my bag, swallowing hard. A good thing I hadn't shared it with Maddie.

* * *

The clinic was warm, comforting air making the wait worthwhile. I didn't need to be seen for my cold. I had had worse colds and lived through them, but Maddie might come back. She might never come back, but maybe she'd be there.

Fabric screens had been pulled into the waiting room to allow a nurse to examine patients. Assisting an older street woman to remove her blouse, the nurse touched the wrinkled face of the patient. Her voice matched her gentleness.

The nurse saw me watching and pulled the screen closed again, but the area couldn't be well concealed. In a few moments she left, returning with the old doctor who looked into the weary woman's right ear with an otoscope. Watching his mouth, I could tell he said the word *infection*. Then, he placed the lighted instrument into her left ear without replacing the disposable cover. No short cut was too bad for this crowd of patients. The old woman could count on an infection in both ears, without a doubt. My head shook almost involuntarily. The doctor left without looking in the woman's mouth.

Twenty minutes later, my turn came to be ushered into the small examining room. There was no record for Dr. Stein to read and he asked no questions. He listened to my chest. Then, with the same poor procedure, he examined both my ears.

In two minutes, the exam was complete. He took an antibiotic from the closet, holding it in front of me.

"Are your eyes good enough to read this writing?" he asked.

"Yeah. It's penicillin, but I have a reaction to it."

"Sorry, Puccini, that's all I can give you. I can write a prescription, but suspect that won't help much. You have any money?"

"Not enough to pay for medicine."

"Typical."

"Didn't medical school teach you to be respectful to all your patients, even the lowlifes?"

"Sorry, it's been a long day after seeing some forty patients. I apologize. You seem to know something about drugs and doctors. How come?"

"I read the papers."

"Do you want the penicillin? Taking it could be dangerous, but maybe you could trade it on the street. I know how you people operate."

"The reaction would be worse than the infection."

Dr. Stein smiled for the first time since I walked into the examining room. Relaxing, he sat on the metal swivel stool. "Mr. Puccini, you speak well. What's your background?"

"I've come and gone through a few things. This and that."

"You don't lie well, but it's none of my business."

I ignored his comment, because my past wasn't his business, but changed the subject. "This is tough work. Why are you here, doctor? I mean, why do you give your time?"

"I'm retired. Lived the good life and have all the money I need. Why not?"

"We're not your best clientele." I had to laugh, but the lightness in my voice came from a reasonable conversation with an intelligent man. I wanted to continue, searching for a subject. "Do you have a modern autoclave in here?"

"No, we use a steamer when there's someone to run it. Sometimes we cut corners, Puccini. What's your first name?"

"Mark." I was glowing with pride for a moment that someone of his stature wanted to call me by my first name. The depth to which I had fallen burst on me.

"Mark, time for the next patient. Sorry there's no

antibiotic for you. If you continue to feel bad, come back, we'll think of something else. Don't wait too long."

"No, I won't." The reason for not saying thank you was too complex for me to understand, but I felt badly. The words didn't come out. *Thank you* had to be reserved for very special people.

CHAPTER 3

Hearing the soft humming of an electric razor, I buried my head deeper into the pillow. My body luxuriated in the warmth of blankets and comfort of a mattress. Sun was streaming through the motel windows. Briefly disoriented, I remembered running into Jake while leaving the clinic the night before.

Jake was one of my preferred customers. A long distance truck driver, he was in his late forties. We met a year ago in a coffee shop near Lafayette Park. When I got my tab, I realized I was a measly thirty-five cents short. Jake, who was sitting next to me at the counter, quickly figured out what was going on, and slapped a dollar down to help pay my bill before we struck up a conversation.

He wasn't the best looking guy I'd ever seen, but he wasn't the worst either. It was easy for him to figure out that I lived on the streets and he invited me back to his motel to spend the night. Picking up a six-pack, he surprised me by wanting to talk when we got to his room. Jake, divorced with grown children, came into DC once a month hauling office supplies and equipment. For some reason, he liked me. Before the night was over, it was obvious he wanted sex. Like reading a script for an audition, I verbally tossed my requirements at him . . . fifty dollars up front, no kissing allowed and no condom, no sex. He reached into his pocket, placed a fifty-dollar bill on the bureau and held up a shiny foil packet. When I awoke the next morning, lying next to the fifty was another one just like it.

When Jake was in town, he always found me. Sometimes I'd even find myself looking for him. Hell, a guy who didn't expect kinky sex and gave me a warm bed for the night was easy to take.

"Hey, Babe, ready for coffee? I've gotta leave shortly and head to Boston, but you know the routine. The room's paid for till two o'clock."

Stretching, I swung my legs to the edge of the bed. Running my hands though my curls, I smiled—loving the feel of my hair after a fresh shampoo.

"Yeah, thanks, Jake. I'll have some coffee and then might indulge myself in another shower before leaving."

I sat watching him as he poured two cups from the Mr. Coffee, a motel standard. Walking toward me, he held out my cup and smiled. "So, are you feeling better after seeing that doctor yesterday?" he asked.

Taking a sip of the hot, black liquid, I nodded. "Yeah, I think so. The doctor gave me ten days worth of penicillin."

He stood drinking his coffee, looking down at me thoughtfully.

"What? Why are you looking at me like that? Do I have a curl out of place?"

Jake laughed, shaking his head. "Not much you can do with those curls. They kinda have a mind of their own. Just like you do."

"What do you mean by that?"

"Maddie, you know what I mean. Why don't you get yourself off the streets? I know you're educated. Clean up your act. Get out there and get yourself a good job. You have the smarts to do it."

"Oh, yeah? Says who? Maybe I never went beyond the eighth grade in school."

"We both know that's a lie. I can't understand why you'd choose a life like this instead of something decent."

Putting his coffee cup on the bedside table, he began filling his small tote bag with shaving gear along with some dirty clothes.

"Nobody said you're supposed to understand. It's part of our deal, remember? You ask no questions. Besides, who the hell would hire me? Some posh finishing school? Yeah, I could teach politician's daughters how to be proper ladies." My laughter was followed by a coughing spell.

Jake turned, shaking his head at me, but said nothing.

I poured another cup of coffee, positioning myself Indian style in bed, as Jake finished gathering his belongings.

Zipping the tote bag, he walked over, quickly kissing the top of my head. "You take care, hear? I don't wanna come back next month to find out something's happened to you. Be careful out there, Maddie."

I nodded as he walked out the door, sighed, and flung my head back on the pillow. Jake's a nice guy, I thought. Probably too nice for me. I got up, walking to the bureau. The usual two fifty's were there along with an extra fifty-dollar bill placed beside a scribbled note. *Be good to yourself, Maddie. Take care of that cold and buy yourself a hat and mittens to keep you warm . . . Jake.* I felt moisture in my eyes, while holding the bills to my chest.

* * *

Blazing hot water felt good as it coursed down my body. How lucky can a girl be? I giggled while washing my hair with generic shampoo the motel provided. Two showers in less than twenty-four hours. No matter that this shampoo was a far cry from the $20 salon ones that used to perch on my shower shelf.

I dug through the black canvas bag that contained everything I owned. Pulling out a bra, panties, clean jeans and a sweatshirt, I realized I'd have to make a visit to the coin laundry soon. My supply of clean clothes was just about depleted. Hooking the black lacy bra made me remember that it was one of the few items I took with me two years before, when fleeing Boston. The bureau drawers and closet filled with designer labels flashed before my mind. Most of it left behind, while beginning a new life on the streets of DC.

Zipping my jeans, the sight of my image in the mirror made me pause. There was a time I couldn't pass a reflective piece of glass without stopping to inspect my hair or makeup. Now I went months without bothering to glance at one. But today I was drawn to the woman looking back at me. Reaching out to the shiny reflection, my fingertips touched a deep and ugly scar that ran from the tip of my ear lobe to just below my bottom lip.

"You're right, Garret, I can't ever forget you," I whispered, spinning away from the mirror.

The bedside clock read twelve noon. Still two hours left to enjoy the creature comforts. Turning on the TV, I stretched out on the bed, fluffing pillows behind me. Reaching for the remote, I tuned to the local news while leafing through a magazine that had been left in the room. Hearing *Pope* I glanced up. Bryce Pope's handsome face flashed across the screen as I turned the volume higher. He was being interviewed in relation to the proposal of a new bill.

A perky, attractive anchorwoman was concluding her interview. "One more question, Senator. After two years, are there any further leads on the disappearance of your secretary?"

Pushing myself to the edge of the bed, I delighted in his obvious discomfort. "No, I'm afraid not. There've been no leads at all," I heard him say. You smug bastard, I thought. Aren't you happy I so conveniently removed myself from your life? He hadn't lost an ounce of his charm. Flipping off the TV, I threw myself across the bed.

Charm. Had I really lived that charmed life in Boston or had it all been a dream? Was it me that had attended all those fancy fundraisers at the Park Plaza, that flew to Washington more than some people drove their cars, that carried Bottega Venata handbags and wore Manolo Blahnik boots? Rolling onto my back, I stared at the ceiling. No, it wasn't *me*. That person didn't exist anymore.

All of a sudden, Mark's face flashed before my eyes. With a haircut, shower and clean clothes, he'd be better then average looking. About seven inches taller than my five feet five, Mark appeared to possess genes that originated in Italy. Thick, wavy, dark hair curled up on the edges above his neckline. Intense eyes that resembled black onyx conveyed a softness that belied his tough exterior.

Giggling, I wondered if the poor fool was still waiting at the clinic for me. Bad girl, Maddie. That was a mean thing to do. So what? Just because he walked me to the clinic, I'm obligated to be nice? I don't think so. Besides, I don't do nice. Where the hell did nice ever get me anyway? Exactly where you are right now, girl.

I jumped off the bed, pulling the curtains open, while recalling the conversation with Mark the night before. He certainly hadn't been like the other street guys I'd met. He was different. Also mysterious. Said he had worked around. What the hell was that supposed to mean? But it had felt good to sit there for a while having a normal conversation. It had felt even better when he held my arm as we walked to the clinic. Give it up, Maddie. You don't need getting involved with another person. Especially one as bad off as you are. Besides, at the moment I'm probably better off than he is. I've got a hundred and fifty bucks to my name and I'm going shopping for a new hat and mittens, thanks to Jake. I'm also buying myself a couple bottles of wine to stay warm tonight.

* * *

Standing in front of the thrift shop window, I gazed at my reflection. Definitely you, Maddie. The bright red, velvet hat fit snugly on my head and the floppy visor concealed my eyes. Pulling on the black, wooly mittens, I congratulated myself on the dual purchase for the mere sum of $10. Quite the frugal shopper, with more money for that wine.

Turning around, I started down the street, enjoying the

sunshine. Laughing to myself, I realized that the hundred and fifty dollars that made me feel so cocky was what I used to spend on one pair of shoes. Now it stood between me and starvation. I felt the rumbling in my stomach. Maybe I'd grab a bite to eat before I got the wine and found a spot to settle into for the night.

Looking up, I saw Mark heading toward me further down the street. Shit. Maybe he didn't see me, I thought, ducking into the small restaurant frequented by homeless in the area.

CHAPTER 4

Panhandling around Lafayette Park was more difficult than usual. Government employees always seemed cynical or cheap, I couldn't tell which. There were fewer lobbyists and staffers on a cold afternoon, so patience was necessary. Calling out for coffee, my stomach rolled and rumbled. I was clapping my hands to restore the blood circulation, eyeing the passersby, when a man tapped my shoulder from behind.

"Cold out today, isn't it?"

"Damn cold," I said. "A few bucks would keep me in a cup or two of coffee. We street people don't get free refills."

He was a tall man, wearing designer clothes. The topcoat could have been from the pages of GQ magazine. His suit reminded me of the Armani I used to wear. My thoughts went to my current wardrobe, and I laughed at myself.

"What's so funny?" the tall man asked.

Before I answered, his face captured my attention. Facial features in perfect symmetry matched his tall frame. His face was smooth, with smile lines adding to his good looks.

"Just a private joke. Most of us street bums are nutty anyway. You should know that."

"Listen, I'm looking for someone and she could be around here. A friend, a dear friend, I've been trying to find for months. I have a twenty for you."

He had a large roll in his hand and he peeled a twenty-dollar bill off the top. His ritual reminded me of the city punks in New Jersey who sported their mob earnings to impress friends and enemies with the size of their stash that somehow equated to the size of their pricks.

"What do I have to do for it?" I asked, while lighting another cigarette.

"Keep your eyes open." He took a photo from his pocket. The worn, poor quality newspaper picture was of an attractive woman.

I stared at it, feeling sensations in the pit of my stomach. The image was Maddie, but there was no scar on her face.

"You want me to look for this woman?"

The man nodded. "Keep your eyes open and call me if you see her. It's worth fifty, if you do."

"Fifty?"

"A hundred."

"Give me the paper, make it two hundred and we have deal."

"You've seen her before, haven't you? I see it on your face."

"No, don't think so, but I won't be able to know her without a picture, to be sure."

He took a small pad from his coat pocket, writing a phone number on a page, before tearing it out to give to me. "This is my number. Wait here and I'll give you a copy of this photo. Don't go away."

This was an order. I sat on the nearest bench, waiting about a half-hour before he returned. He handed me a new page, the photo being even worse quality and graininess, but it was Maddie.

"What's your name?" I asked, now seeking to discover the real connection to Maddie.

"George."

His coat was open and his old fashion tie bar had the engraved letters *G D* on it.

Looking down at my face, he snarled, "Don't screw around with me. What's your name?"

"Marty." I wasn't sure why I didn't use my real name. Perhaps it was fear for Maddie—or me.

"Okay, Marty. I'm counting on you. Want to help this girl? She's not a friend; she's my sister. I've got to get her away from the streets. All right?"

"Yeah."

He walked away with a strange gait, as if he had been injured or had polio as a child.

* * *

Money in hand, I headed for the only restaurant that tolerated guys like me on a regular basis. The thought of hot coffee and eggs brought a smile to my face as I picked up my stride. Then, I saw Maddie going into the restaurant. Without thinking, I was running toward the door. She looked a lot different.

Maddie was sitting in the farthest corner, facing away as if she were talking to someone in the booth, but she was alone.

"Maddie?"

"What do you want?" Anger ruled her voice.

"Can I sit with you? Like to buy you a coffee."

"I have my own money. Keep yours, you'll need it."

"Please, Maddie, I need to tell you something."

"So, sit down and tell me."

The waitress stood looking at us. Maddie ordered bacon and eggs with black coffee. My order was an egg sandwich and coffee.

"Two checks or is this big man going to spring for it?"

"Two, I pay for myself," Maddie said, spilling the anger she was feeling.

I looked around the restaurant, not wanting to see Maddie's face until I'd framed my words, but she spoke first.

"You still look dirty."

"You look terrific. Clean and sparkling, even. Where'd you go last night?"

"Are you my keeper?" She fumbled with her coffee cup as she stared at me.

"No, but you could've told me you wanted to be alone instead of leaving me at the clinic to wait for nothing."

"True, but I had business." Maddie's voice was raised causing other patrons to turn toward us.

"You slept in a hotel last night, didn't you?" I asked in a hushed tone.

"Don't question me, Mark. You have no right to judge me, either."

"Didn't you? Where'd you get the money?"

"It fell out of the damned sky. None of your business."

Seeing her shiny hair and smelling the scent of lotion drove me to persist. "Maddie, did you turn a trick?"

"What's it any business of yours what I do?"

"Do you have a brother?"

The food we had ordered came and we were asked to pay on the spot. Too many walked out without paying.

"Do you?" I asked again.

"No, I was an only child."

Watching her anger grow, I needed answers before the conversation was over. "Maddie, I'm not interfering with your life, but tell me the truth."

"I ought to know if I have a friggin' brother or not." Maddie stabbed a fried potato with her fork, followed by a scraping sound on the plate.

"I think you're in trouble." My words weren't sinking in.

"You're so damned pitiful. You'd do anything to get close to me."

Before Maddie got up to leave, I took the photo page from my pocket and handed it to her.

"Where'd you get this?" In a span of a second, she changed her hard expression, while her lips dropped on the ends. Her eyes opened wider and there was a quivering in her cheeks and lips. "Oh, God." Her eyes filled, as tears rolled down her shiny face.

"A guy was looking for you in the park. He was asking other people about you, too. A guy named George."

"Tall? Good looking? Well dressed?"

"Yeah, and he walked with a limp."

"Jesus, how did he find me?" Her head fell lower, almost touching the table.

"Why's he looking for you? Are you running away from

something? Is he your husband? Maddie, tell me. I want to help you." Now my anger took over because I needed answers.

"No one can help me."

I had gone too far and Maddie stopped listening to me as she wrung her hands. "I can. I want to . . . be your friend. How'd you get in the paper, and who's George? Why's he after you? Did you do something to him?"

"I'm leaving," she said.

"You don't have to. I'll leave. Don't expect me to ask you again, because I don't give a fuck anymore." As I stood, anger flushed my face, replacing every good thought about this goddamned hooker. Being a friend wasn't enough for her to be truthful with me. I had some pride, too. The last drops of coffee warmed my throat as I looked down at her in the dirty plastic booth. My teeth were clenched.

"Sit down," she said. This wasn't an order. "Please, sit down. It's a long story."

CHAPTER 5

Before speaking, I glanced across the table at Mark's face. He showed no emotion while waiting for me to answer his questions. Looking at him more intently, it was easy to see that a haircut and shave would enhance his basic good looks. Just what I don't need. A good looking guy to complicate my life further.

I tried to figure out what I'd tell Mark. "The reason my picture was in the paper is because I'm considered a missing person. I have no family, but according to the article that went with the picture my co-workers reported me missing."

Mark seemed to believe this, so I continued. "Senator Pope was also questioned and he claimed he had no idea why I would disappear or where I'd go. He was one of the major reasons I left Boston. Men with power are the worst kind to be involved with. They think they can have whatever they want with no regard for the female."

"So he was sexually harassing you?" Mark questioned.

Nodding, I lit up a cigarette. "Yeah and after two years of this he made it very clear either I accommodated him or I'd be replaced. I decided to leave before he got the chance to replace me."

Mark looked at me doubtfully. "That's no reason to take up a life on the streets. It also doesn't tell me who this George is."

Taking a drag off the cigarette, I blew smoke in his face. "I don't owe you any explanations, but I will tell you he's not my husband and his real name isn't George. He's got a violent streak, so I'll leave it up to you if you wanna tell him you know me."

"Is that who put the scar on your face?"

I shook my head as my hand automatically reached up to the side of my face. "No, it was an accident," I said, not sure if he believed me.

"So why didn't you blow the whistle on this senator?"

The sarcastic edge to my laugh filled our table space. "Oh, sure. I don't think you realize how powerful he is. I was his secretary, but I had no concrete proof to back me up. He was very cautious to make sure our conversations and his advances were always in private. There wasn't a leg to stand on if I reported him."

Mark remained quiet as I prepared my exit. "Enough of this confessional shit. I need a drink. See you around."

Glancing over my shoulder as I headed toward the door, I ignored what appeared to be a look of concern on his face.

* * *

Turning the corner, I saw Sylvia. Only morning, but she already looked high.

"Hey, Maddie," she hollered to me. "How's tricks?"

"Not bad," I said, walking up beside her. As pathetic as I looked, she looked worse. Mid-twenties, but her years on the street had aged her quickly. Way too thin, her straight blonde hair begged for a shampoo. The cotton fabric jacket she wore wasn't nearly warm enough. Despite her hardened facial features, if one looked close they could still see the remnants of a once beautiful girl. Unfortunately, her stepfather saw the beauty and began sexually abusing her at age twelve. She ran away from her family by the time she was sixteen, making the streets her home for the past ten years.

"Damn, but it's cold this morning," she said, hopping from one foot to the other.

I felt guilty for my warm hat and mittens. Putting my hand through her arm, I led her down the street. "Come on," I said, "let's get you something warmer than this jacket."

Her face brightened. "No shit?"

I laughed as we headed to the thrift shop. "No shit," I told her.

"Wow! You must have scored big last night."

We found a warm fleece coat, hat and mittens for a grand total of thirty bucks. Back out on the street she admired her reflection in the store window.

"Hey, thanks, Maddie," she said, hugging me. "I owe you."

I shook my head. "You don't owe me anything, Sylvia. Just make sure you don't trade the clothes for drugs." Her face flushed as I could tell she had considered it.

"I won't. I promise," she said. "Got any extra though for some crack? There's some good stuff around right now."

"No. I'm trying to get away from that shit. But I'll share some wine with you. Come on, let's go get a bottle."

We found a sunny spot on the edge of the park. Leaning against a huge tree provided a backrest for us. I unscrewed the cap, took a sip, then passed the bottle to Sylvia.

"Syl, do you ever think about cleaning up your act? You know, getting off the streets?"

She took a long drink of the wine, then laughed. "Oh, sure. I think about it all the time. What the hell would I do? I never even graduated high school. Now you . . . you have class. It shows right through your street dirt. I never had class and I never will."

"They have places that would help you. Get you enrolled in school; maybe train you for something."

Her laughter had an ironic edge to it. "But I *am* trained. I'm trained to be a hooker and I do it well. You know that, Maddie. I have a good share of customers."

I shook my head at her. "Yeah, and that one last year damn near killed you from the beating. Think about it," I said, sadly. "Give it some thought, Sylvia. You deserve better than this. We all deserve better than this."

I took another gulp of wine and we remained quiet for a few minutes. "I need a favor, Sylvia."

She looked at me intently. "Anything, Maddie, you know that.

You've been good to me from the first time we met."

Nodding, I recalled two years ago. Sylvia was getting knocked around by some scumbag in the park. Cops don't usually pay attention to the street people, but I was able to convince one that he needed to help her. He chased away her attacker and she'd been indebted to me ever since.

"Somebody's looking for me, Sylvia. Tall, good looking guy. He walks with a limp and dresses very upscale."

Her immaturity came out as she giggled. "Now, I would think you'd want to hold on to this one. Sounds mighty nice to me."

"He's not nice. Far from it. He has a newspaper photo of me that he's showing around. Can I trust you to tell him you never saw me?"

Humor was replaced with alertness, as she stared at me. "You know you can, Maddie. I'll also put the word out to everyone. We never saw you before. Don't worry, we'll look out for you."

* * *

That evening I saw him, almost coming face-to-face with him on the sidewalk. Garret Dawson passed within inches of me and had no idea who I was. Turning down another street to get away from him, I was grateful for my metamorphosis. He glanced at me, paid no attention, and kept walking.

Ducking into a pharmacy, I noticed my hands were shaking. How long before he found me? Why hadn't I been more honest with Mark that morning, neglecting to ask for help? Maybe he could provide the assistance I needed.

CHAPTER 6

Cold coffee was worth drinking. Besides, I didn't want to leave the restaurant until I got Maddie out of my head. The waitress came back and a coffee refill earned the dirtiest look imaginable. Nothing was free.

"So, why're you working at your age? You aren't such a hot shit," I said. The sarcasm came from the knowledge that Maddie had lied to me. She was beginning to affect me in ways I didn't appreciate.

"I'm not a street hustler like you," the waitress said. "What keeps you from working, smart ass?"

"A shower and a street address."

She seemed to be evaluating my comment, then said, "Yeah, heard that sob story before. Get a life."

The old bitch was right. Maddie got cleaned up sometimes, like today, becoming almost respectable. Hell, she worked, even if she sold herself, but I was a panhandler. Why wouldn't Maddie lie to me? I'm worthless and can't be trusted. She knows me, so piss on her. Damned liar.

The piping hot coffee tasted good. Staring at the cup reminded me of the strong coffee I used to drink at the orphanage. There was no recollection of having milk when I was there. Another dark image came to mind, paralleling my dream of the night before. A black gemstone, swinging in front of my face. Other kids were allowed to play, but I watched a black stone and listened to music. My favorite music, Beethoven's Fifth Symphony, always made me feel good. In the daylight, I miss the music as much as yearning for intelligent conversation, without lies, but at night even the music haunts and terrifies me. The dreams intimidate me.

* * *

Walking along the street, the cold air made my lungs ache as I coughed. I needed that antibiotic after all. My chest hurt.

The clinic was full of poorly clothed people. Signing the register, I noticed Maddie's friend, Rudy, moving among the waiting crowd. About half of the patients were street dwellers; the rest, judging from their clothing and restrained conduct of their children, were struggling poor.

Rudy paused by several people to conduct a transaction with four of them. The bastard was selling drugs. I watched as a young woman holding a baby seemed to be begging him for a packet. Rudy said something too far away to hear, but the woman nodded, placing her palm flat against his pants. He smiled, putting something in her hand. I hated the prick.

A seat was open in the front row. Taking it, I continued watching Rudy over my shoulder. He strode in front of me as I stuck my leg between his. Flying forward, he knocked a small table askew and hit the linoleum-covered, concrete floor with the splat of his open hands.

"You son-of-a-bitch," he said, as he rose to his knees. "I'm gonna kill you."

Before he could get up, I kicked him in the stomach, missing his groin. He was at me in a second. We wrestled on the floor as women cried out and a man shouted, "Give it to him." I hoped he was talking to me. We exchanged a few good punches, one feeling like he broke my jaw, before the doctor and two nurses separated us. Rudy brushed his fairly clean clothes off as he went out the door, cursing in a loud voice.

"Everyone calm down, it's over," Stein shouted. Looking at me, he shook his head as if I were a juvenile. Clenched lips showed his disgust at my violence. "Mark, come in and let me treat the cut on your chin. Pick up your stethoscope."

I felt my pocket, realizing my stethoscope had fallen out during the scuffle.

"We have some medicine for you, too," Stein said. "It's better than penicillin."

"Thanks," I said, accepting the small bottle of capsules, "but I can't pay."

"A sample, several samples, in fact. Didn't you give samples to your patients?"

My face went slack. As I started to leave, he pushed my shoulder down.

"I haven't finished with your chin. Sit down."

Blood was dripping from my chin, so I followed his orders.

"Did you lose your license to practice?"

"No."

"Pass your boards?"

"Certainly."

"Can you practice in the District?"

"Virginia, Maryland and D.C," I said, feeling a sense of pride, which I hadn't felt for a long time.

"What was, I should say, what *is* your specialty?" Stein continued his questions as he sutured my chin.

"I was a surgeon, specializing in oncology cases."

"What the hell are you doing in this disreputable state? A doctor and you let yourself come to this?"

I looked away from him. The fleeting pride was gone.

"Listen, Mark, I can help you, but I have to know the circumstances of your downfall. There's a small grant intended to hire a technician or two for a year. I could arrange for you to be hired. This job wouldn't pay much money, far below what a doctor should earn, but I'm not being paid anything to be here." Stein peered at me intently as if he could will me to submit to his interrogation.

"I can't." Feeling shame now, my gaze went to the floor.

"Why not? You're needed here and seven bucks an hour is more than you have now. There's a supply room in back that you can sleep in. We can pick up a bed from Goodwill. There's a shower here and you'd be off the street. Most of all, you'd be applying your skills to help these people. What do you say?"

I stared back at the Good Samaritan. Perhaps this was a chance for Maddie *and* for me. "Maybe, if you got two beds. I have a friend on the street who could use a place to lay her head."

"Well, I don't know about a woman." His head shook slowly as he considered my request and his frown said no.

"Is that a moral judgment you're making, Dr. Stein?"

"No, of course not." With widening eyes, Stein reconsidered my potential as a doctor in the clinic. "Sorry for that remark, but I have to know why you lost your practice or can't in good conscience allow you to treat these people."

"I can't be trusted." Turning my head away from him again allowed me to say the words with less shame.

"Meaning?"

"I leave at inappropriate times."

"Sorry, Dr. Puccini, but I don't follow you."

"Once while operating on a young woman with stomach cancer . . . I left the OR in the middle of the operation."

"For God's sake, why'd you do that? Did the woman die?" In astonishment, his mouth opened and his brow rose.

"No, my assistant took over. That incident wasn't the first time, though. I missed a scheduled surgery, as well."

"Why did you do such things?"

"I have no idea."

The doctor grimaced, not believing me. "You pass out or something?"

"I walked out."

"Where'd you go? For God's sake, Mark, don't make me pull it out of you."

"I don't know, but when I returned my hospital privileges were gone. I was blackballed in the state. Couldn't operate any more. The hospital didn't take formal action against me, because they were afraid of being sued. Everything was hushed up, but I was out."

"Why don't you know where you went and what you did?

Amnesia? A mental disorder of some kind?"

Raising my palms upward, I tried to explain. "There are periods when I can't account for my whereabouts. That's all I know."

"Mark, Dr. Puccini, you can do well at this clinic. Can't you? Think about it. If you walk away after a few weeks, and never come back, we still get three weeks of badly needed help. We can watch you and maybe help."

"I think so."

"I'm going to request the grant be activated. The process will take a while, maybe a week or two, but you can begin sleeping here any time you want. I'll see to a bed, I mean two beds, tomorrow. No need to thank me," Dr. Stein said, as my mouth opened to form the words. "Thank *you*, Doctor. The clinic needs a partner here, very badly."

"I'm sure that's true for you to accept *me*."

"One other question?" he asked. "Doctors earn a lot of money; what happened to yours?"

"Like others in my generation, I lived high and had everything I wanted; my wife wanted two of everything. For the things we desired, we went into debt. There was a million-and-a half dollar house, two Mercedes, a sixty-five foot boat, credit card balances and designer clothes, all justified by the prospects of even greater success. When I deserted my wife, she didn't have much left after the bills were paid. We both started from zero again, only I'm still there."

"I appreciate your honesty. Welcome aboard, Dr. Puccini."

* * *

Richard Witton was the last man to enter the large conference room at International Holding Company. He took his place at the head of the broad table, nodding to the man on his right.

Charles Lester opened a folder lying in front of him before speaking. "Related Research, Inc. is nearing a solution to the mutating AIDS viruses. This startup company has only one researcher of merit—the principal developer and owner. When he's gone, the company's doomed, but the research data must also be destroyed."

"Is this the only company we know of that's approaching a breakthrough?" Witton asked.

"Yes, sir."

"Our statement, Charles, please," Witton said.

"The Infinite Hope Society, supported by the moral men of this Earth, believes that AIDS is transmitted by evil men who sin against God's most basic laws. Providing a cure will only encourage immoral behavior. God in his wisdom will see that our path is made even. In the name of the living and true God, we condemn the saving of evil men, instead demand the damnation of those who blaspheme society. God give us the wisdom and strength to carry out our mission."

"Who do you recommend for the mission?" Richard Witton asked.

"Beethoven, sir."

"Are we in agreement?" Witton asked the group.

Seven heads nodded.

"This meeting is adjourned. Call Beethoven to duty."

"Yes, sir," Lester said.

CHAPTER 7

Rain pelting against the window woke me up. I opened my eyes to survey the dingy, gloomy room . . . cement block walls, with a high solitary window preventing any view outside. My glance fell to the twin bed separated from mine by an ugly green four-drawer bureau. Mark's bed was empty, with no sign of having been slept in.

Turning on my side, I pulled the warm blankets tighter around my body. Thanks to Mark, I was actually among the gainfully employed again. If you considered minimum wage being gainfully employed, but it also included having a roof over my head. A roof that wasn't supplied by a shelter or in exchange for sex. I recalled bumping into Mark the week before. Even more surprising than his offer of the job and sleeping arrangements was learning that he was a doctor. The surprise was greater the next day when we both showed up to work at the clinic.

I did a double take when I saw that the tall, good-looking man smiling at me was Mark. Gone was the grimy beard, replaced with a killer smile I hadn't noticed before. His dark, wavy hair was still a bit longer than conventional, but clean and I had to admit the slightly longer style looked sexy. Over his jeans and sweatshirt he wore a white lab coat with a stethoscope dangling around his neck. It gave him validity as he projected the image of a physician.

No doubt about it. He looked good and made me feel good. Laughing, I put my hand out toward him. "Dr. Puccini, I presume?"

He caught the joke, returning both my laugh and the handshake. Nodding, he said, "And you are?"

Not releasing his hand, I replied, "I'm Madeline Chapelle, Dr. Stein's new Gal Friday. But you may call me Maddie."

As I pulled my hand from his, he became serious and said, "It's my pleasure to make your acquaintance, Maddie. I think we're gonna be one hell of a team."

He was right, I thought, pushing the blankets off me while on the edge of the bed. We had worked exceptionally well together for almost a week. He assisted Dr. Stein with seeing the patients while I assisted both of them by keeping track of who was next, transcribing the brief summary of each visit from the doctor's voice recorder, and trying to help Barbara, the nurse, in any way I could.

Pulling on a pair of heavy socks, I got up to turn the electric heater a little higher. Damn, it was cold in this room. I glanced at Mark's empty bed again. Where the hell was he? Today was Wednesday, a day off, because the clinic was closed on Wednesday and Sunday. He certainly didn't owe me any explanations, but it seemed strange he hadn't said a word last night after dinner about not coming back.

Mark had gone out of his way all week to be nice to me. I smiled, remembering our first night sharing this room. He had even offered to hang a blanket between our beds to give me some privacy. Chuckling, I told him a hooker loses her modesty mighty fast, so that wouldn't be necessary. Besides, I was sleeping in sweatpants with a sweatshirt to stay warmer. From the first night after we finished our duties at the clinic, we'd gotten into a routine of having supper together. I had to admit I enjoyed it. His company and conversation were luxuries I'd missed the past few years. I also liked the fact that I didn't have to fight him off. Agreeing to the sleeping arrangements, he assured me he wasn't looking for sex in return. He'd been true to his word. But where the hell had he been all night? I realized I was concerned for his safety. These streets could be fatal.

"Hey, not my problem," I said out loud, reaching into one

of the bureau drawers. Pulling out clean underwear, jeans and a sweater, I headed for the small bathroom across from the supply room.

I remembered how Mark acted a little weird the evening before. We had finished supper at the cafeteria-style restaurant, enjoying a cup of coffee as we talked. I was telling him about Sylvia and how she worried me. When I looked at him, he had a dazed look on his face. Like he hadn't heard a word I said or wasn't interested. I wasn't sure which. All of a sudden, his eyes cleared. He jumped up, threw on his jacket and left without another word.

After I finished dressing, I walked out front to the clinic area. Barbara was in one of the examining rooms standing next to the med cabinet. She turned and smiled at me. "Hey, Maddie. Big plans for your first day off?"

I liked Barbara. She had retired from hospital nursing a few years before, helping out at the clinic for the same reasons that Dr. Stein donated his time. They wanted to give back to the community. They also worked well together, and if I wasn't mistaken there was a definite attraction between them.

Returning her smile, I replied, "No, I'm afraid not. I was just heading out to get some breakfast. I thought we were closed today. What're you doing here?"

"Just came in to straighten out some of these meds. Most of them are donated to us from drug reps and people in the community. Docs switch meds so often on people, and they can't be returned to the pharmacy, so many patients are kind enough to drop them off here. We can use everything. But sometimes they're expired, so I usually come in for an hour or so on Wednesday to check through them."

I nodded. "You're a good person, Barbara. The patients are lucky to have you. By the way, any chance you've seen Mark this morning?"

She looked away from me and started replacing some of the bottles into the cabinet. "No, I haven't. Why?"

"I haven't seen him since after supper last night. He just took off from the restaurant. Said he had something to do and never came back here all night."

Still not looking at me, she said, "I guess he wasn't lying when he told Dr. Stein he disappears sometimes."

"What? Disappears where? For what reason?" Surprise was in my voice.

Turning around, Barbara faced me. "I don't know, Maddie, and please don't tell Dr. Stein or Mark that I told you. Dr. Stein told me that sometimes Mark might not be around, but not to be concerned. I have no idea what it's all about. Strange, isn't it?"

Strange? More like bizarre, I thought. But all I said was, "Yeah, very strange. Hey, thanks, Barbara, and I won't say a word to either of them. I'm going to get some breakfast. See you tomorrow."

* * *

Stepping outside, I would have given anything to have my own apartment complete with kitchen to cook breakfast. The rain had increased in intensity, the wind was blowing, and the bitter cold only added to my discomfort. The street was deserted. No sane person would be out in this weather unless absolutely necessary. At least not without an umbrella.

"Shit," I said. "No choice, Maddie. You wanna eat, get moving." I made a run for it around the corner to the cafeteria where Mark and I had eaten supper the night before.

Pushing my shoulder against the glass door, I stepped inside. A welcome blast of heat surrounded me as I shook water from my hair and clothes.

From out of nowhere I felt a hand groping my backside, making me spin around. "Get the hell away from me," I snarled at the man standing there grinning. I had no idea what his name was, but vaguely remembered him from a night of sex and drugs.

"Aw, what's a matter, baby? Too early in the morning for ya? I'll buy you breakfast first. How's that for a deal?"

"It sucks. No deal. Leave me alone." I ignored the stares from some of the customers and walked toward the buffet area. Turning around, I saw him shrug his shoulders as he walked out the door. Picking up a plate, I began filling it with scrambled eggs, bacon, and home fries. Getting a cup of steaming, hot coffee, I paid the cashier.

Making my way to an empty table in the back, I draped my rain-soaked jacket over the chair. Once again, my mind drifted to Mark. Maybe he's a drug dealer. But he doesn't fit the profile. By the time my plate was empty, I was no closer to finding an answer for his sudden disappearance.

Reaching into my backpack for cigarettes, I lit one. Well, Maddie, I thought, how do you choose to spend your first day off work in two years? I surprised myself with the disappointment of being alone. Usually, I enjoyed being alone. Admit it. During supper last night you assumed you'd be spending today with Mark. He had mentioned possibly catching a movie, but it hadn't been confirmed.

I liked being with him, because when we were together, nobody else bothered me. That jerk this morning never would have touched me if I had been with Mark. It was an unspoken code on the streets. The females belonged to nobody, but if they were with a male, johns looked the other way. A hooker alone on these streets was fair game for anyone.

I crushed the cigarette out in the ashtray realizing the only male in my life that had taken care of me and protected me was my father, but he had died of a massive coronary when I was twenty. Being with Mark gave me the feeling he wanted to look out for me. Yeah, right, Maddie. He can't even take care of himself. Get real. Lighting another cigarette, I waited for my jacket to dry a bit more.

Checking my cash, I saw I only had fifty dollars left from the money Jake had given me the week before. Then I laughed to myself. But hey big spender, you're getting your first paycheck from the clinic tomorrow. You're on easy street.

Dodging the raindrops, I headed to the thrift shop. Twenty-five dollars got me an umbrella, floppy rain hat with a matching raincoat and a heavy pullover sweater.

About to open the door and step outside, I saw him across the street. His limp was unmistakable. Turning back into the thrift shop, I smiled at the cashier mumbling I'd forgotten to look for a pair of jeans.

Walking down the aisle of the shop, I realized my hands were shaking. What the hell was he still doing in this area? He had questioned Mark weeks ago. Was he that desperate to find me?

Mark, a typical man . . . never around when you need them. Where the hell was he?

CHAPTER 8

Draft from the trains came roaring up the stairs as I walked into the lobby of Union Station. Like waking from a dream, I struggled to understand being there. The smell of smoke raided my senses, because the odor clung to me, but why did I stink of smoke? Darkness surrounded me and was frightening. My last memory was in the evening, not yet dark, at dinner with Maddie.

I glanced at my watch, seeing it was almost midnight, but what day was it? Dr. Stein had given me a basic watch that didn't display the day as a welcoming present. Clearly, the day mattered now that people were counting on me at the clinic. Perhaps this was a workday and I wasn't there. What about Maddie? What'll she think of me?

The Metro subway map showed the trains would stop soon; I needed to get home. My legs skipped stairs down to the deserted platform. Christ, was there another train tonight? The whoosh of a train approaching in the tunnel brought relief.

Metro Central station was fairly close, a few blocks walk to the clinic building. Running, a feeling of loss crept over me as I arrived home. The side door was locked with the chain probably in place. I knocked softly at first, then louder.

"Who's there?" Maddie asked.

"Me, Mark."

The chain slid in the plate, followed by the door opening. Maddie must have run from the hall, as she was under the covers when I got there.

"Don't you want to talk to me?" I asked, searching for a sign of her mood.

"Glad you're home," she said. Her words chilled the room.

"Maddie, I'm sorry. What day is this?"

"It's Wednesday. No it must be Thursday morning by now." She turned away before finishing her sentence.

"Thank God. I didn't miss the clinic."

"Where the hell were you and why didn't you have the grace to tell me you were going away? Damn you, I was worried." Maddie slapped her fist into her hand for emphasis. In a louder voice, she asked, "Where were you?"

"I don't know."

"Yeah, right, don't tell me. Go to sleep. The doors open in six and a half hours." She pushed the covers back and stared at me from the edge of the bed.

"Can we talk about it tomorrow?" I tried to hold her arms, but she pulled back and stared at me.

"Why would I care, doctor? You're your own man."

Climbing into the small bed, I began to shiver from having been cold and afraid. Maddie now knew for sure that she couldn't trust me. I had no idea where I'd been or what I had done for over twenty-four hours. Finally, I drifted off to sleep. My legs were sore from running, working, or something.

* * *

The walk to the restaurant was silent because Maddie's normal light conversation was missing and she avoided looking at me. I didn't intend to bring up the subject of my disappearance, apparently she wouldn't either.

She took a table with an abandoned *Washington Journal* lying on it and leafed through the front section. I took a seat across from her and ordered coffee.

"Can I see part of the paper?"

"Yeah, but look at this," she said pointing."

The bottom of the first page had an enticing leader.

Fire Destroys AIDS Cure Hopes.

An arson fire destroyed an AIDS research lab and killed the leading contender for an early cure credit. The laboratory in the Maryland suburb of Hagerstown was burned to the ground during the evening hours. Doctor Rudolph Obermann, President and CEO of Related Research, Inc., was found bludgeoned and burnt after an attack occurred when he was apparently working alone. The police have called the death a homicide, but there are no suspects at this time.

"Horrible," I said. "Why would anyone kill a man doing AIDS research? The article says that he was close to a breakthrough. Jesus, the killer destroyed research notes and may have stolen data media from the computer in the room."

"I read it," Maddie said, not looking at me.

"So, they may have to start from scratch. There was only one other medical researcher on the project."

"I read it, Mark," she said, with more emphasis.

"Sorry, Maddie, that I made you angry yesterday."

"Forget it, will ya? Why would anyone give a shit if you want to run off."

"But, I didn't . . ."

"I'm heading back to the clinic. See you there," she said, her sharp tone signaling her disgust with me.

* * *

The day was extra busy. New patients flocked in since they learned there were two doctors. Unfortunately, or fortunately, depending on perspective, Dr. Stein greeted my arrival as a reason to take some time off. Therefore, the clinic was packed and I had a brisk schedule. The ten-minute appointment rule had never held water for me. I took as long as each patient needed, and no insurance company was going to tell me how to do my job. But that was history; there was no insurance for any of the people who came to our clinic.

The factor that impressed me most was the number of working poor who wanted to be seen. Maddie asked each patient a few questions to determine need, but most of the patients displayed *a need* far beyond what any more rigorous interrogation could assess. We turned no one away; after all, who would come to *me* if they didn't have to? I was regaining some of my self-respect, but obviously had a long way to go.

My skills returned faster than I anticipated they would. A boy with a knife-inflicted cut got my suturing talent almost back to peak. Honestly, I enjoyed sewing him up.

We worked through closing until all who needed help were seen. Now, there was time to break the ice with Maddie. "Let's walk to the deli and have some pizza," I said.

"I'm awfully tired, besides I don't want to be seen." For the first time since my absence, Maddie seemed more afraid than angry.

"Maddie, did George come back?"

With her head bowed, she quietly offered the worrying truth. "Yeah, he's been hanging around the area asking questions. Sylvia made sure she let me know."

"Sorry I wasn't here to help you."

"Well, if I end up dead, maybe you'll wish you had," she retorted, walking outside.

"Maddie, please, I feel bad enough. Please." A cigarette sticking out of my pack was meant as a peace offering.

"Do you want a medal for disappearing when you could've been looking out for me? Not that you're needed, but it would've been nice to have a friend who cared."

"Care? God, I care. What happened to me is beyond my control."

"Yeah sure. Beyond your control? Like a bottle of cheap wine and a joint is beyond your control?" Maddie inhaled deeply on the cigarette, with her pace five steps ahead of me.

"I don't know where I was or what I did." My voice was too loud, but my control came back as Maddie's face softened toward me.

"You were sleepwalking?"

"No, I don't think so." Reaching for her hand, we moved to a bus stop bench. I patted the seat and she sat.

"Why did you get up from the table last night?"

"All I know is the music started."

"What music?" Disbelief, then new anger crossed her face.

"Beethoven, my favorite symphony. Beethoven's fifth."

Maddie's brow wrinkled and her eyes closed to slits. She didn't have to say what she was thinking. My story wasn't convincing, but she wasn't going to challenge me. Beethoven didn't play in the restaurant—not *that* place. I knew that, too.

"The same thing happened before, in surgery. I've gone off a few times instead of caring for a patient. Because I just take off, I'm not a doctor any more, not rich and driving a Mercedes."

"Are you all right, now?"

"Yes, but would you do me a favor?"

"Depends what it is."

"If I go off, you know . . . disappear, will you follow me? Then you could tell me what I did and where I went."

"How often does this happen? That is, if I believe this crazy story."

"Not often—I'm not certain. Not being on a normal work schedule for so long, I may have been away without knowing it. Some nights after too much wine, I haven't known where I had been, but maybe that was only drunkenness. Will you help me, Maddie?"

"You're a good doctor. You may even be a good man, but I can't promise to just follow you God knows where. Let's see how it goes."

"Fair enough. How about a pizza? I'll spring for it."

"Oh, big spender from . . . where? Where was your home? Where did you graduate from?"

"New Jersey and I graduated from Rutgers."

"No shit?"

"Really." I smiled with pride at perhaps my only true accomplishment.

"I'm impressed. And you're a street person. Incredible. I'll follow you next time it happens, but it works both ways. Will you help me with George?"

"It's a deal."

We shook hands as if we were business partners. I guess we were.

"Maddie, will you tell me the truth about George?"

CHAPTER 9

Mark knew I was nervous walking around our usual area, so he suggested catching a subway to the outskirts of Washington where we found a casual Italian restaurant. The hostess seated us in a booth, complete with red checked tablecloth and candle-filled wine bottle. Amazing what a little bit of money and clean clothes will get you. The waiter even presented Mark with a moderately priced wine list. I could tell by the way he studied it that he knew his Italian wines well. He selected a Chianti, telling the waiter we'd wait a few minutes before ordering

"Okay," I said, looking across the table at Mark, "time for confession, I guess. First of all, the guy that's following me, his name isn't George. He's Garret Dawson." I waited, but Mark's face remained impassive. "I met Garret about five years ago at a political fundraiser in Boston and was attracted to him. Tall, good-looking, well dressed, educated. When he approached me and we started talking, I found myself enjoying his company. He asked me out for the next weekend."

The waiter returned to the table, poured a bit of wine for Mark to sample, then filled our glasses. Lifting mine, I touched the rim of Mark's. "Here's to honesty," I said and Mark nodded.

"So we dated for about six months. No doubt he had money— lots of it. He always managed to get the most expensive seats at the opera or theater. We dined at all the top restaurants in Boston. He tried to give me very expensive gifts. Jewelry, mostly. But that's where I drew the line. I didn't love this guy and the longer I dated him, I wasn't sure if I even liked him. So I wouldn't accept the gifts.

He'd try to get me to take them, but then he'd back off. Our relationship was strictly platonic. We kissed, but I never slept with him. He seemed okay with that too."

"Sounds like a pretty good guy," Mark said.

"Oh, yeah, every woman's dream." I could hear the bitterness in my voice. "More like every woman's nightmare. After dating for a few months, I began to suspect that he was dealing drugs. Many times before going to the theater or wherever we were going that night, we had to make stops at various shops in a seedy part of Boston. I'd wait in the car. He always said it was business. I didn't ask questions and he didn't elaborate.

After about six months, I was almost positive he was a drug dealer. When I began to decline his dates, he called me at work constantly, left messages on my cell phone and home phone all hours of the day and night. He was frightening me and I wasn't sure how to handle the situation. I finally decided we needed to talk and agreed to let him come to my condo so I could break off the relationship. That was my first mistake."

Reaching in my handbag, I lit up a cigarette. Recalling the memory of that night, fear surged through my body. Mark said nothing for a few moments, reaching across the table to squeeze my hand.

"Go on. What happened when he got there?"

"He was pleasant when he first arrived. Even brought a bottle of champagne. He poured us each a glass and then asked what was this foolishness that I didn't want to see him anymore. I tried to explain that I was getting busier at work with less time for socializing, but he wouldn't accept it. Finally, I told him it wasn't anything personal. I might want to date other people.

"That's when he went nuts. He started screaming, yelling, and saying it *was* personal . . . very personal. He threw the champagne bottle across the floor, saying I knew way too much about his personal business. Before I knew what was happening, he shoved me on the floor and raped me. When he was finished, he grabbed a shard of the broken glass from the bottle and dragged it down my face. Yeah, this is a lasting memory from Garret. He said the injury was so I'd always remember to keep my mouth shut." My hand trembled as it reached up to stroke the scar embedded in my face.

"Holy shit. This guy's a psycho. Did you report this? Didn't you press charges against him?" I saw the horror and empathy on Mark's face.

Shaking my head, I let out a disgusted laugh. "Oh, I tried. But I didn't get very far. He had a great alibi for that night. The police told me they didn't believe him and I could push the case, but they doubted I'd get very far. Besides, it could get nasty at a trial. So I decided to drop it and try to get on with my life. I was pretty sure he was following me though. I got a very sophisticated alarm system for my condo and tried to get along day-by-day."

"I take it that didn't work? That's why you ended up in Washington?"

I poured more wine into my glass and took a sip. "Funny enough, it had nothing to do with the rape. A few months after that happened, he was arrested for drug dealing. I was called to testify against him and wasn't going to at first. But then I realized he'd already gotten away with a rape, why the hell should he get off on drug charges? So I testified—my second mistake. Based on my testimony, he got jail time. Apparently, I knew more than I thought I did. Names, places, dates, and times. They pulled him from the courtroom screaming and yelling that when he got out he'd finish the job on my face. I was terrified, but figured with him behind bars, I was safe.

"Two years later, a phone call came from the prosecutor's office. They wanted to warn me— Garret was being released after only serving two years. There's no doubt he had connections in high places. Between the sexual harassment with Bryce and Garret being back on the streets again, I went over the edge. With nobody to turn to for help, my plan was to relocate somewhere and start over. But I knew Garret could trace me through credit cards, bank accounts, all of that. He had his ways, which left me no other choice but to pack a few things leaving everything else behind. I simply walked away from my other life. I'd been to Washington a lot on business and felt comfortable here. Crowds of street people made it easy for me to get lost among them. Taking the train from North Station in Boston avoided any record with an airline ticket. These streets have provided my anonymity for the past two years."

Mark's face looked incredulous as I finished telling him my story. "And I'm not even sure you can help me, Mark. But if Garret finds me, I'll be lost forever."

Mark remained quiet after I finished telling him about Garret. His expression changed to impassive, making it difficult to know his thoughts. What did it matter? He couldn't help me anyway. On the ride back in the subway he began to converse a little more, avoiding any mention of Garret. We mainly talked about the clinic. But I noticed he was extra attentive to me. Taking my elbow as we boarded the subway, trying to make general conversation and even trying to make me laugh. As much as I hated to admit it to myself, I enjoyed his company.

When we got off the subway near the clinic, Mark told me to take the scarf from around my neck and drape it over my head to conceal the lower part of my face. I saw his eyes darting in all directions as we walked back to our room at the clinic. For some reason, I didn't feel scared walking with Mark.

We went around the back of the building toward our entrance. Walking along the alley, I saw the figure of a person standing at the far end. I stopped short, but couldn't make out who it was. Mark's arm slipped around my shoulder and his body stiffened in anticipation.

"Maddie? Is that you?" We heard a voice say.

I let out a breath I hadn't realized I'd been holding. "Sylvia? What the hell are you doing here scaring the shit out of me?"

She ran toward me, laughing. "I'm sorry," she said, giving me a tight hug. "But I wanted to warn you. That guy. The one you told me about? He's been around all night looking for you. Showing everyone your picture. I thought you'd wanna know."

I was glad Mark hadn't released his arm from my shoulder. I felt weak. "Oh, God. Has anyone told him they knew me?"

Sylvia shook her head forcefully back and forth. "Hell, no, Maddie. I told you we'd all cover for you. As a matter of fact, he might be heading to Boston in the morning. He mentioned this to Blind Tony. He knew Tony couldn't see your picture so he described you. But Tony said no, he didn't know who you were. This guy seemed real mad and said something about he had been positive you'd be here and was pissed he wasted his time. He told Tony to keep his ears open, cuz he was going to Boston tomorrow, but he'd be back."

I leaned over and hugged Sylvia. "Thank you. Thank you for putting the word on the street." I reached into my handbag. "Sylvia, here's five dollars. Promise me you'll get a meal or something with it? No drugs?"

She hesitated for a second, then nodded. "Yeah, okay. I'm starved anyway. I appreciate it, Maddie. And you just be careful. Hear?"

We stood for a few seconds watching her walk away. "Well, I guess I get a bit of a reprieve. If I'm lucky, he won't be back. But I've never been a lucky person."

Mark pulled me toward him. "Come on. Let's get in our room. It's freezing out here."

He always let me use the bathroom first at night. I was still lying there awake when he came into the room. Dressed in sweat pants and a sweatshirt, he looked like a suburban husband who'd just returned from a jog around the neighborhood. He was a good-looking guy. Why was I trying to avoid this fact? I looked up as he smiled down at me. He even had a killer smile, although he didn't smile very often.

"Are you okay?" His voice softened as he looked down at me.

"Yeah, for tonight I am. We'll see what tomorrow brings."

Mark shut off the light and springs creaked as he got in bed. The spotlight from the parking lot lit the room just enough so I could see his face emerging from the blankets. Once again, he smiled at me.

"Mark?"

"Yeah?"

"I think I forgot to thank you. Thank you for the nicest evening I've had in a long time. Goodnight."

CHAPTER 10

Three months passed since Dawson left Washington. This time was one of change and good fortune for Maddie and me. We became partners in a way difficult to describe to my friends at the clinic. We shared an understanding—unspoken, but always there. I admired her, without ever telling her. Maddie understood anyway.

Her looks became beauty for me. The scar on her face was a detail never seen. Her new clothes revealed her body and the feminine lines previously hidden became an attraction. At first, there was an admiration, now I saw the sexual Maddie. She was beautiful and my closest friend.

To my sorrow, I didn't believe Maddie had the same feelings for me, so I was careful never to cross the imaginary line we had set up in our room.

In a way, I gained notoriety by accident. A haggard looking woman was sitting on the examination table waiting for me. She looked familiar, probably another street person who had passed in my travels, but the woman smiled. I recognized her immediately. "Connie? Connie Height?"

"Hello, Mark. I never would've thought of you as the *Street Doctor*."

"Street doctor?"

"Yeah, the locals are calling you the street doctor and they're telling their friends. Were you really homeless?" Her face lit up as we began to renew our friendship.

"Yes. Still am as a matter of fact. We're living in the back of this clinic at the good will of Dr. Stein. What about you? You look like you're down on your luck."

"There was a problem, my problem. Got caught taking drugs from the ward cabinet. The end of a great career as an R.N." Connie moved about on the examining table where she sat, looking away to escape my eyes.

"Are you clean now?"

"Yes and no. I kicked my pill habit, but got stuck on booze."

"Sorry."

Connie reached for my hand and the comfort she needed. "Me, too. I'm very sorry—pitiful really." She couldn't go on. Her tear-filled eyes gazed away. She smiled before speaking again. "Never thought I could be out of control like this. Ashamed is the operative word, but I did stay clean from drugs and got my license back. A job in the medical field is open to me, if I ever get it all together. Have to submit to random testing, but I'm not black-balled. You know the term—*impaired nurse.*"

Connie had a urinary tract infection, which we treated with drug samples from a company salesman. The only salesman who lowered himself to come to our clinic, even though we never purchased any of his drugs.

On her second visit, we talked about her situation. Unfortunately the story was familiar. Working at a very low paying job because of her heavy drinking and unable to afford medical care. No insurance, but not poor enough to be on welfare. Her experience in the field gave us much to talk about. We had a common interest in poor people who deserved health care, but didn't have it. Neither of us would have considered the subject five years ago.

Dr. Stein was moved by my description of Connie and her abilities, so he scoured the community and nearby universities for additional grant money. Failing in that search, Stein secured $50,000 from a philanthropic endowment. Thereby hiring Connie to work as a nurse; however, she possessed the skills to work independent of us as a Physician's Assistant.

By a trick of fate, our clinic was staffed by three street people, a volunteer doctor and a part time LPN. When we changed the name of the clinic to *The Street Clinic,* Jerry Wells, a local reporter noticed the change and interviewed our staff. For about two weeks, the series that ran in the *Washington Journal* was picked up by the wire services and distributed across the country. Wells, who was very liberal, asked me questions about health care when he ran out of local interest items. One could say I was forced to recall my discussions with Connie and ideas from my days as a young impressionable doctor. In those days, paying off a student loan created a real burden.

"How can the problem be fixed? How can the poor and working poor be given a reasonable health safety net?" Jerry Wells asked, leaning forward on his feet. "We have hundreds of thousands of readers who care."

"Seven years after I passed my boards, I paid off my student loan, but considered myself lucky because I also had a scholarship to Rutgers, so my loan was fairly small."

"So?" Jerry searched for the point I was making as he frowned.

"I'd have been happy to work a few hours a week or more and accept credit against my loan for the time worked. That would have been the cheapest way any government could offer health care to the underprivileged."

"And individual doctors could contribute to the local community while they lowered their loan principle?" Jerry asked.

"Exactly. Furthermore, local clinics could be staffed by volunteer health professionals, if they weren't petrified by lawsuits. Believe it or not, most doctors are generous people who appreciate the gifts they were born with. Doctors do pro bono work now, but in an unorganized way. With clinics established by government and a single administrator, the staffing could be all volunteer *Pay Back* doctors. The law would need to be changed to protect the professionals from civil suits."

"*Pay Back*—PB Doctors. I like the sound of that."

Thus ended my second interview, which wound up on the bottom of the front page of the *Journal.* Jerry Wells had done his homework. He supplemented my ideas with other options, such as hourly working doctors paid directly by a government agency. Again, a low cost way to bring care to the working poor and indigent. Locally run volunteer clinics were on the lips of the educated in the nation's capital.

A homeless doctor, *The Street Doctor*, had made the front page. Whether by coincidence, mystical plan, or philanthropy, each of the former homeless professionals began receiving a better living wage. Maddie and I could almost afford to rent an apartment.

* * *

After the series ran its natural life and the reading public switched to another issue, health care for the poor and uninsured remained unresolved, and Barton James came to our room.

Maddie and I had returned from supper at a small, inexpensive restaurant in the area. We were reading with the aid of a single light between our beds when the knock came. I opened the door to the extent of the chain lock until I observed his stylish, formal suit.

"Dr. Puccini?" he said. "I'm Barton James."

James was short and stocky with a double chin, probably the result of too many political dinners and booze. His face had a slight reddish glow.

"Come into our home, humble as it is. Mr. James, this is Maddie Chapelle." He barely looked at Maddie as my arm gestured him into the room.

"I didn't believe it. I read the entire series, talked to Jerry Wells, and still thought it was a conservative trick. You're really living in a room in the back of a clinic? This is Hollywood stuff," James said.

"No, this is *life*. We're happy to be here, but you surely couldn't understand that," Maddie said.

"What can we do for you?" I asked.

James stared at us for a moment, taking stock of us as if we were for sale. "I'm Counsel for the Senate Committee on Health, Education and Welfare. That makes me the senior staffer for the committee chairman, Senator Bryce Pope. Senator Pope is for the little man. No one cares more than my boss for the health of poor Americans. Bryce is a champion of the downtrodden." He raised his chin to end his speech.

"So . . ." I said

Glancing at Maddie, I noticed that she looked shocked and pale. She sat on her bed, her back hunched and taunt with fright plainly visible on her scarred face.

"Are you okay, Maddie? Come on, head between your knees." I stepped into the doctor role.

Maddie's face regained its color, but she retreated to a corner of the room where the light was dimmer.

"So, I need your help. As you probably know, when we draft a bill, we normally find professional people who have an interest in the legislation. Lobbyists, corporations, health professionals, consumer advocates, environmentalists, and so on. Your input to a draft bill to be sponsored by Senator Pope is needed. We've been working on it a long time. Then later, you would be a witness before our committee."

"Christ, why me? I'm only a step above being a bum."

"Because you've captured the imagination of a lot of liberals who want to fix the health problems of this country." Barton moved his hands in animation as he spoke of the subject he loved.

"Anything political here?"

"Don't be naive, Puccini." His sneer made the point.

"It's either Mark or doctor, but not Puccini."

"Sorry, Mark. No intention to offend you."

"Guess I was a bit defensive, too." No question, this man was used to talking down to people from his lawyerly platform. I didn't like him.

"Doctor, we can do this work on your schedule, most of the time. In fact, politically, it's important that you continue to work at the clinic, as you're a model for the country. We can work early in the morning, at night, or during the day when you have time. Working every weekend isn't new to me, so it's no skin off my nose."

"I'll think about it," I said, nodding my head.

"Good, I'll be back or it would be better if you called my office? We can do some good here, doctor." He handed me his card.

"Mr. James, I've been interviewed with Mark using an alias, Ann Miller. Can I trust your discretion to keep my identity a secret? You know how it is with us homeless people," Maddie said.

"Of course. Frankly, I'd already forgotten your name," James said, as he turned to leave.

The flush of Maddie's face reflected the contempt Barton James had for ordinary people. She remained silent, but her blood was boiling.

CHAPTER 11

Looking in the mirror, the woman staring back looked like an old friend I hadn't seen for awhile. I knew her once, then she disappeared, only to return with a regenerated image. My investment in make-up had paid off. Eyeliner and mascara added increased definition to almond-shaped eyes. Bronze blush enhanced my cheekbones, radiating a soft glow. Red liner and gloss on my lips gave them a sensual appearance. But the most striking change was my barely discernable scar. Skin care products can cover a multitude of imperfections.

Walking away from the mirror, I looked around my bedroom. *My* bedroom. I chuckled out loud as I realized this fifteen by fifteen space was all mine. Not like the streets, motel rooms or shelters I'd had to share over the past two years. This was mine and nobody could cross that threshold unless I agreed to it. I silently admitted that during the previous week of living here, there were one or two times I wished Mark had taken that step.

Through the kindness of Dr. Stein, we found an apartment to rent. The owners, an elderly couple, were patients of his before he retired. When Mark and I arrived at the two family home, I prayed we'd be able to afford it. Set back from the sidewalk, the white clapboard house was well maintained with colorful spring flowers dotting the walkway to the front porch.

Mr. and Mrs. Kaminski were friendly and their home reminded me of my grandmother's when I was a child. Heavy mahogany furniture, lace tablecloths, family photographs displayed on the mantel, and the fragrance of lavender in the air. Before taking us upstairs to see the vacant apartment, they insisted we join them for coffee and pastry.

A worn but sparkling linoleum floor, enamel sink, organized spice rack above the stove, and the aroma of freshly baked apple pie brought back more childhood memories.

Mark and I sat at the rectangular wooden table covered with plastic to protect the lace beneath it, smiling at each other. If one didn't know better, we were a married couple visiting grandparents on a Sunday afternoon. But the Kaminskis did know that we weren't married and worked together at the clinic. The apartment had two bedrooms so they didn't question our sleeping arrangements. They didn't even question either of us in regard to our personal life.

"I think you will like the apartment," Mrs. Kaminski told us. "The kitchen gets the morning sun and the living room has the afternoon sun. The porch in back is very nice on summer evenings to have supper." Even after almost sixty years in this country, she still retained her Polish accent. Small and spry with snow-white hair fixed in a chignon, she bustled back and forth in the kitchen refilling coffee cups and offering more pie.

Mr. Kaminski was tall and slender with large, calloused hands that attested to many years spent as a carpenter. He was a quiet man, allowing his wife to do most of the talking. With a simple glance at each other, love passed between them. Finishing his final piece of pie, he wiped his mouth with a linen napkin, then cleared his throat.

Smiling he asked, "Do you like to cook?"

Cook? I hadn't even had my own kitchen for two years. "I haven't done much of it lately," I replied, "but yes, I do enjoy cooking."

He nodded his head. "Then you're sure to love the kitchen upstairs. Our daughter had that apartment when she was attending Georgetown and I did all the carpentry work in the kitchen. I like to think it's a cheerful place for a woman to prepare meals."

Mark laughed and said, "I occasionally dabble in cooking, so I'll probably enjoy it also."

* * *

From the aroma filling my bedroom, Mark had been right. He had offered to cook dinner for us tonight and it was easy to see he took his job seriously. I'd been banned from the kitchen all afternoon. Curled up on the sofa with a magazine, culinary sounds had drifted to me—no doubt Italian sauce had been simmering for hours.

Reaching for the bottle of perfume on the bureau, I sprayed my neck. A far cry from the French scents I once owned, but a light floral odor filled the room. Mark had said we'd have a glass of wine before dinner, which he planned for eight o'clock. The bedside clock read seven ten. Walking into the living room, my eyes spotted a large vase on the coffee table that hadn't been there earlier. Filled with yellow daffodils, it gave a cozy appearance to the room. The Kaminskis had been generous in leaving the sofa, two chairs and tables that their daughter had left behind when she moved to the west coast upon graduation. Mark and I visited local thrift shops to purchase beds, bureaus and a small kitchen table and chairs.

On the opposite side of the living room, his bedroom door opened. Mark stood there for a moment staring at me, as if not quite sure this was the Maddie he worked with at the clinic. Wearing casual slacks and open collar shirt, his image was not the one I was used to either.

"The flowers are lovely," I said. "Nice choice."

"Good. I'm glad you like them. How about a glass of wine on the porch? It's such a nice evening; I thought we'd eat out there."

Following him to the back of the apartment, I was impressed with his decorating ability. A worn red tablecloth covered the round patio table, mismatched dishes and silverware indicated two place settings and a tall, tapered candle dripped along the edges of a wine bottle.

I smiled at his obvious effort to make the atmosphere pleasant. "Very nice," I said. "I can see you have a flare for entertaining."

He expertly uncorked a bottle of Chianti and poured two glasses.

"Here's to new beginnings."

"New beginnings," I repeated, touching my glass to his.

I could feel Mark staring at me across the table. "There's something very different about you tonight. You look terrific. You have an air of mystery about you."

For the first time in over two years, my emotions were at ease as I started laughing.

"Ah, you noticed. Well, perhaps you can call me Mysterious Maddie."

"Speaking of mysterious," he said, "I really don't know you at all. Where did you grow up? Do you have any family? How did you get that position with Senator Pope?"

Taking a deep breath, I launched into my past. "I was an only child and grew up in the White Mountains of New Hampshire. Quite scenic and lovely, but after high school I had to spread my wings and see the real world. I got accepted to Boston College, majored in political science, so after graduation I worked at various small jobs at the State House. I attended numerous fundraisers and that's where I was introduced to Bryce Pope. About a month later, he called me personally to tell me he was losing his secretary of five years."

"A secretary?" Mark questioned. "You had a degree in political science."

Nodding, I explained. "Yes, but he informed me my position would have the title of Administrative Assistant. I reported directly to him and had my own secretary."

"I see. So where are your parents now? Have you been in contact with them?"

I shook my head. "My mom passed away from cancer while I was in high school and I lost my Dad to a heart attack a month after graduating college. I've been on my own since then. How about you? Where's your family?"

Mark paused before answering. "I don't have any either. I was raised in an orphanage." Standing up from the table, he said, "Just give me a few minutes to get the food out here."

I started to get up, but he put his hand on my shoulder. "I'm waiting on you tonight. I can manage."

Sounds drifted from the kitchen. Water running, the grating of a knife against a cutting board, a spoon tapping the side of a metal pan. I took a sip of my wine and smiled. I liked Mark. I knew very little about him, but I knew I liked him.

He walked onto the porch carrying two salad plates. "Capresi," he said. "I hope you like it. It's Italian."

I looked down at the artfully arranged plate, with slices of bright red tomatoes and basil interspersed with pure white mozzarella, all of it moist with oil.

Sampling my first bite, I smiled and nodded. "It's delicious. I love it. Where did you learn to cook Italian? I could smell the spices simmering all afternoon."

"I'm glad you like it," he said, avoiding my question.

Following the salad, Mark brought out a bowl filled with spaghetti and another with sauce, meatballs and sausage. The garlic bread was perfect for scooping up the delicious sauce.

"I have to confess, I cheated and went to the bakery for dessert," he said, placing a slice of tiramisu in front of me.

Although I had to be quite insistent, Mark did allow me to help with the dishes. He washed while I dried. I'm not sure if it was the satiation of excellent food, but we were both quiet as we worked. My thoughts wandered to places I hadn't thought about in a long time. Something as simple as a home cooked dinner eaten on a back porch and the sharing of doing dishes touched me deeply. These small but significant moments made me realize that maybe I still had a chance to make a life with another human being. Not necessarily Mark. I wasn't sure how he felt about me, except as a co-worker and roommate. But he made me aware that possibly the fear I had lived with these past two years was diminishing.

After we got the kitchen cleaned up, Mark suggested another

glass of wine in the living room. He turned on the old radio that Mr. Kaminski had found for us in the attic. A Strauss waltz filled the room and Mark moved closer to me on the sofa. Taking the wine glass from my hand, he placed it on the table and brushed his lips against mine.

"I like you, Maddie. I'm glad we met," he whispered.

His hand stroked the side of my face as his lips increased their pressure on mine. I felt myself responding. The past two years being with strange men for survival no longer existed in my mind. Only this moment was reality. And this moment felt so right.

Mark gently eased me back against the sofa pillows, his tongue hesitantly entering my mouth. Both passion and desire—two emotions that had been dead during my years on the street—bubbled to the surface. My breathing increased as Mark's hand slid under my blouse creating an electric current on my skin. His hands were on my breasts, and I wanted them touching my entire body. I never wanted to stop kissing him, yet I pulled away. Unlike so many of the men these past few years, Mark followed my lead and waited.

Standing up, I ran my hands through my hair shaking my head. Taking a couple of deep breaths to slow my breathing, I glanced at Mark. "I don't want you to think I didn't enjoy that, because I did. I'm just very confused right now."

Mark stood up, putting his arms around me. Being hugged felt warm and secure. In addition to shame, the thing I hated most about being a hooker was the lack of pure and simple affection. I couldn't remember the last time a man had held me only for the closeness of an embrace.

He pulled me tighter to him and said, "It's okay, Maddie. I understand. It's been a great evening with you, but maybe we need to say goodnight."

Reluctantly I pulled away and stared into his face. "You're right. Thank you for a wonderful dinner and evening."

I closed my bedroom door behind me, leaning against it. "You have to be very careful, Maddie," I said out loud. "When fear disappears, love can step in."

CHAPTER 12

Last night with Maddie was a bad dream come true. My coming on to her was ill timed at best and stupid at worst. The signs she gave me led me to believe that we had something special, sexual, between us, but I must have been wrong. How the hell could a doctor be embarrassed by a hooker? The truth was I didn't think of her as a hooker, just a person who had to survive and now wanted a new life. If she didn't, why were we living in the same apartment? Understanding women hadn't been one of my strong points anyway, so chalk it up to experience, but I wouldn't be embarrassed again.

* * *

The day began well with an office full of patients accompanied by plenty of honest work to do. Maddie manned the front desk with her usual vigor, making everyone feel welcome. Almost everyone, because Barton James arrived about three o'clock, issuing his usual orders. He wanted to see me *now*. I smiled as Maddie returned some expert bureaucratic bullshit, but I wanted to talk to him.

I appeared in his view and he walked past her. She had a glint in her eye, the look of a woman going to trip a little man, when she saw me approaching.

"It's all right, Maddie," I said.

"Dr. Puccini, nice to see you again." James walked toward me with an outstretched hand, ignoring Maddie.

"Same here, Barton. What brings you to the best part of

town?"

"I want to discuss your student loan idea."

Previously, I had written a long exposition about doctors trading their working hours for credit against their outstanding student loans and sent it to Barton's office. James had talked to his staff and he seemed loaded with questions.

"Is this a good time?" James asked, being more courteous than seemed natural to him.

"Yes, we've run out of cases for my attention. We can go to my cubicle. Some dressings are being done by the nurses, but I'm free for the moment. Let me be frank, you aren't used to waiting for anyone, especially a skid row doctor. What's up?"

"You're very important to my boss. He wants to author substantive health changes before the upcoming election. A Democrat needs ideas like yours."

"Christ, you're honest—at least on this subject."

"Direct, but not afraid to lie for a good cause. The ends justify the means. Don't forget it, that belief is what Washington runs on. You may have to lie when you appear before the committee, but lying is no big deal."

I shook my head in disbelief. "It is to me."

"Okay, Mark, let's not get into it. I respect your beliefs. Do whatever you have to do." His upraised hand told me he was finished discussing the morality of truth.

"What are your questions?"

"Why would any successful doctor, or nurse for that matter, contribute their time to serve the poor?"

"Your staff understands that nurses are important to this effort, too. That makes me happy. Good. Remember, our oath includes helping the sick. So there's a humanitarian component to start with. There's the obvious need. Look around you; I saw over forty people today. Many of them are working at respectable jobs, but without insurance, they're working poor. Doctors and druggists alike take a hell of a lot of money from patients. Maybe doctors and nurses will see that they owe something back for the good life they lead in this country. Then there's the practical side. A smart person can give hours and gain cash in the form of loan relief. Seems like a good deal for everyone."

"And the poorer segment of the population can win. Senator Pope loves the idea, but I suspect the insurance industry isn't going to support it. They'd rather have an insured answer that they run for the Feds. That's another problem we don't have to solve now. Look, Mark, I've got about thirty questions here, for you to answer. My staff will fold your responses into the text."

"What text?" James was always planning things without consulting me. I guess he knew my place in the scheme of things.

"We're writing a speech for you. All you have to do is read it before Senator Pope's committee."

"When?" The idea didn't thrill me.

"As soon as the bill is placed in the hopper. Since Bryce is committee chairman, there's no question about the bill's longevity. But . . . we need more."

"More what?" I wondered where all of this would lead me.

"Ideas to fill out the legislation."

"Okay, I'll work on it. I'll answer your questions and write them up."

"Good man. You're going to be famous, *Street Doctor*."

"Being famous isn't my goal."

James smirked at me. His was a look of disrespect. Something like, *lying shit*.

"Mark, take taxis. When you come to the hill, take a taxi, even though it isn't far. We want the press to have lots of opportunities to see you. Play the game—okay?"

"Okay, but . . ."

James took ten twenties out of his wallet. "For taxi fare. Don't worry, it's legal and from campaign contributions. The senator wants you to go in style."

* * *

The next day was Saturday so we tried to have a half-day schedule at the clinic. This day, we were free by one o'clock. I wanted to do something with Maddie. Clearly we needed to talk. Hopeful that she hadn't been to the Washington Arboretum, I asked her if she wanted to spend a quiet day with nature. She was almost giddy at my suggestion, and dashed to her room, wanting to change into comfortable jeans.

"Maddie, let's take a taxi," I said.

"Can't we take a bus? It's cheaper."

"We could, but let's go in style."

"I like your ideas, Dr. Puccini." Maddie took my arm and flashed her warm smile.

While Washington wasn't as convenient as New York to hail a taxi, there were many around the streets. After a few minutes, we were seated in a very clean Ford with garish orange paint and lettering saying it was a yellow cab. Someone was a colorblind entrepreneur.

Maddie took my hand, almost absentmindedly, as she looked out the window. I admired her face. She was beautiful and I knew joy just looking at her.

"Where to, buddy?" the cabbie asked, his furled brow seeming to signal a puzzling dilemma.

"The arboretum."

"We have a great one here. You been there before?" the driver asked, turning to look at us again.

Before answering, I looked at the identification picture found in every cab.

"No, Robert, we haven't been there yet." My eyes were drawn back to the picture and the name listed under the photo. *Robert Mozart.*

"My friends call me Robbie." The oversized man was as friendly as a puppy. "Where're you from?"

"New Jersey, originally," I said.

"Me, too. Where? What city?" He burst with enthusiasm.

"Northern New Jersey. I don't know exactly where I was born. I'm an orphan."

Robbie Mozart turned hard right, coming to a sudden stop at a curb in a no parking zone. He stared at me. His eyes scanned my face as if he were trying to compare me with an image from the past.

"What's going on?" Maddie asked, her eyes wide and dark.

"It's all right," I said, "Robbie thinks he knows me."

"What's your name, sir?" He twisted until his arms draped over the front seat.

"Mark Puccini."

"Were you in the Holy Right School for Boys?" His eyes were as big as quarters waiting for my answer.

The hair on my neck and arms stood up as a ripple zipped up my spine. My eyes bore into his face, searching for some recognition. "Yes." I couldn't say anymore. My tongue felt constricted, but a smile emerged on my face. "Robbie, I know you, too."

"What do you do? I mean, you look as if you're doing all right."

Maddie smiled broadly. I could tell from her raised eyebrows what she was thinking about my recent homelessness, but she kept her thoughts to herself. I patted her hand.

"I'm a doctor. I work in a clinic here in the District."

"Congratulations. Not many orphans make it like you have. Great, real great . . . doctor."

"Mark. You've always called me Mark. How long have you been driving? Is this your cab?"

"It is. I've been here for about seven years. Doing all right."

"I'm sure you are. There are so many questions to ask. Maybe we could get together to talk old times. What do you say?"

"Do you and the lady have to be at the arboretum any special time?"

"No, we have all day. Right, Maddie?" Robbie and I looked at her for approval.

She nodded, smiling at us.

"I want to talk to you. I mean right away."

"Sure. Where?"

"A block up the street there's a small park." Robbie didn't wait for an answer. He spun rubber and sped to the park. We got out, then sat in the sun for a few minutes before anyone uttered a word.

"I have dreams. One dream really." Robbie hesitated. "Someone's cutting me open and you're in my dream. The boy, Mark, I should say."

My heart was pounding as sweat ran down my face. For an instant, fainting was possible.

Robbie continued speaking at a fast, New Jersey pace. "Do you ever have a dream where doctors operate on you?"

My first thought was to see what Maddie was experiencing. She looked to be in awe of the whole conversation. Her eyes were wide and her jaw was slack, perhaps not believing what she heard.

"Do you have kids? Are you guys married?"

"No, we're co-workers, that's all," Maddie said.

The words *that's all* made me feel small, but there was nothing I could say.

"I don't have any kids. Divorced," I said. "Why?"

"Because, *I* don't have any kids. I've had a vasectomy. Don't know when I got it—it was a gift. I believe the home sterilized all of us. We weren't good enough—not select enough—to continue the line. That's what I dream about." He paused again, maybe waiting for my response. "Have you had the operation?"

My head thought he had thrown something at me. The answer was embarrassing. I didn't know if I'd had a vasectomy. A doctor who didn't know about his own body. Were my hated dreams because they stole my ability to produce a child? Why talk about this? I was uncomfortable and changed the subject. "How did you end up driving a hack?" I asked.

Robbie looked at me in disbelief. I turned away, unable to provide a good answer to his important question, but my out-of-context question got us to the heart of the matter.

"When I came to from a blackout I have sometimes, there was an envelope of money in my pocket and a note saying the dough would buy a taxicab. I didn't ask what taxi. I bought one to become an owner/operator."

His words hit my chest and my breathing surged. "You have blackouts? Periods of time you can't account for?"

Maddie's face became pale. I held her arm for a moment. She crinkled her lips, but tears still filled her eyes. "Mark, this is like you," she whispered.

Robbie heard her. "What's like you?" Robbie asked, with a panicky surge in his voice.

"I have a habit of going off to places, not remembering where or why I went there."

"Jesus Christ. Mark . . . Mark, do you hear music?"

I couldn't find the words. I nodded.

Robbie gave me a bear hug that took my breath away. He didn't let go, clinging to me in what seemed to be some sort of relief.

"Doc, I'm not alone. We can beat this."

"We will, Robbie. You have a business card?"

He gave me a card and I waved my fingers until he handed me a second card. I wrote our address and the phone number of the clinic on the back of one card, and gave it back to him, keeping the second.

"I'll be back to you. Need to think this thing out and check my privates. Do you hear Mozart?"

"Yeah. You get Puccini?"

"No, Beethoven's Fifth."

CHAPTER 13

Staring at the 8x10 white paper in my hand brought a feeling of relief and skepticism. What it contained could have been a death sentence or redemption. For now, it was a reprieve.

Following dinner with Mark, I approached Dr. Stein about having an HIV test done. Without judging me, he kindly agreed to draw the blood. I glanced at the word *negative* again and wasn't sure if I was more relieved or surprised. Although I had always been adamant about the use of condoms, I think deep inside I worried that eventually my lifestyle of the past two years would catch up with me and I'd be punished. For the moment, the gods were looking down on me kindly. As suggested, I would have another test done in six months to confirm the first one.

Today was our day off from the clinic, but Mark had agreed to go in for a few hours to see an overflow of patients. Everyone seemed to be suffering from allergies caused by springtime in Washington. I tucked the lab slip into the pocket of my bathrobe as I walked into the kitchen. Reaching for a cup in the cabinet, my glance went to the note Mark had left earlier in the morning. *Maddie . . . If you have no plans today, meet me for lunch around 1:30 at Alberto's. Hope to see you then. Mark.*

Smiling, I placed the note on the table, then poured my coffee. I'd been feeling guilty the past week about my behavior the night of our dinner, unable to explain to Mark my hesitation had been caused by fear—fear of getting involved with him, but primarily fear for his safety. He seemed to overlook the fact that I was a hooker. He never made me feel uncomfortable, always treating me with the utmost respect. I cared for Mark a lot and didn't want to cause further damage to his life. Having the test wasn't an option. Now the time had come to explain why.

The morning was spent cleaning up the apartment. We had a mutual agreement that we'd share the chores and Mark was a joy to have as a roommate. Both of us being neat and organized enhanced sharing our residence.

Going down the hall stairs to answer the doorbell, I saw Sylvia standing on the porch nervously jumping from one foot to the other.

"What's up, Sylvia?" I asked, hugging her in greeting.

"I need to talk to you, Maddie," she said, returning the hug, then following me up to the apartment.

"Sure. Want a cup of coffee?"

I could tell she was stressed, but wasn't sure if it was from drugs. She shook her head. "No, no coffee. Maddie, I think I'm in trouble."

"Drugs?" I questioned.

"No, I've been clean for awhile now. Honest. I see what you've done and I'm really trying, Maddie. I even signed up to start classes next week to get my GED. I need a high school diploma before I can do anything."

Without warning, she began sobbing and clung to me. Hugging her tight, I tried to calm her.

"What is it, Sylvie? Tell me. I'll help you," I said, stroking her hair. Sylvia was the younger sister I never had.

Trying to compose herself, she choked out the words, "I'm pregnant."

Oh, God. She can barely take care of herself, never mind a child. Taking a deep breath and trying to find a strength I didn't feel, I said, "It's okay. We'll figure something out."

She broke our embrace as I heard bitterness in her voice. "Oh, yeah? Like what? I'm not even sure who the father is. I have no education, no job, no home. What the hell kind of world is that to bring a baby into?"

She was right, but I knew she was very fragile now. "Come on, let's sit down and talk about it." I said, leading her to the sofa.

Christ, what were her options? Not many from what I could see. "What do you want to do?"

"Me?" she questioned, like that was the last thing to consider. Like her life was so worthless that this situation wasn't about her. "I just want it to be over. All of it."

"You mean the pregnancy?"

"I don't know what I mean. Maybe my entire life. Maybe I want it over."

I reached for her hand. "Sylvia, don't say that. Please don't even think it. I know you're upset right now, but that's not the answer."

"Why not? My knight in shining armor lost his way a long time ago. He's never coming to rescue me. Why kid myself?"

"Listen to me," I said, hearing the sternness in my voice. "No, he's not coming to rescue you. You have to rescue yourself. We all do. And we all take different paths to do that. Do you want this baby? Yeah, it'll be tough raising a child alone, but you can still get your GED. You can get a job and have the means to support yourself and a child. What do *you* want, Sylvia?"

She reached for a tissue from the box on the coffee table and wiped her nose. "I'm not sure. This baby inside me doesn't seem real. But I do know one thing, I can't kill it. I can't get an abortion. I just can't."

Sylvia's gentleness and sensitivity poured out of her with the force of her words. The kid who had been abused had no abuse inside her. Somehow, despite the horror in her life, she had managed to hold on to the emotion of caring.

"Then you won't," I said. "You're not having an abortion. Now that we have that settled, have you seen a doctor yet? How far along do you think you are?"

She nodded. "Yeah, I went to the clinic for my pregnancy test. I'm about three months, Dr. Stein thinks. They gave me some vitamins to take, but I'm sick to my stomach in the morning. Do you think it's the vitamins?"

I smiled, reaching over to hug her. "No, it's not the vitamins, Sylvia. Being sick in the morning is natural. It'll go away in another few weeks. You know what we need to do? If I'm going to be Auntie Maddie, I have a vested interest in this child. I'm off work next Wednesday. I'm treating you to lunch and a day at the bookstore. We're going to find a few good books for you to read on pregnancy. This will all seem more real to you if you understand the changes your body is going through. You're gonna do just fine, Sylvie."

She stood up and smiled. "I do feel better, Maddie. I hated to bother you with this, but I didn't know where else to turn."

"Hey, what are friends for? By the way, where are you staying at night? You need to be taking good care of yourself. Getting good sleep and eating proper meals."

Sylvia laughed. "You sound like a nervous aunt. I'm still going from here to there. Some nights at the shelter, if I can get in. I'm staying away from the guys, so no more motel rooms."

"Let me think about this," I said, having no idea what I was going to think about. I reached for my handbag. "Here, be good to yourself and that baby. Have a good lunch, Sylvia. Something nutritious," I said, passing her a twenty-dollar bill.

"Maddie, no. That's way too much."

I pressed the bill into her hand. "Take it, please. Consider it a gift for my future niece or nephew."

She looked at me gratefully and I saw the tears in her eyes. "Thanks, Maddie. You're the best.

* * *

No doubt about it, spring in Washington was a riot of color. Everywhere I looked I saw the pale pink cherry blossoms. Their scent lingered in the air as a floral perfume. Being early for lunch with Mark allowed me to stroll along and savor the April day. My mind wandered to the encounter Mark and I had had with Robbie. I still had no details on what it was all about. Mark was evasive on the subject so I didn't pressure him. *He* wasn't quite sure what was involved, but he knew I'd listen if he chose to share it with me.

Mark was seated at a table for two at the back of Alberto's. His face lit up when he saw me walking toward him and his smile made me feel good inside. I had to admit it. I was definitely attracted to this man.

"I'm sorry you had to wait. Sylvia dropped by the apartment."

Mark's smile broadened. "No problem. I finished up at the clinic a little early. How's Sylvia?"

Sitting down, I took a deep breath, deciding to share the news with Mark. "She's pregnant. Pretty upset about it and needed somebody to talk to."

Mark shook his head. "Shit, just what she doesn't need. Is she keeping it?"

I nodded. "That's the one thing she's sure about. She doesn't know why, but yes, she's keeping it. I'm not sure if that's good or bad, but it's certainly not up to me."

"I understand what you're saying. Where's the poor kid living? Still on the streets pregnant?"

"I'm afraid so," I said. "She tries to get into the shelter when there's room, but if not, she spends the night on the street."

Mark paused for a few minutes before speaking again. "This is probably none of my business, but I know how you care for Sylvia. Maybe we could find a spot for her at our apartment, if you think it's a good idea."

Overwhelmed with his generosity, I wasn't sure how to respond, but had hoped that perhaps Mark would suggest something like this. "Are you serious? You wouldn't mind? She couldn't afford to contribute to the rent or anything, Mark."

"I know that. We're doing okay financially. You and I split the costs and so far it's working. What's one more mouth to feed? Well, technically two."

He grinned at me and I felt my heart turn over. "This would be great, Mark. I hated the thought of her on the street all alone. The poor kid has no family. Nobody to look out for her."

"So we'll be her family. How do you feel about sharing your room with her? We could pick up another twin bed at the thrift shop. Or I suppose she could bunk out on the sofa."

"I have plenty of room for another twin bed. No problem.

God, she's gonna be thrilled when we tell her. Maybe we can tell her together and try to find her after lunch."

"Sounds good to me."

"Mark, I have something else to tell you." His face became alert at the serious tone in my voice as he waited for me to continue. "About that night after the lovely dinner you cooked for us. I need to explain why I pulled away from you. I need you to know it wasn't you. It was me." I suddenly seemed at a loss for words and wasn't sure how to explain it to him.

Reaching into my handbag, I passed the lab slip to him. "I hope this will explain my caution. Pulling away from you certainly wasn't from lack of desire."

Mark read the lab report carefully, then looked up at me with a tender expression on his face. "You got tested because of me? You needed to be sure you didn't test positive for HIV before we made love?"

I nodded. "Yeah, I did. I needed to protect you so I couldn't take a chance without knowing for sure."

"You're a pretty special person, Maddie Chapelle. Do you know that?"

CHAPTER 14

Charles Lester carried a folder into the expansive office, going directly to Witton's desk.

"That was fast, Charles," Richard Witton said, not looking up.

"I've been giving this situation all of my attention, sir."

Witton counted on Lester for many things in the business, but nothing was as important as the moral obligation. Looking up after forcing an uncomfortable wait on Lester, Witton opened the folder and scanned it. He prided himself on being a quick reader, comparing his ability to John F. Kennedy.

The decision to be made was easy. The Surgeon General of the United States was planning to desert the right wing of Congress and the President's administration by instituting procedures to make abortion easier to obtain in federally funded facilities. Since there were few hospitals and clinics that weren't dependent on some federal funds, the procedures would be far reaching.

Witton pondered the impact for a moment. "This will set the movement back quite a few years after the gains that have been made. Does anyone know why Admiral Brown is making such a stupid move?"

"Only that he's had a change of heart, being dead set on standing up for his version of women's rights," Lester said.

"Have our people talked to him?"

"Yes, sir, but he's determined, so I'm told. Do you want me to review his procedural changes with you?"

"Is it a move toward the abortion crowd?"

Witton's question was rhetorical, but Lester answered anyway. "Yes, sir."

"That's all I need to know. Who should receive the assignment?"

"There are two music lovers available. Either will be competent."

"Suggest one, please," Witton said, annoyed at Lester's lack of initiative.

"Mozart will be close and has been superb before."

"Fine, call the board together tonight. Seven thirty."

Charles Lester smiled, walking away from the desk. His eyes sparkled with pride in what he was doing for the good of the greater society. No ordinary person would ever know or understand his critical role in the International Holding Company, but his masters would know.

* * *

Maddie's concern for my health told me more about her than health issues. I thought she was pushing me away that night, but she was acting to bring us closer. My instincts were good and I was doing the right thing, because Maddie was as special as my soul thought she was.

Knowing more about Maddie's feelings brought me greater responsibility. Talking with Robbie the other day opened up the subject of my disappearances again. While I had told Maddie about blacking out and losing my memory, there were things not said. My dreams were as real as life, but I didn't understand their significance. How could I explain what I didn't understand? As Maddie learned to trust me, would I be able to trust myself? Talking with Robbie was a breakthrough for my own knowledge, but I needed to ask him many questions. I called his dispatcher late that evening.

"Robbie isn't on the job. Christ knows where he is. How about another taxi? They're all the same, buddy," the dispatcher said.

"No, I want Robbie. It's a special run and he could use the

money. Thanks anyway."

* * *

Sylvia and Maddie were busy setting up the room to accommodate both of them. The twin bed from the thrift store was the perfect solution to Sylvia's housing needs, and they seemed to be enjoying making the room homier.

I didn't lie telling Maddie that I was going to talk to Robbie, but had no idea where he might be. Taking the subway got me close to the address on his business card. Once there, I rang his doorbell many times before giving up. The neighborhood wasn't sterling, but there were worse in Washington. I sat on the steps of the building where I could see his taxi parked across the street.

Without a book to read, I watched the people passing by. Many were startled when they came abreast of me in the dark, realizing I was looking at them. I got a strange feeling—making people uncomfortable just by being there. If I were walking by, I'd be wary as well. We all have our demons to fight and conquer. The lucky ones conquer; others hope to survive with a lot of fear in their hearts.

My patience was rewarded. After about an hour, Robbie came walking at a fast pace around the corner. He crossed the street, heading to his taxi. Fumbling with the lock, he angrily slammed his hand to the door. Robbie sat in the driver's seat, placing his head on the steering wheel. He didn't move for many minutes, but then his head slammed back to the headrest. Something was very wrong.

Robbie was an old friend, but I knew him when we were just kids. I wasn't sure there was a connection between us any more. My steps were hesitant as I walked to the passenger side of the taxi and knocked on the window. The big man jumped; his eyes opened wide.

"It's Mark. Are you all right?"

Robbie ran his hand through his hair, adjusting his jacket before he clicked the lock switch.

"Can you talk for a minute?" I asked, looking for a way to ease into the cab.

"Sure, but why the hell are you here?"

"I came to talk. You didn't answer your phone, even your dispatcher had no idea where you were. You didn't report for duty, he said." I sat on the passenger seat filled with papers and fast food napkins.

"What time is it?"

"Just eleven."

Robbie looked tired, perhaps troubled by my visit. "What day?"

"Monday." For the first time since our conversation in his taxi a few days ago, I felt chills caused by memories of not knowing where I was or what days had passed. "Are you okay?"

"Sure."

"Where have you been that's shaken you so?" I touched his shoulder remembering a lecture in medical school about the closeness of friendly touching.

"I have no idea."

"You heard the music?"

"It must have been this afternoon when I heard it. I woke in the train station a little while ago. Woke? That's a laugh. I haven't been sleep walking or asleep, but I woke up. God, Mark, this scares me. Maybe I should go to a shrink."

"You have something on your shirt," I said, when I noticed a dark red stain covering his lower chest.

Robbie reacted by touching the spot with his open hand. "Christ, it's blood, I think," he said, staring at his outstretched palm.

Leaning toward him, the distinctive color and stickiness of blood became apparent. "Are you injured?"

He opened his shirt, pulling up his tee shirt. There were no injuries. At that instant, he realized he was touching someone else's blood. His face squeezed up and wrinkled in driven stress. Eyes betrayed a fear that caused him to breathe in gasps. "Mark, where was I? What happened? What did I do?"

"Nothing. There has to be a simple answer, but let's get that shirt off and clean you up. Can we go upstairs to your apartment?"

The tension in his face was stark as his legs reluctantly mounted the stairs. I took his key to let us into the apartment. His eyes seemed glassy.

"Don't sit down. The blood might get on something. Take your shirts off and put them in a plastic bag. I'll take it to your trash can and you get a shower." In Robbie's state, he needed someone to tell him what to do.

"If I did something wrong, you'll be an accomplice."

"You didn't do anything wrong; someone wronged you. We'll sort this out. Now get cleaned up, will you?"

Rather than put the bloody clothes in the trashcans next to the garages, I wrapped them in newspaper and lit them, watching them burn almost completely leaving an odor that began to turn my stomach. Then I placed the few scraps in the emptiest can before going upstairs.

Robbie was changed and looked a bit more settled sitting at the kitchen table. "Thanks for your support, doc."

"No sweat. You feeling better?" I sat too, trying to smile.

"Yeah. How come you're here tonight?" There were tears in his eyes, but he managed to keep them from falling.

"I wanted to talk more about the orphanage and your dreams . . . and mine."

"You have dreams about an operation, too?" His hyper hand movements started again.

"Yes and I have a vasectomy scar on my scrotum. They sterilized me as well."

"Christ, what in the name of God did they do that for?" The man was losing his composure again. Tears meandered down his face.

"I wish I knew. Can you tell me anything about tonight? Do you have anything in your pockets that might give us a clue to where you were?"

Robbie searched his pants pockets, producing a subway ticket. He had passed through a turnstile three times. That didn't help.

"Did you have this ticket before today?"

"I always drive my cab. Why would I have a subway ticket?"

"No memory for over ten hours?" I knew he had the same experiences I'd lived with for years.

"No. Should I go to the cops?" He searched my face with his eyes, begging for a good answer.

"And tell them what?"

"I had blood on my shirt." He betrayed his emotion by shouting at me.

"You know how many people will be killed or injured tonight with the blood type on those shirts? A lot. The cops will pick some killing or mugging and charge you. You probably didn't do anything, but you'd be dead in the water without a defense."

"But there's DNA. That's better than blood typing. They'd know."

"I burned the damned shirts and hope there's not enough left for a DNA test. Robbie, you have no idea what you did or where you were. Why would you let some cop or D.A. decide for you? You need to see a doctor, a psychiatrist. Have you told your doctor about the memory gaps?"

"Sure. He doesn't know what could cause them. Wanted to send me to a neurologist, but not having a lapse for a long time, I didn't make the appointment."

Leaving Robbie became easier as he gained control of his emotions. He said he was sure we could work it out. He wasn't a bad guy, so there had to be a rational explanation. We agreed to talk tomorrow and set up an appointment for him to see me at the clinic. A thorough checkup seemed to be in order.

* * *

The old, small screen TV that we had in the apartment was blaring as I woke. I was pissed because I had at least an hour left to sleep.

"Hey, you guys, what's going on?" I yelled out my bedroom door.

Maddie held a tissue to catch the tears rolling down her face.

"The Surgeon General was mugged last night. They got his wallet, rings, and gold watch. Someone stabbed him twice, and they even killed his dog." Sylvia said, in her childlike way.

I walked into the small living room. "Did you know him, Maddie? Why are you taking it so hard?"

"The police found a man in his taxicab this morning. He shot himself through the mouth. His name was . . . Robert Mozart. I'm so sorry, Mark."

With tears streaming and her breath coming in gulps, Maddie held me tightly as I tried to grasp what she had said. Robbie was a good man. He would never have done anything as wrong as murdering a person.

CHAPTER 15

Meeting Robbie and seeing him in personal, haunting misery changed my life. He also made my budding relationship with Maddie suspect. Telling Maddie about the blood on his clothing, then his suicide, laid *my* life open. For the first time, I didn't know myself, and she certainly didn't know me. Even with the horrors of my blank spells, why would I think I'd been involved in any wrongdoing? The thought never crossed my mind, but if Robbie was so torn as to take his own life, there was good reason for me to worry. Knowing myself wasn't enough anymore. I had to know about someone else, if Robbie's death was to mean anything. There were too many similarities between Robbie and me to ignore the possibilities. Maddie was a special worry. What must she think of me?

After working on various subjects for my presentation to the senate committee, I was tired and hungry. Coming out of my bedroom, I watched Sylvia heading to bed. She wasn't keen on working the johns since she became pregnant. The responsibility for her prenatal health was mine, but I always insisted that she come into the clinic for any consultation. Seeing her going to bed early made me feel good.

Maddie started reading in the weak light of the old floor lamp where she was just settling into a comfortable position. Looking at her was a pleasure for me; I stared at her until the energy of my eyes caused her to look up.

"You truly have a way with that girl, Maddie. She respects you and needs your counsel."

"Sylvia has come to rely on you, too. Don't you know how kind you've been to her?" She smiled in a way that melted me like ice in August dog days.

"I'm only her doctor. There's nothing I've done that she shouldn't expect from any other doctor."

"Any good doctor."

"Thank you. It's been a while since someone told me I was good at anything," I said, still smiling at her compliment. "Can we talk for a minute or are you talked out after Sylvia?"

"Did you eat?" she asked, without answering my question.

Searching her face for a clue to her motive, I said, "No, I've been busy writing. I'm meeting the senator's staff tomorrow. Barton said they want to get to know me. If you're hungry, we can walk down to the café."

"Can we just stay here? A sandwich will do me. How about you? We have some nice wine, too. I could use a glass, then we can talk."

I watched her prepare the sandwiches. Maddie was so feminine, with her hands moving in a gentle way. Fingers displayed their tactile strength by barely touching a sandwich as she cut it in half. She smiled at me.

"What? Why are you looking at me like that? Where's my wine?" My gaze embarrassed her.

"I've already poured it. You make me feel good looking at you. No intention to make you uncomfortable." As I uttered the words, I realized her discomfort was about me and my situation. Maybe the whole mess created a wall between us, because she really knew little about me. She didn't want to talk about it.

We sat at the small kitchen table with paper wadded up under the leg to hold it steady. For a few minutes, we ate silently until I raised my glass to make a toast. "To our friendship."

"Cheers." Maddie lowered her eyes to avoid mine.

"This is difficult for both of us, but please hear me out."

"Is it about Robbie?" She took my hands, surrounding my wine glass.

"Robbie and me." I thought she knew the connection I felt

with Robbie, but couldn't be sure the bloody violence of his life and death hadn't branded me in her eyes.

She seemed to read my mind. "You must know I'm not afraid to stay here, Mark. Otherwise, you'd be alone in this apartment. I'm not great at handling fear. Remember, I run."

"There's plenty of reason to run from me. Thanks for at least staying until this chance to try to tell you what I believe."

"Tell me about the orphan's home."

I nodded, pausing to be sure my thoughts were straight. "There isn't much to tell. Robbie and I were part of a group of boys who were treated differently. We didn't get to play ball or join athletic teams. I had a tutor. The guy told me what my IQ was, but I wasn't impressed at the time. I'd be more impressed finding that out now. Pretty high. There's a theory that the line between genius and being a mental case is thin, indeed."

"Are you considered a genius?"

"No, but I belong to Mensa, so you know my IQ is high. Anyway, our group of about ten kids was more studied and disciplined. My dream about an operation and Robbie's recollection being so similar means, to me, that we were surgically changed. We were both sterilized. Why?"

"Maybe the custodians of the home thought orphans are less . . . somehow."

"Maddie, these same people picked smart kids, had them tutored, and educated us at the best schools. I graduated from Rutgers, number one in my class. That doesn't seem as if they intended to restrict our seed because we were less than other people. This isn't about discrimination or personal rights. There are no similarities to the sterilization of mental patients or slow learners of seventy-five years ago. We weren't being weeded out of society, we were being groomed, but for what?"

Maddie shook her head probably not understanding how specialized training and permanent birth control could make sense.

"How about the music?"

"What about it?"

"I've heard of people going to the dentist to have a tooth

filled, then hearing a radio station in their head. But that occurred constantly, until they did something to the teeth again. How do they put music into your head? And who are *they*?" Maddie asked with a pained expression.

"The same questions are in my mind. When I realized that the music was related to my absences, I thought I was being hypnotized, or had been a long time ago, and was reacting to some preset condition."

"Could that be true?" She took my hand again, pressing it hard to relieve her own stress about my hypnotic response.

"Yes, I think so. There's a memory of one time when my tutor, Mr. . . . I can't think of his name . . . hypnotized me with a large gold coin on a chain."

"Only one time?"

"Perhaps, that one time, he didn't tell me to forget being hypnotized. That's the way they do it in nightclub shows. The hypnotist always says that you'll not remember any of this when you wake up. I just don't know, but I was under a spell at least once. Besides that, there's a dream that drives me crazy a couple times a month. A large coin swings before my face and it frightens the hell out of me. It's as if the damned thing could harm me. I see blood dripping from it."

"Was Robbie doing something very wrong? Is that why he committed suicide?" Maddie's voice was raised an octave.

"I don't know, but the blood on his clothes worries me. Every night there are muggings, robberies, and murders in Washington. He could have been helping someone who was hurt at the hands of a criminal or at the scene of an accident. I told Robbie not to go to the police."

Maddie got up from the table and began to pace. She watched me as I continued.

"The cops would find some crime to match his period of absence and he couldn't defend himself. It would be like saying to society, here convict me of something. But what if Robbie killed someone? What if I left surgery years ago and killed someone? Where did I go when Garret threatened you?"

"Maybe a doctor can help. A shrink." Maddie moved behind my chair and placed her hands on my shoulders to comfort me, but didn't respond. She started walking again.

Shaking my head, I said, "At least it's a place to start, but did you ever hear of a shrink who treats the indigent?"

"You're not a street person any more. You have an address, Mark." She stopped pacing to watch my response.

"Not much money, though. This mess is contrived enough that I might be able to find someone who'd give me treatment as a professional courtesy."

Maddie came close to me, kissing my cheek. I wanted to take her in my arms, but knew her fear was an impediment I had to deal with first. "It's a good thing you had second thoughts the night I tried to seduce you," I said, feeling sorry for myself.

"No, Mark, I made a mistake, but I can make up for it."

"Maddie, will you do something for me? Something difficult?"

"Tell me."

"Follow me the next time I hear the music."

* * *

The taxi stopped in front of the Senate office building. Just as Barton James had predicted, a press photographer took a few clicks and another camera whirred at me. I smiled, trying to look the part.

The small room, decorated in modern mahogany-accented walls, contained a large wooden table with many faces looking at me. The staff turned out to be four men and three women, ages about thirty to fifty. I was seated opposite all of them, something similar to what the arrangement would be in the senate committee room. Barton came in last to begin the session.

"Welcome, Dr. Puccini. We're pleased you could find the time to let us get to know you," James said. He didn't shake my hand or make the session personal in any way.

"My friend said you'd be grilling me."

"Of course not," James said, but before the words were out

of his mouth, the youngest woman spoke.

"Were you actually living on the street?" she asked.

"Yes, for about four years."

The room intrigued me. Expense and power were illustrated everywhere starting with the solid mahogany. The table, too, was made of the same solid wood, not a cheap veneer. The place rivaled the excess of a lawyer's office.

The staff eyed me like I was a specimen on show at a circus. The smirks pissed me off from the first words the young woman spoke.

"How does a doctor end up on the streets of Washington of all places?" She twirled her glasses making me think she took the whole situation very lightly.

"The luck of the draw."

"Why should the committee members believe anything you have to say about the medical needs of the indigent?" the oldest man asked.

"And the working poor, as well. I've been there and I know what causes people to become detached from the health care system in this country."

"Dr. Puccini, you were going to talk about other improvements we could offer the committee," James said. He leaned toward the people on either side and whispered in their ears.

"In addition to volunteer personnel in free clinics, the idea should be extended to cover all government programs. For example, a doctor could volunteer his time given to a Medicare patient or a Medicaid person. He'd also gain value toward his student loan. I see no reason why the same couldn't be done in any clinic where a person or family couldn't afford the costs of the treatment."

"Such as in a general or county hospital?" James asked.

"Exactly. The idea is two-fold. First, use the accumulated loans as a trade for service to the poor or uninsured working poor. Secondly, never establish a new program. The organizational costs of new programs make them prohibitive in many cases. By extending the demographic base of eligibility, a greater segment of the needy can be accommodated. The Children's Health Insurance Program is a good example. By extending support to the single mothers of the entitled children, we cover a broader base of genuine need; then single fathers. Giving prenatal care to a child in the womb will also allow care for the mother in need and help the lifelong health of the child."

"But that's an attack on the right to choose," a red-haired woman said.

Not being introduced to each person was taking a toll on my effectiveness to make points. My frustration was beginning to show as I glared at her, feeling the pressure of the inquisition. "Madam . . ."

"Evelyn Rosen," she said, smiling for the first time.

"Ms. Rosen, I'm not a political person. These are suggestions to improve care without building new bureaucracies. You'll have to decide what's politically prudent."

She nodded probably thinking I was a political neophyte. How true.

"Any other thoughts, Mark?" James asked.

"Set up pharmacies in poor neighborhoods. Staff them with volunteers. The government would purchase all the drugs distributed. Use an existing agency as the buyer—never set up a new agency. The Veteran's Administration, for example, could be the purchasing agent for the volunteer pharmacies."

Discussions went on for five hours. Subjects moved from substantive to my personal life many times. Did I have a drug habit? Was I married? Properly licensed? Had I ever been arrested? And on and on. I answered all questions honestly, even the embarrassing ones.

Finally, all the questions were answered and the session adjourned. Barton James came over to shake my hand. "You did a great job, Mark. Now these smart people are going to finish writing a script for you to deliver to the committee. If there's anything you don't like, we can talk and change it. We just want to make it easier for you since you have a free clinic to run."

Walking out of the building, I felt that I was going to accomplish something for the first time in my life. Nothing would keep me from testifying before the committee because helping to pass the bill would truly do some good. I also had to meet Senator Pope to gain his confidence. Passing this health bill had become a crusade for a poor street doctor.

CHAPTER 16

A solitary woman sitting at the bar glanced up when the tall, good-looking man entered the room. He looked vaguely familiar—probably either a politician or news anchor. The bar at the Ritz in Boston was a frequent venue for after-hour business meetings. She resumed staring into her martini. The man stood for a minute to allow his eyes time to adjust in the dimness of the room before heading to a table in the rear corner. Extending his hand to the man who stood, he forced a smile.

"I'm sorry I'm running a bit late," he said, with apology absent from his voice, "Friday evening traffic in Boston is murder."

"No problem," the man replied, sitting back down. "You always make it worth my while to wait for you, Senator."

Bryce Pope dispensed with the mutual fake attempt at geniality as he signaled for the waiter. "Chivas Regal on the rocks," he told him. Lighting a cigarette, he stared at the man across the table as blue smoke spiraled between them.

"Thought you gave those things up," the man said.

"And I thought you said you'd stay away from Washington. I'm hearing rumors you were seen there recently," said Bryce. "What brought you to our illustrious capital?"

Surprise registered on the man's face. "You do have your connections, don't you?"

"You ought to know that better than most people. Answer my question."

"I was looking for somebody. Heard they might be in the area."

Bryce passed his credit card to the waiter, as the drink was placed in front of him. "Did you find the person you were looking for?"

"Nah, no luck. Mighta been a false lead."

The senator took a couple of quick gulps of Scotch. "Make sure it was. I better not hear about you slithering around Washington again. Stay in Boston where you belong. Understand?"

The look on the man's face indicated assent and he nodded as the waiter returned for Bryce's signature.

"Have you got the package?" A bag with a Barnes and Noble logo was passed across the table. Bryce reached for it, then removed three hard cover books—French classics. Nodding, he reached inside his suit jacket, passing the man a thick white envelope. The man took it, flipped open his briefcase, and placed it inside.

Standing up to leave, the senator said, "Don't forget, Dawson. Stay put in Bean Town."

Garret Dawson's grin evolved into a smirk. "You don't need to worry about that, Senator. I never screw up a good deal. See ya in three months—same time, same place."

* * *

With the preparation complete, I placed the casserole dish on the counter. The clock above the table read 6:05. Sylvia had left for her classes at the local high school and Mark was due home from the clinic any minute. Walking into the living room, Bob Seger's voice greeted me on the small stereo with the lyrics *Like A Rock*. Hearing the downstairs front door close, I smiled. Funny how easy it is to get accustomed to comfortable sounds. Mark was home.

"Hey there," he said, smiling at me. "I like your choice in music."

My smile matched his. "Would you like some wine before dinner?" Then I noticed a bag he was carrying. "Oh, did you bring some home?"

Mark reached into the bag, removing a small bottle of cognac.

"Actually, I brought a little something for after dinner. The wine sounds great. Just let me jump in the shower and I'll be back in no time."

"I'll get dinner in the oven now. Perfect timing," I said, heading into the kitchen. After placing the casserole into the pre-heated oven, I searched through the drawers for a corkscrew, a smile forming on my face. The cabernet I'd purchased earlier was a far cry from the cheap twist cap wine I had consumed on the street. Drinking then had been a means of forgetting—a good bottle of wine was now the social experience I'd previously enjoyed. Living on the streets morphed a human being into ways most of society didn't understand.

Mark returned to the living room wearing a fresh pair of jeans and sweatshirt. Sitting beside me on the sofa, he lifted his wineglass, inquiring how my day off had been.

"It was good. I got the housecleaning done. Did some laundry. Spent some time helping Sylvia with a homework assignment and even managed to squeeze in some reading on a novel I picked up at the library. How was your day?"

"Busy. It's amazing how many people need our services at the clinic. I hope Senator Pope will be able to do something to remedy the situation."

"I know. Well, as much as I can't stand the guy, I have to say if anyone has enough clout to get that bill through, Bryce does."

"What's his background, Maddie? Did he come from money himself?"

"No, far from it. His father died when he was a child. The mother had no education or training and raised her only son in the projects in Boston. But she was determined he'd have better. He was brilliant in school, which earned him a scholarship to Harvard. He became an attorney with a top law firm in Boston and ended up marrying the senior partner's daughter. This is where all the money came from. The rumor was that daddy had been the major campaign contributor that helped get Bryce elected."

"Really? Interesting. What's the wife like? You've met her, haven't you?"

I nodded. "Oh, yeah, many times at various events. At Christmas, they'd host an elegant dinner at their home in Beacon Hill. Lila Pope is one sad, lonely woman. I always felt bad for her. She's exceptionally beautiful, almost in a classic sort of way. But obviously, it was never enough for Bryce. She's well educated, stunning to look at, but you can see the emptiness in her face. Rumor had it that she had a bit of a drinking problem. I remember she disappeared for a few months and Bryce said she was on an extended holiday in Europe. But the office was buzzing that she was probably in some fancy rehab facility."

Mark shook his head. "What a shame. His professional background is well regarded. Too bad his personal life wasn't on the same level. With his rough beginning, I can see why he's so intent on getting this bill passed for health care."

"And I have no doubt that he will. Dinner's just about ready. Hungry?"

"Starved," Mark said, following me into the kitchen.

Swirling the amber liquid in my glass, I was enjoying the after-effects of a good meal, pleasant company, and Mark beside me on the sofa.

"I haven't seen much of Sylvia these days. It's hard to believe she's been with us a month already. How's her night school coming along?" he asked.

"Very well. I think she surprised herself with how well she's doing. The poor kid never had anyone who cared enough to encourage her. She's also taking a typing class three days a week, so I don't see much of her either. I guess she really likes it though and is leaning toward taking some business courses."

"That's great," Mark said, as he moved a bit closer to me. "Business colleges have excellent placement programs, and in Washington, she could end up with a very lucrative position. What time is she due home tonight?"

"Later than usual, probably around 11:00. She's met a nice fellow in her class who invited her out for coffee after school tonight. She said Ben is in his late twenties, has been working at the university doing maintenance work, and now realizes how valuable his diploma and more education would be. Since her pregnancy will be showing in the next few weeks, she felt it was only fair to tell him about it tonight. That way she figured it would give him a chance to back away from her gracefully, if he wanted to."

"I think she might be very surprised that he probably won't," Mark said. "She's an attractive girl with a lot of potential that she's yet to discover about herself."

"You could be right. I hope so, because she's been excited about having a friend. Except for me, I'm not sure she's ever had one."

Mark placed his hand on my knee. "You're a good friend to me, Maddie. I hope you know that, but I think you also know that we've moved beyond friendship in the past few months."

I nodded. He was right. Almost from the beginning, I liked him as a friend. But now it was more. I wasn't sure what the emotion was, but I knew it had grown. His arm slipped around my shoulder, as his head bent to kiss my lips. Instantly, my desire increased and for a brief second I recalled how for the past two years, despite having sex, I had never once experienced the sweet sensation of passion.

His tongue slipped into my mouth as he pressed his body closer. Mark's desire was obvious through his jeans. Urging me back against the pillows, our kisses intensified. His hand radiated heat as it moved from my face, slipped along my shoulder, to my breasts. Emptiness of the past two years receded with the merging of our combined passion.

"Oh God, Maddie," he whispered. "I want you so much. Let me make love to you."

When I nodded, he took my hand, leading me toward his bedroom. We continued kissing, touching, searching, as he positioned his body alongside mine on the bed. I couldn't recall such a heightened awareness of my own body. The entire world slipped away as he undressed me and then himself. I was grateful when he momentarily paused to reach for a foil packet from the drawer in the night table. When Mark slid his body on top of mine, I could see his face perfectly in the dim lamplight, and reached up to trace my fingers across his lips as he entered my body. The sensation he created was surreal. Unsure if the moaning and sounds of passion were coming from me or from Mark, I heard him scream my name. Perhaps the emotions of love echoed from both of us, resulting in a powerful wave of ecstasy.

Lying in Mark's arms, I understood the definition of afterglow. All of my senses had been made love to and I felt a serenity that consumed both my soul and my body. Mark pulled the sheet snug, holding me tight. "God, Maddie. That was incredible. What an experience. I can only hope it was as good for you," he said, softly.

I snuggled deeper into his shoulder. "It was even better." He kissed my forehead and cheek. "Any chance you'd want to spend the rest of the night in here with me? Or do you think maybe it wouldn't be right with Sylvia staying here?"

I turned on my side, touching his lips with mine. "I think Sylvia would understand. I have a feeling she's seen the chemistry between us that we've failed to acknowledge. She hinted the other day that she wouldn't be concerned if she awoke to find my bed empty. She'd know I was with you. I'm just going to get a nightgown and bathrobe for the morning."

"I'll keep the bed warm while you're gone," Mark said, kissing me.

"Take my robe on the chair to go to your room so you don't have to get redressed."

Slipping into the oversized bathrobe, I looked at him stretched out on the bed. He was definitely one good-looking man. Reaching for the doorknob, I turned around. "Hey, I just realized something. How come you got the queen size bed in this apartment and I got the twin?"

"Because since we moved into this apartment, I've been hoping to share the extra space with you."

I laughed. "Touche, Dr. Puccini. No wonder you're such a brilliant doctor."

CHAPTER 17

A prestigious trail of two limousines sped through the New York streets escorted by many police. United Nations Plaza saw many such travels everyday; it was commonplace for a high official to stop traffic, causing backups. This time was no exception. Horns blared as police gave the U.N. priority. The difference was that it was eight o'clock in the evening; most U.N. people were home enjoying their luxurious American life.

Stopping at Wingate Towers, bodyguards flocked to the second car. The tall man who rose from the car had an air of royalty. He smiled at and patronized all those he passed as he swaggered through revolving doors. Reddish brown hair and bright green eyes marked his face for attention. The eyes were riveting, somehow eerie. Passersby stared after him, wondering what high position he might hold.

Bodyguards positioned themselves at the ground-level elevator door and at an exit on the thirty-second floor.

Charles Lester met the man, offering his hand, but was rebuked by the swiftly moving official.

"Sorry, sir. For the inconvenience, I mean. I know it's late," Lester said.

"You don't suspect that I maintain long hours at the U.N.?"

"Yes, sir, but . . ." Lester bowed slightly at the waist to emphasize his grievous miscalculation of an apology.

"Please."

"Yes, sir."

They entered the large, well-appointed conference room and

each of the eight seated men rose, turning toward the door. Some bowed their heads in recognition of the visitor.

"Gentlemen, permit me to introduce Ronald Esterward Owens, Deputy Secretary General of the most important organization in the world," Lester said.

"Welcome, Ron, I apologize for the inconvenience of the late hour, but there were few choices open to me."

"It's good to see you, Richard. Have you prepared the room?" Owens asked, preferring not to heap scorn on Witton's apology.

"It has been guarded since it was swept this morning. We're able to speak freely."

"Good." He approved.

Owens sat at the head of the table while Richard Witton took a seat at his right. Each of the other seven men stared, seeming to capture the moment for their memory. No one dared to speak or introduce themselves. Silence reigned as Owens rolled his eyes over each person.

Witton reviewed his notes, waiting for permission to begin. The delay was tense because Owens used time to visually survey each man, causing some to lower their gaze or wipe their brow.

"Begin, Richard."

"There are two critical subjects for your consideration. First, is the situation with Queen Christa. The court has used every means possible to dissuade Her Majesty from revising the divorce rule. She is immoveable. Sir Lionel can provide details, if you wish."

A short, stocky man dressed in dark blue pinstripe pants and a solid-colored jacket stood at attention, waiting to speak.

"Yes?" Owens said.

"The Church of England will be severely injured by this theological error. A religion in descent will lose its final hold on its member's morality. Loss of membership could be catastrophic. It's a moral decline without question and loss of control matching the sexual devastation occurring today. The Queen will not reconsider."

"How would it be done?" Owens asked, leaning back in his chair. He had total control.

"A drug could be administered that would cause seizure of her heart muscle. It would appear to be a heart defect, but there would be no trace of the stimulant."

"Who would administer the drug and by what means?"

"I would place it in Her Majesty's food myself. I have daily contact," Sir Lionel said.

"Prince Edward has a different view of the marriage law?" Owens raised his eyebrows awaiting confirmation of what he knew to be a fact.

"Yes, sir. King Edward wouldn't violate Church or membership discipline."

"Richard, proceed. We have no option here; there's a moral imperative," Owens said. "What's next?" His tone was impatient.

"One of our choir members committed suicide after he carried out an instruction. Possibly, he had some recollection of his mission or his preparation for it," Witton said.

"A shame, but that's a long paying investment. Even our men must die, so what's the issue?"

"Before his last instruction was completed, he met another choir member."

"And how would we know that?"

"The satellite positioning system placed them together, sir."

"So, it was a coincidence. They may have even spoken, but so what? Are you losing confidence in our technology and methods?"

"They met again, and I'm certain they shared information. Beethoven was traced to Mozart's home where he stayed, so Beethoven met him the night before the suicide. There's a good probability they exchanged information about our methods. We've never had choir members speak before. The risk is too great that something about their condition has changed," Witton explained. "If they violate one rule why wouldn't they be capable of other transgressions?"

"Beethoven's a good performer?"

"Yes, sir. Flawless."

"Do what you must. It's troubling that such a vast investment of money and time should be wasted, but there can be no mistakes. Whatever method you use, insure that the mechanism is removed and surgery is not visible. Is that understood?" Owens' eyes protruded, emphasizing his direct order.

"Yes, sir."

"This is the first time we've had to eliminate one of our own. Isn't that true?" Owens asked.

"That's why I asked you here, contrary to our long standing procedure, sir," Witton said.

"Well done. Do all country representatives agree with these courses of action? Did you explain to your leaders?" Owens asked, as if any man would have the courage to disagree with him, but it was all part of the control philosophy.

Each of the men nodded.

The meeting was over.

* * *

The clinic was busy and I was working as hard as when the big bucks were coming in. However, there was no fancy wife to spend my money quicker than I earned it, even though I was making only a pittance now. We were crowded all day and two staff members from Senator Pope's committee observed for a few hours. They added to the bedlam, but were able to see a no-fee clinic in operation. Surely, there were some who didn't believe it could work smoothly. Perhaps one of the staffers was surprised to see that poorer people were actually as human as he was. He seemed to have that look of superiority.

I wasn't comfortable with the occasional photos they took, but they insisted they were important to passage of the health bill. All in all, I was very tired when we arrived home past seven o'clock.

Maddie was immediately pounced upon by Sylvia, who apparently had a bad day. Although Maddie was street savvy and understood a lot about Sylvia, I had the advantage of a medical education. Despite going to school and setting goals, getting off a drug habit was very difficult, even if Sylvia was pregnant. The drugs can possess one's soul. Maddie would have to do the counseling.

I bowed out of the conversation, laying down on my bed for a few quick winks. The sound of crying woke me from a deep sleep. Cracking the door, I could see Maddie scolding the girl with a waving index finger.

"Is everything all right, ladies?"

"I'm good now—well not good, but better," Sylvia said. She laughed at her gentle joke and walked into her bedroom.

"Maddie, do you need help with something?"

"No, I'll tell you all about it though. Sylvia didn't do well today. She used all the money she had to buy hashish or some kind of pot, I'm not sure to be honest. I told her before about the danger to the baby and she promised that there were no drugs in her life. She failed her baby. I told her in no uncertain terms and probably was too hard on her."

"You couldn't have been too rough. Jesus, she knows what can happen. I'll talk to her if you want me to."

"No. She's upset and I made my point. You can save your ammunition for a time if she falls again or goes after the hard stuff, but I don't think she will. Sylvia is very impressionable and knows she did a very serious thing. Thanks, though. Want some supper? We have a good store bought pizza in the freezer. I'll do the honors."

With that, she went into the kitchen to begin preparing the meal. I read the paper, still needing some sleep. Minutes later, Sylvia was crying so loud that we both heard her through the door. Maddie was first to run into the room.

Sylvia's blood was running down her left arm from the incision made across her wrist. She was hysterical still holding a razor in her right hand. Tears were rolling down her face. Her voice was shriek and unsettled, quavering with emotion.

"You know you can quit. Why are you punishing yourself for one false step?" Maddie shouted. "Don't do this to yourself, for God's sake! Think about your baby."

"I'm only thinking of myself. There isn't a good bone in my damned body. Remember, I used to sell myself to sick slobs on the street." She slid off the bed and landed with a thump on the floor. Maddie knelt next to her rubbing the tears from her own cheeks.

"Let's treat the wound," I said, stepping between the two women. "Luckily, it isn't a deep cut. We don't need to worry about stitches. I'll do a butterfly dressing and you won't even have a scar." My words seemed to calm her.

As I was tending to the wound, Maddie held the young girl in her arms. "You're like my younger sister, Sylvia. You have no right to take that away from me." Maddie's sobs partially obscured her words.

"Are you doing anything else to cause your mood shifts?" I asked.

She shook her head. "I'm not even on uppers and downers, honest. I still get so depressed. I lose it, Mark. Can't seem to help it." She trembled at the thought that she was out of control.

"You'll be all right. Come on, let's have some pizza and talk. I've finished with your arm."

Maddie's smile made me feel very good. I liked being needed and successful at my work.

The pizza was hot, just the way it was best. In the middle of a too large bite, I heard the music. I stood.

* * *

My head was pounding. The lump on the back of my scalp throbbed. Trying to get up from the sofa, I fell back as Maddie pushed me down.

"Stay put, Mark."

"What happened? My head's killing me."

"You got that way out look in your eyes and put your jacket on. I tried to talk to you, but you wouldn't listen. Then I remembered the promise I made. My promise to you was to follow you, but I couldn't do it. Sylvia couldn't be left alone." Maddie was in tears.

"What did you do?"

"I hit you."

"With what?" My head hurt more when I spoke.

"A frying pan—a cast iron skillet. I'm so sorry, but you wouldn't stop. You were going out . . . and I had to keep you here. Do you understand?"

"No wonder my head hurts so much. How long have I been out?"

"Almost a half-hour."

"I'm glad that I didn't go into a coma. God, you're tough. Thanks. I owe you, Maddie. Thanks for keeping me here." I closed my eyes and leaned back on the sofa in an attempt to stop the throbbing pain.

"Oh, Mark, I didn't want to hurt you."

Maddie's arms were wrapped so tightly around me that I had to make an effort to breathe.

"I'm all right, but I'll never get in a fight with you. You're mean." Despite the pain in my skull, I smiled at the woman who may have saved my life by stopping me.

Finally, a smile broke out on her face, while Sylvia looked relieved for the first time.

"Remember your promise, if you can't follow me, use the frying pan again, but not so hard next time."

* * *

The High Council was forced to meet again as a result of the first system failure experienced by the organization. Mr. Owens wasn't able to attend, but his instructions were absolutely clear. Witton had little patience as he reviewed the technical aspects of the failure. The satellite positioning system locator was operating normally, but Beethoven didn't answer the musical call. There were several possibilities. The circuit could have been malfunctioning and may be useless in the future. Interference could have temporarily caused the music to be lost or distorted beyond the point of recognition. The subject could have been incapacitated. Lastly, the scientist explained that the controlling mental powers built up over time could have somehow been overcome by the subject.

Witton found no comfort in any of the possibilities, unless Beethoven was dead. He looked to Charles Lester.

"What about the article?"

"It was in the *Washington Journal*, complete with photos of Dr. Puccini working with the disenfranchised at the clinic."

"And why should I worry about this?"

"The good doctor will be appearing before Senator Pope's Health, Education and Welfare Committee."

"Good God. What for?" Witton's calm demeanor cracked in a moment of surprise.

"He'll be supporting a bill to expand health care for the uninsured and indigent."

"I always thought he was too damned smart to fully trust. The chance of coming out of his role and exposing the program is too high, so we must act soon. When is the committee appearance?"

"Not scheduled, according to the *Journal.*"

"Well, find out. There can be no slipup here. Beethoven's a critical risk. We must retrieve the apparatus, but he can't be killed in any situation where there will be an autopsy. Do you understand?" Witton drilled the words toward Lester, causing the little man to step back.

"Yes, sir, but I'm thinking that killing him, given his prominence, will bring undue attention to our organization, however we do it," Lester said. "It could open a window on the entire situation. Perhaps establish a connection to the Queen—somehow." He took a deep breath after having the nerve to disagree.

Witton considered his aid's advice and impertinence before issuing revised orders. "The first priority is retrieving the apparatus. Second is eliminating him without connection to the organization. It's better to let him live if we could totally block his mind. I'm not sure we can eliminate him cleanly. Understand? I'll clear it with Owens, but you get right on it."

CHAPTER 18

I glanced out the window at the Victorian structure that stood beside others lining the street, while Ben maneuvered the car away from the curb into the Georgetown traffic. A serious look on his face told me how difficult the past two hours had been for him. I liked Ben. No doubt he was very fond of Sylvia, wanting only the best for her—even if the best didn't include him. We both remained silent, lost in our thoughts. I felt hopeful with a tinge of apprehension.

Following the terrible fight with Sylvia the week before, it became apparent that she needed professional help to kick her drug habit. When she moved in, she had tried to convince Mark and me that she wanted to be clean and wouldn't do anything to jeopardize her baby. But she had. At least she was wise enough not to say, "It was *only* a joint I smoked."

* * *

When I came out of Mark's room the following morning, Sylvia was gone, but her bed had been slept in. I felt a surge of relief when I saw her backpack was missing from the hook in the kitchen and her breakfast dishes had been rinsed. Despite the fight the night before, she was at her typing class.

The clinic was exceptionally busy that day, leaving little time for Mark and me to discuss Sylvia or what might be done. I arrived home from the clinic at 5:30 to find Sylvia at the living room desk practicing her typing. Still angry from the encounter, I nodded on the way to the kitchen to begin preparing supper.

A few minutes later, Sylvia came in and reached for her backpack. "I'm sorry," she said, softly. "I'm really sorry, Maddie. I'll be home from my classes by ten." I heard the door close behind her.

* * *

Ben broke into my thoughts. "Where should I drop you off, Maddie? Are you going back to the clinic?"

"No, I have the rest of the afternoon off. Could you drop me at the coffee shop down the street from the clinic?"

"Sure, no problem," he said. "She's going to be fine, you know. I think she's a lot stronger than she even realizes."

"I hope you're right, Ben. Because she's going to need a hell of a lot of strength to get through the next year."

He nodded and we resumed our silence.

* * *

I took a sip of the hot, dark liquid. Funny how coffee can restore me in a way no other beverage can. The coffee shop was deserted. As I sat in a rear booth, my thoughts wandered to Sylvia.

I wanted nothing more than to see her succeed—because of Mark's help, she just might. He had been instrumental in getting her placed at a private rehab facility in Georgetown. Sylvia's name had been added to the waiting list, but Mark had no qualms about pulling a few strings by drawing on professional courtesy to speak directly with the administrator.

Grace's Retreat operated with a very unique concept. Open for twenty years, it had been the idea of Dr. Gray Norton. He purchased the sprawling Victorian structure with a determined vision in mind. The home would be a place of residence for pregnant females addicted to drugs. His lucrative practice enabled him to get the project off the ground. Within months, colleagues in the community volunteered financially. Various fundraisers over the years and continuous donations kept the project growing. After a complete renovation of the three-floor structure, *Grace's Retreat* opened its doors to the first resident—Grace Norton, Dr. Norton's sixteen year old, drug addicted and pregnant daughter.

The small staff of twenty years ago had grown to include RNs, drug counselors, social workers and volunteer lay people who offered various services. Grace Norton-Oxford held the position of administrator and psychologist. Recovering from her drug addiction, she gave birth to a healthy daughter, acquired her high school diploma, and graduated from Boston College with a PhD. in psychology. When Melinda was nine years old, Grace married Neil Oxford, obstetrician on staff at *Grace's Retreat*.

The facility admitted a mixture of girls from wealthy families as well as street addicts, without discrimination. However, the exceptionally stringent rules and regulations were discussed with the girl before admission, followed by a signed contract. The girl must be pregnant and have a willingness to conquer her drug addiction. She must agree to attend classes toward her high school diploma, if she didn't possess one. Participation in parenting classes was listed on the contract as mandatory. And the final agreement was that after the girl became drug free and gave birth, she must in some way give back to the facility for five years. Volunteering as receptionist, cooking, working in the laundry, or doing household chores for a minimum of eight hours a week. Over twenty years, many of the girls went on to further education, returning in the capacity of nurses, social workers, and drug counselors. The success rate of girls who stayed at *Grace's Retreat* was impressive, and each year more names were added to the invitations sent out for fundraisers.

I took a bite of the apple pie I had ordered and glanced at my watch. No wonder I was hungry—past three and I had skipped lunch. After interviewing Sylvia the day before, Grace explained to Mark and me that she would be accepted and we were to have her there today at eleven. Grace also explained that we wouldn't be able to visit Sylvia for the first four weeks of her six-week stay.

She would be allowed to telephone us one evening a week during the first four weeks. We could drop off personal items, candy, magazines and little gifts for her, but no visiting was permitted. When Grace found out that Ben had offered to drive us to the facility and that he was a friend of Sylvia's, she explained it was important to speak with him also. Anyone involved with Sylvia's life needed to understand what a difficult task lay ahead for her. Positive encouragement was needed from everyone in contact with Sylvia.

I signaled to the waitress for another cup of coffee, recalling our arrival at Grace's Retreat earlier that morning. Stepping into the foyer of the Victorian brownstone with Sylvia and Ben beside me, I heard the soft strains of a Mozart symphony coming from a large sitting area to my right. A few girls sat on sofas and club chairs reading as music from the stereo filled the room.

A young girl sitting behind the polished oak desk looked up and smiled as we walked toward her. Her smile widened as she said, "Hi, I'm Eileen. You must be Sylvia. Welcome to *Grace's Retreat*. I'll let Ms. Norton-Oxford know you're here."

Sylvia visibly relaxed as the girl's friendliness touched her. When Eileen replaced the phone, I glanced down to the side of her desk and was surprised to see an infant sleeping in a carrier next to her. She caught my look and laughed.

"This is my son, Aaron. He's four months old. It's nice that we can bring our babies with us when we return to work our hours here."

I saw Sylvia lean over the desk for a better look, but she remained silent. "He's gorgeous," I said, with truthfulness. "And looks like a good baby."

"Oh, he is," Eileen bragged. "Aaron's been sleeping through the night since he was three weeks old."

Grace's heels echoed down the corridor as she approached the three of us with a warm smile and handshake. Then she leaned over to peek at the sleeping baby. "Gosh, you should be proud of him, Eileen. My Melinda never slept as well as Aaron does." The compliment radiated Eileen's face.

Grace asked Ben to wait in her office while she escorted Sylvia and me upstairs to her room. Without conversation, we walked along a thickly carpeted hallway. Each closed door had a creative nameplate attached—oval shaped wood with the girl's name painted in bright colors. Surrounding each name were various items, also painted, according to each girl's hobby or interest. I saw a piano, ballet slippers, a book, an ice cream cone, and a rose before we came to Sylvia's room at the end of the hall.

"Once you decide what you'd like on your plaque, we'll have it painted for you," Grace explained. "One of our former residents, Cathy, is an artist who does all the lovely artwork."

Stepping through the doorway, two things surprised me. The room was larger than I had imagined it would be—comprised of a twin bed, bureau, desk, and a cushioned loveseat placed in an alcove, with windows behind. The other surprise was the obviously very pregnant girl sitting there. She got up as quickly as her bulk would allow, smiling at Sylvia.

"Hi, I'm Vanessa," she said, her voice filled with pleasure. "I'm going to help you get settled in."

Sylvia smiled, but had a bewildered look on her face.

"We have a sort of buddy system here," Grace said. "The last two weeks of each girl's stay is spent helping a new resident learn the ropes. Today Vanessa will take you around the house, show you where things are, introduce you to the other girls, and answer any questions you might have. And for the next two weeks, she'll be available to continue helping you. Your next two weeks, Sylvia, will be spent with you learning to be independent. Nobody will remind you to set your alarm for school, nobody making sure you attend the parenting class, and nobody checking to see if you've completed your required chores for the week. Your final two weeks will be spent giving back to another new resident."

Sylvia smiled, nodding at Grace and Vanessa. "I understand."

"I'm going to take Maddie back to my office now," Grace said. "So we'll give you a few minutes to say your goodbyes. Vanessa and I will be right outside."

I watched them close the door softly as tears stung my eyes.

Oh, great, Maddie. You're supposed to be the strong one here. I took a deep breath, pulling Sylvia into my arms. We clung to each other for a few moments, then I held her away from me, while looking at her face. God, she was so young with so much ahead of her. I saw the moisture in her eyes and forced a smile.

"You're going to do wonderful here, Sylvia. I'm going to miss you around the apartment, but I want you to work harder than you ever worked before. Do you understand me? I'm so proud of you for taking all the steps you have. You are one very brave and strong girl. Do you realize this?"

She nodded, moving into my arms again. "I love you, Maddie. Thank you for everything. Will you tell Mark I said thank you, too?" she whispered into my ear. "I'm going to choose Wednesday evenings to call you guys, because I want to be able to speak to Mark too, the one night I can call."

I moved out of her embrace and said, "I love you too, Sylvia, and will definitely tell Mark what you said. We'll be waiting for your phone call Wednesday evening."

As Grace and I walked back to her office, she explained she'd like me to stay when she spoke to Ben. She felt he might need someone to talk to during the next six weeks who loved Sylvia and could share what was going on. Grace explained to Ben about the rules of visiting and phone calls as he sat quietly listening. She also told him that right now he was a friend in Sylvia's life and she was confident he was important to her. But she wanted to make sure he understood that when a person was drug free, sometimes things changed. He had nodded sadly and said yes, he did understand, but he'd also be hoping that their friendship would remain.

I looked up as the waitress approached my table. "More coffee, hon?" she asked.

"No, thank you. Time for me to go." I was surprised to see it was already four and Mark would be finishing up at the clinic. We had made plans to meet there, then walk to our favorite Italian restaurant for dinner. I knew he'd be anxious to hear about the events of the day.

CHAPTER 19

The clinic was becoming almost famous as a good place to obtain medical treatment. Dr. Stein continued to work long hours and between the two of us, we were able to leverage the skills of nurses and technicians to treat many more people.

Work I had done as a surgeon paled to working at the clinic. Somehow, I felt good about seeing every patient, including some poor souls suffering from terribly debilitating illnesses. Unfortunately, ten percent of my patients had AIDS or HIV symptoms. Most of those patients were women. A check of the records revealed that thirty percent of my patients had no address. No wonder I was feeling good about my work and colleagues. Where would these people have gone if we weren't there?

Some patients must have been very interesting, at least to the two men who had been sitting in a car across from the clinic for over two hours. Connie noticed them first, telling me about their vigil. I paid no attention to them and had a laugh with Connie, accusing her of being paranoid. She wasn't amused, so I watched them through the mini-blinds to make her feel better.

Both men were well dressed in suits and ties, suits that were out of place for the area they were in, even in Washington. The BMW must have cost $75,000. What the hell were they doing watching our clinic?

"Connie, they must be with the committee staff," I said. "Maybe they're counting bodies coming in here or something as asinine."

She looked through the blinds again, maybe wishing for a clue to solve the mystery. "If they're staffers, why don't they come in like they did the other day?"

"You think they're after you?" I said and laughed. "I'll go out and run them off."

"No, Mark." Connie's face grew pale, absenting her smile, a rare condition for this trooper. "I'll call the police."

"No, what are they doing—sitting in their car?" I had to grab her arm to keep her from a phone.

"They're watching us and for what?"

Holding her shoulders, I smiled and nodded, working to calm her nerves. "Okay, Connie, go back to work. I'll check them out."

"Mark . . ."

"For God's sake, don't be such a worrywart." I walked out, still in my white coat, going directly across the street.

A bald, heavyset man who was behind the wheel, started the car the second he saw me, pulling into the street. I hadn't seen a big BMW burn rubber before. As I scratched my head at the antics of two grown men, the car disappeared.

Connie had been watching me. "So." Her arms went to her waist to complement her smile of self-satisfaction.

"Must have been CIA."

She hit my arm with an open hand. "Cut it out, doctor. Why should those guys be checking on us?"

"They're probably IRS agents seeing who's taking advantage of the system in our clinic."

"Damn it, be serious."

"I don't know what's going on, but whatever it is probably has something to do with the hearings coming up. Don't worry."

* * *

Maddie was on time, but had to wait while I saw one last patient, a street boy with advanced AIDS. Three telephone calls later, I completed arrangements to have him hospitalized. The cocktail of drugs he was being treated with had become ineffective and he was slipping fast. Being on the street didn't help.

An ambulance arrived in fifteen minutes and the young man reluctantly agreed to go with the technicians. Before leaving, he shook my hand, tears streaming down his cheeks.

"Thanks, doc. If I'd come to you a lot sooner, I might have made it," he said.

"You'll make it, Joe." I lied.

Maddie was holding my arm, feeling the lad's emotion. Her face was drawn into an unnatural strain, perhaps to fight back the tears. At that instant, Maddie's beautiful face projected the goodness in her soul, allowing her energy to flow into me.

For that moment, I knew we were in the right place, doing the right thing. Getting the health bill passed became my primary goal.

* * *

"I'm starving, Maddie, do you want to go? Sorry, I kept you waiting," I said, trying to leave the emotion of the boy's pain behind.

"I love you, Dr. Puccini. You're such a good man."

"Cut that stuff out. Don't you feel some ravioli coming on?"

Arm-in-arm, we walked to the restaurant. Carmine's Trattoria was the best Italian restaurant in the slummy area where we lived and worked, even better than any fancy white tablecloth place in Washington. All I could think of was good pasta and red wine. Then, I saw the car.

The BMW was parked across the street from us facing in the same direction as we were walking. Maddie didn't know about the car and I hesitated to frighten her, so I ignored it. After putting sunglasses on, I was able to keep my eyes on them without being noticed. I speeded up my steps noticeably.

"What's the hurry, Mark?" She put pressure on my arm to make me slow the pace.

"Nothing, sorry. How did it go with Sylvia today?" I turned to see the car begin to follow us.

"She did great. I know she's going to be just fine. Thanks for your help. We appreciate all you're doing."

Maddie continued to give me the details of the check-in at the Victorian house and Sylvia's determination to change her life. Despite my interest, my attention was divided. The car kept its distance, tracking us no doubt. I was glad it was still daylight, because that was probably the only reason the well-dressed thugs weren't closer. When the restaurant marquee came into sight, I felt relief.

"Well, I'm happy it all went so well. I'll plan on keeping my Wednesday evenings open for our mother-to-be."

"I knew you would. I like you, my friend," Maddie said.

"You're my best pal, I *hope* you like me." I tried to laugh away the stress I was feeling.

* * *

Dinner was as good as usual, but the wine was better. Somehow, drinking wine, any kind of wine, with Maddie improved the vintage. Staring at her face, she flushed at my attention. Looking away, I saw the car double-parked in front of the restaurant.

"Shit," I said.

"What's wrong?" Maddie turned to follow my gaze.

"Nothing. I'm too full to have dessert and all that dreaming of Italian cheesecake is going to be wasted."

"Take it home to the apartment. They give doggie bags."

I took Maddie's hand in mine and leaned forward to attract her full attention. "Maddie, we're going to leave the restaurant by the back door. Carmine told me that an alley goes to the next street."

"Why?" Her sharp tone matched the frightened look on her face.

"Two guys are following me. They were at the clinic for a while today; when I approached them, they made a fast exit."

"Who are they?"

"I don't know, but I have to think there's a connection to Robbie or my memory lapses."

"Let's just stay here. We'll have some more wine. Maybe they'll leave," Maddie said, with a trembling voice. She leaned back in the booth accentuating her intention to stay in the restaurant. She was shaking.

"Good idea. We'll outwait them." It wasn't a good idea, but Maddie needed to relax before we made a move. Hell, I did, too.

My head had been aching all day, but now it pounded, with my frown transmitting the discomfort. Maddie took my hand to stroke it.

"Your head hurts, doesn't it?" In an instant, her concentration on my pain gave her release from fear.

"Yes, Stein looked at it today and decided I had a concussion. There's a blood clot just below the surface, as you'd expect with a hard blow to the head, but he didn't like the raised bump."

Frowning now, in sympathy for my obvious discomfort, she said, "Do the headaches ever go away?"

"They're pretty much permanent. Don't laugh, but it feels as if I have something in my head. A hell of a blood clot. I need to get some images taken to be sure there isn't serious damage."

We drank more wine, watching the car that appeared to be empty. Christ, they might be coming in here, I thought.

"Maddie, let's go. I'll pay the bill as we go out the back. Let's go *now*." My tone was too harsh. Jumping right up from the seat, Maddie must have felt the negative energy.

We settled the bill with Carmine by telling him what we had, then giving him a handful of bills. He was gracious to let us use the back exit. My heart was pounding along with the pain in my head. In the alley, I pulled Maddie by the hand trying to put some distance between ourselves and the goons, as we ran through the dark spaces with disregard for obstacles in our path. Then my mind became clear. I stopped running. "This is stupid. I'm sorry for frightening you. We don't need to run because those guys must know where we live. They're probably there already."

"What are we going to do, Mark?"

"Nothing. If they intended to kill me or beat me up, they had plenty of chances, but they didn't take them."

"Then, what do they want?"

"I don't know, but I'm not afraid of them. We'll be safe in our apartment. Let's walk home."

The car didn't appear again as we went home at a relaxed pace, but I turned the deadbolt and attached the chain lock when we entered our hallway.

Maddie hugged me, pressing to stay in a bear hug. My body relaxed with a new sensation. After running away from some undefined danger, her arms and warm body were a shelter for my thoughts. I kissed her waiting lips. God, Maddie was so wonderful. She was always there for me. Our kisses became more insistent, and I slowly undressed her. Her smooth legs and waiting breasts seemed to invite my attention. We went to the living room without releasing our hands from each other, making love by scented candlelight. Maddie was the woman I had waited for all my life.

The events of the day argued against an early sleep. Two cognacs allowed us to relax as we rested naked on the sofa, while I admired her beautiful body.

"How about getting some news?" I asked.

Maddie switched on the television, surfing for a news channel as we sipped our extravagant drink.

We break into our normal programming to bring you startling news. The Queen of England has died of a heart attack in Windsor Castle. She was found by her husband after a rare late night meeting with members of her staff. The courtiers told the BBC that matters relating to her trip to visit the cathedral of the Archbishop of Canterbury required a last minute discussion. Her Royal Highness was seventy-nine. The country is in deep mourning after the Queen's sudden death.

"What a shame," Maddie said, admitting she was a bit of an Anglophile. "She had so much to live for."

"It's a shame for another reason. I was looking at one of those religious magazines some church puts in our waiting room at the clinic and read that the Queen was considering some milestone changes in religious doctrine, but can't remember what they were."

"You'd think with all her money, she'd know she had heart problems. They said that her condition hadn't been diagnosed," Maddie said. Her nakedness contrasted her empathetic thoughts for the Queen. She pulled a lap blanket over herself.

"Right, someone's head'll roll."

"Are you going to be able to sleep tonight, Mark?"

"Sure, don't worry about the goons; we have nothing to fear. In fact, I'm tired, so let's go to bed."

"I'll stay up and catch all the news reports about the Queen."

Maddie seemed lost in the images on the television screen. I found her robe and brought it to her. "Goodnight, Maddie. Have I told you how good you are to love?"

"No, tell me."

"You're terrific. I didn't know it could be like that." Kneeling in front of the sofa, I wrapped my arms around her and felt the warmth of our lovemaking still on her skin.

"I love you, Mark."

I pulled back. "Hope you don't mind, but I asked Dr. Stein if he had a problem with you taking off work to go to the hearings with me. We don't need the money. We're doing fine and . . . well, I'd like to know that you'll be with me in case I hear the music again."

"I don't mind. I'm flattered that you trust me so. I do love you." She kissed me softly.

"I love you, too. Goodnight."

"I'm coming to bed now. I can't stand not being next to you, but we're going to sleep now, right?"

Her broad smile provoked a laugh from me. "Yeah, we have a lot of work ahead of us tomorrow and the first hearing is the following day. We need a good rest."

CHAPTER 20

By noon time there was a lull in the steady stream of patients walking through the door. Mark had paperwork to catch up on, suggesting I take at least an hour for lunch to bring a sandwich back for him.

I decided to browse in the shops to purchase some items for Sylvia. Not being allowed visitors for four weeks was going to be difficult, so I thought it might be nice to drop off little gifts for her once a week.

In a small candy shop, I found a box of hard candy I thought she'd like. At the bookshop, a book on baby names seemed appropriate. I had no idea if she hoped for a boy or a girl or even if she had any names in mind.

Coming out of the bookshop, I heard my name called. Turning around, I saw Jake walking toward me. "Maddie? Is it really you? God, I've been worried sick about you. You look terrific."

His concerned words caused me a mixture of embarrassment and happiness. Jake had always been good to me, but I had pulled a disappearing act on him. Never bothering to let him know when I got off the streets.

"Hi, Jake. Gosh, it's good to see you. I'm fine. Very good, actually."

"You certainly look good. I almost wasn't sure it was you. I really have been worried, Maddie. You cleaned up real nice."

I laughed, noticing the blush moving across his face. "I took your advice, Jake, and finally got off the streets. I work over at the clinic near the park. Have myself a nice apartment that I share with a doctor at the clinic. Yeah, things are going pretty good for me now."

"I'm real happy for you. You're not cut out for street life. I'd love to take you to lunch, but I'm behind schedule getting out of the city and heading to upstate New York. I'd really like to see you again though—just as friends. I'll look you up at the clinic sometime and we'll go for coffee or lunch. Would that be okay?"

Jake was a decent human being and I smiled, nodding my head. "That would be nice. I'd like that. You take care, Jake. It was great seeing you again."

He leaned toward me, giving me an awkward hug. "You too, Maddie. Keep up the good work," he said, walking away.

*　*　*

Although I missed Sylvia around the apartment, the privacy that her absence gave Mark and me was welcome. From the first time we had made love, every night was spent falling asleep in his arms. I enjoyed the freedom of waking up beside him in the morning, being able to share my affection with him without trying to be proper in front of Sylvia.

Both Mark and I were apprehensive about the hearings the next morning. We had dinner at home, followed by an old movie from the forties on television before turning in early.

Climbing into bed beside him, I smiled. His right arm was stretched across the bed, waiting for my body to fit there. Pulling me to him, he kissed the top of my head. "I love you, Maddie. I'm glad you're going with me tomorrow. Are you nervous about seeing Pope again after two years?"

"I love you too, Mark." I traced his lips with my fingertip. "Yeah, a little bit. I shouldn't be. I'm not the one that did anything wrong. There's certainly no law against a person giving up their job, their home, and all their belongings to begin a new life. Crazy maybe—but no law against it."

"You're right. He's the one that ought to be worried when he sees you. You could always press those charges for sexual harassment. There *is* a law against that. But I imagine he'll be quite shocked to see you at a senate hearing, after you literally fell off the face of the earth."

I nodded. Mark was right. My option to file suit against Bryce was reasonable, but I knew it would never come to that. I removed myself from the situation, therefore he wasn't a threat to me any longer. Garret Dawson was the danger that loomed over me. Knowing he was still out there somewhere offered no reassurance that he'd given up his search. Garret was the last thought in my head as I finally drifted off to sleep.

* * *

Every spare minute that I wasn't doctoring in the clinic was used to study and revise the text of my testimony for the committee meeting. My continuous changing was a source of consternation for the staffers who foolishly believed that I was going to read the statement just as they had drafted it. They didn't know me very well. First, I had to be comfortable with the phrasing, in particular the medical terminology and references to the indigent and Medicaid. Then, I had some new ideas that expanded the concepts of the bill, which had been put in the hopper just two weeks before. While the existing draft legislation wouldn't be changed until committee discussion, I knew that my ideas could gain new life in the give-and-take of two-party system compromises.

Whenever I called with a revision, a staff secretary dutifully came to the clinic in a taxicab to pick up the text. She then made the changes and distributed the new copy to each of the applicable staffers, including me. This activity was a compromising process with my giving in only grudgingly when the politicos assured me that my position aided foes of the legislation.

The foes were many; more than I had considered. Barton James did yeoman work in educating me about the lobbies that had something to lose from my testimony. My feelings were crushed to learn that the American Association of Medical Doctors didn't consider me a worthy representative of other physicians.

No *Street Doctor* could represent them. They also opposed the voluntary aspects of the bill because they believed that when government got its foot in the door, volunteerism would soon become mandatory for every practitioner with an outstanding student loan or other debt to government.

Health insurance companies were opposed to major portions of the legislation because the free and expanded clinics fell outside the governing principles of current managed care. No fee meant zero payments for the company, but also reduced the need for insurance. The industry believed the large body of uninsured would, over time, eventually become insured with the help of federal legislation keeping the indigent in a private health insurance mode. Everyone seemed to have an angle without concern for the basic health needs of many indigent persons and working poor.

The pharmaceutical industry was livid over my proposal to establish existing agencies as drug purchasers for free clinics. The overall impact of the government contracts would be to drive the price of drugs down. Drug manufacturers were apparently seeking to trade extended patent periods for large-scale government-purchased drugs.

The foes were giants of the health industry and I felt like a formerly homeless David facing the Goliaths of Madison Avenue, Park Avenue, and Wall Street.

During a busy period at the clinic the day before my testimony, I received a call from the big man himself. I made him wait while I finished applying a dressing for a drunken homeless man who had been assaulted the night before. Pope's secretary was livid.

"Dr. Puccini, I've been waiting to connect you with Senator Pope," she said.

"Thank you for waiting. You're very kind, but I had a priority patient."

The woman must have been beside herself because she didn't speak for at least twenty seconds.

"Hold for the senator, doctor," she said curtly. I had no option this time, waiting a few minutes for him to come on the line.

"Hello there, my friend. Are you feeling nervous yet?" the senator asked in an upbeat jovial tone.

"No, sir. I feel fine. This is a cause worth speaking for."

"We chose the right man for the job. I'm impressed with your presentation and my staff is impressed with your determination. There's a minor sticking point that I should discuss with you myself, Dr. Puccini. May I call you Mark?"

"What's that, Senator?" I didn't answer his question. He was being falsely polite.

"The AAMD, and some of the other opponents to my bill as it stands, are going to challenge you—your reputation. Some colleagues of mine will stall the testimony to inquire about your bona fides. That will cause us to run over our allotted time, so there will be other sessions. Do you see what I mean, Mark?"

"This sounds a bit nasty, Senator. Why should they attack me rather than my words or ideas?"

"There's a lot at stake, son, and this is Washington. They've already developed a thick dossier on you, I'm told."

"That explains the well-dressed goons who are following me." A sense of relief came over me. I had been worried over nothing but snooping politicos.

"I don't think that's normal, but they may have something they think is damning. Trying to catch you red-handed, so to speak. Are you clean, doctor? Can I be proud of you and your ideas?"

Questions like this were to be expected given my former life, but I resented them anyway. "I'm clean, but worried about the continual tail."

In a deep, almost pensive voice, Senator Pope counseled me. "Don't break any laws, hire prostitutes, or use illegal drugs. I need you to help me win passage of my bill."

"I need you to help a lot of folks who need medical care. We're a team. Thank you for having a conscience about the health of ordinary citizens, Senator."

"I look forward to meeting you tomorrow." He hung up without a goodbye.

Respite followed the thought that I was being watched by

legislative foes rather than someone connected to Robbie or God knows who.

* * *

Dr. Stein took over clinic responsibilities so that Maddie and I didn't have to come in early on the morning of my testimony. We slept until seven, the last hour in each other's arms as we enjoyed the pleasure of unhurried lovemaking. The morning was a continuation of the warmth we had shared the night before.

I grimaced as I moved on the pillow.

"Your head's still hurting?" Maddie asked. "Doctor, you wouldn't let one of your patients go so long without further treatment."

"Yes. You don't know your own power, girl. I need to have an MRI or CAT scan, but not today."

Maddie ran to the shower and I started the coffee. The newspaper featured heavy coverage of the budget discussions and early fact-finding on major bills fighting for life. Senator Pope, a master of media manipulation, garnered good space with a speech at the National Press Club. He plugged his bill, mentioning me several times as a man who had seen both ends of the economic spectrum and knew how to fix the health care problem. Start by expanding existing government programs and capitalize on volunteerism by health professionals. Hell, you read my speech, I said, laughing to myself.

* * *

We heard the taxicab horn and started down the stairs. Maddie had purchased a suit for the occasion from a local thrift store that looked fabulous. She could have easily passed as an up and coming congressional staffer.

The cab pulled away and a large BMW fell in behind us. Trailing closely, after a few minutes the car burst forward, forcing our cab to the curb. Two men jumped out, then approached our door. The cabby sunk below the level of the seat, making me think he was hiding. Maddie was crying and whimpering as she shook, but my adrenaline pushed me to attempt to protect her. Crossing over her legs, I reached the door, but the cabby had already jammed his door into the traffic lane, pointing a 45-caliber pistol at the men, moving it between them as he told them to back off. He cocked the pistol demonstrating that he knew how to handle the weapon.

Maddie and I sat frozen in the seat. What the hell was going on?

A police car rounded the corner as the two men ran to their BMW. The sound of spinning wheels with the smell of burning rubber stole the scene. They were gone before the policemen arrived at the cab.

We agreed that the cabby should file the report at the police station later, thereby avoiding having to explain what I didn't understand. Blood seeped down my neck as a result of the quick stop and hard turn that had thrown us to the right taxi door, further injuring my sore head.

"Damn, I'm going to have to testify in a soiled shirt."

Maddie, now less frightened, told me that was fitting for a street doctor. I fit the role. Seeing her laughter dropped my anxiety level. "The senator's people will have a first aid kit. We can put a dressing on the wound," Maddie said.

The remainder of the trip to *The Hill* was uneventful giving me an opportunity to mentally prepare for the most important testimony of my life. As we exited the taxi, a few reporters fired questions at us.

"Sorry, fellows," I said, "we're late for the committee room. Catch us later."

One young reporter walked along with us shouting questions. "How did you get off the street, doctor? Are you board certified? Why doesn't the AAMD support your plan? Are you clean?"

"Get the hell away from me, you leech," I shouted at him. He backed off—must have been a freshman.

The staff secretary who had done my typing, but had never

introduced herself to me, waited at the entrance.

"This way, doctor." She ignored Maddie and pissed me off.

Barton James was at the door of the large committee room. There were few seats available, but James had reserved a seat near the back row for Maddie. "Sorry I couldn't get you closer to Mark, but this was the best I could do with the late notice."

I had called James the day before.

"Go right up to the witness table; your materials are at your seat," he said.

"I brought my material with me, but thanks. Wouldn't want anyone to have changed my words." I smiled at him, being a little smart-alecky and ungrateful for his help. In this city, a man had to be his own man.

Some spectators from supportive groups introduced themselves to me, as I kept my eye on Maddie. I was concerned about her reaction to seeing the senator and his reaction to seeing her in attendance at his committee hearing. That is, if he noticed her at all.

The NAACP representative shook my hand, wishing me luck. She was a gorgeous woman with a distinctive Boston accent, which sounded strange issuing from her chocolate-colored face. When thinking about Boston, I remembered Irish, English, Poles, Frenchmen, and Italians, not African-Americans.

Congresswoman Mary Brosky, Democrat from California, spent minutes urging me to establish volunteer clinics in her district. I was flattered, but taken back. God, why didn't she take action in her own territory?

Senator Pope arrived five minutes late, waving to me in a near-salute. I took my seat, glancing at my notes as he began the proceedings.

"Ladies and gentlemen, worthy colleagues, friends of justice in the United States, we are pleased to welcome Dr. Mark Puccini to our hearing. He has demonstrated his strong sense of duty to this country and our community by his tireless efforts on behalf of the indigent and working poor at his clinic. Because he's not as well known to some of my colleagues as he is to me, he has consented to a brief period of personal questions before he begins to speak. Thank you for your generosity, Dr. Puccini."

I nodded.

Staffers presented note cards to three of the senators seated on the dais.

"You have the floor, Senator Cummings."

"Thank you, Mr. Chairman. Doctor, I see from your biographical sketch that you have a long period when you didn't practice medicine before you began work at the clinic. Would you care to tell us what you did to earn your livelihood during that time?"

That was the beginning. Senator Cummings sneered at me. I had to admit I left a good practice because of unreliable work habits, that I lived as a homeless person, and had used illegal drugs.

Senator Pope tried to divert questions by asking me about some of the successes in my life: first in my class at Rutgers, a reputation for saving the lives of cancer patients who had been written off, and a record of service to the community.

But the attacks came again. Pope must have known what would happen. The C-Span television coverage was eliminated for this first session. Couldn't have fellow senators looking like shits, even if they were.

Now the strategy was clear. I was to be identified with groups of those who weren't pulling their own weight in society, not drawing large salaries, and expecting a handout. The bill itself was so labeled by the opposition, but why was Pope allowing this to happen? My patience grew short, and in exasperation at one point, I turned to look at Maddie, ashamed of the verbal beating I was taking. What did she think of me?

Pope followed my glance and his face paled, then he signaled to James, who stepped to his side. James looked into the audience and his mouth formed the words, "Is that her?"

Pope was angry. James' face and neck turned red before he went back to his seat. The senator had made the connection between Maddie and me.

"The hour's late. This committee is in recess until after the lunch hour. We'll start at one thirty, promptly," Pope said.

Pope left the dais first, with Barton James racing to keep up with him. My thoughts recalled the pompous James and the chewing out he was going to get.

Maddie came to my side. "He saw me, Mark. I mean he recognized me." She was speaking very fast.

"If he has any intelligence, he'll invite you to meet with him," I said. "I'll be there with you, though."

"I want you there." She hugged me in public.

* * *

The afternoon session had a very different flavor. Senators were friendly and courteous as the C-Span cameras broadcast the event. My presentation was well received, giving me a feeling of accomplishment that was lacking in the earlier session.

Experiencing the vehemence of the opposition to expanding health care, I also knew that the fight was only beginning. Senator Pope needed a street doctor and he could help me. In fact, for the first time, I clearly understood that we would be using each other to reach our goals. Now I had to be certain that Maddie wasn't hurt as we moved toward those goals. She had been hurt enough. Too much.

CHAPTER 21

The phone call from Bryce came the following morning at work. Answering in my customary business manner, I recognized his voice immediately. "Hey there, Beautiful. The disappearing lady surfaces after two years. How are you, Maddie?" Same charm, same self-assured tone.

"I'm fine, Bryce, and you?" I could hear the pleasantness oozing from my voice.

"Good, very good, in fact. I'd really like to meet with you. Any chance we could set that up?"

Smiling, I recalled Mark saying that if Bryce was intelligent, he'd want to meet with me. The senator's brainpower had never been a liability to him. "Sure, we could arrange that. I'm working here till five today."

"How about if we meet in the lounge of the Capital Hilton? Would that be convenient for you? How's five thirty?"

"Yeah, the time is fine. However, that's clear across town and I have no transportation."

"I'll send a taxi to pick you up. The clinic or your place?" he asked.

"The clinic will be fine."

"Great. There'll be a taxi out front at five. I look forward to seeing you, Maddie."

"I'll be ready," I said, hanging up the phone.

I waited for Mark to finish with a patient, then told him about the phone call.

"He doesn't know I'll be with you?" he asked.

I shook my head. "No, he didn't mention it, neither did I. We'll surprise him."

* * *

With the usual assortment of patients, the afternoon passed quickly. Just before five, a frantic mother raced into the clinic carrying a little boy whose screams filled the small waiting area. She was holding a blood-saturated towel to his forehead.

"He was jumping on the sofa," she said, "and hit his head on the edge of the coffee table. Can somebody help him?" Her voice was shaky as she clutched the screaming child to her chest.

Escorting her into an exam room, I grabbed a handful of gauze bandages, telling her to hold them tightly against the boy's forehead. Mark was finishing his last patient, then followed the screams to the child.

"Hey, little fellow," he said, smiling at the boy and his mother. "Looks like you had quite a tumble." Removing the gauze, he nodded. "I'm afraid it's going to take some sutures to close this wound."

"Will he be okay?" the mother asked, with concern in her voice.

"Sure, he'll be just fine," Mark reassured her. "Maddie, can you ask Connie to come in to assist me and I need to speak to you for a moment outside."

Mark proceeded to explain the procedure to the mother, while I searched for Connie. A few minutes later, Mark approached my desk. "I'm afraid I'll have to stay behind for a little while and get this patient sutured. Your taxi's out front, Maddie. Would it be okay if I joined you there within an hour?"

Reaching for my sweater and handbag, I nodded. I had no desire to meet with Bryce alone, but didn't see any alternative. "Yeah, that'll be fine. Promise me you'll come directly there as soon as you finish?"

He leaned over and kissed my cheek. "I promise. I'll grab a cab and meet you in the lounge."

* * *

Traffic was heavy on the drive to the Capital Hilton. It occurred to me that it was ironic that Bryce should suggest this venue for our meeting. Although he probably had no recollection of this, I distinctly recalled his suggestion over two years ago that he could obtain a suite for us at that particular hotel. I had been in Washington assisting him with problems that had cropped up and we had been working late at his office. My plan was to fly the shuttle back to Boston at nine that night. His plan was to get me into bed at the Hilton. After much wasted coercion on his part, I remember boarding my flight, wondering how much longer I could maintain both my position and my self-respect. A uniformed doorman met the taxi as we pulled to the curb in front of the Hilton. The driver turned and smiled, touching his hand to his cap. "The fare and a sizable tip have been taken care of by a gentleman. So you have a good evening, ma'am," he said, the innuendo obvious.

Until entering the lobby of the Hilton, I'd been neutral about my meeting with Bryce. Now I felt uneasy. Glancing at my watch, I headed in the direction of the lounge—five thirty five and Mark should be arriving within a half hour. Immediately, I saw Bryce seated at a booth toward the back of the dimly lit lounge.

He saw me enter and stood up, looking distinguished and confident. "Maddie," he said, reaching for my shoulders in a hug. "Thank you for meeting me. Sit down. What would you like to drink?" he asked, as he motioned for the waiter.

"A glass of cabernet, please."

After the waiter walked away, Bryce smiled—the exact smile that guaranteed female votes.

He shook his head in astonishment. "Christ, Maddie, I can't believe it's really you. When I saw you in that committee room yesterday, I thought I was seeing things. Where the hell have you been for so long? You just dropped off the surface of the earth. Why'd you do it?"

"Well, you were right up there with my number one reason."

"Me?" he asked and had the nerve to sound incredulous. "You left a well-paying position, a lovely condo, everything you owned, because of me?"

Maybe this man wasn't as intelligent as Mark and I had assumed. "Things have changed quite a bit in the work place for females since I worked for you, Bryce. We even have a label for it now—it's called sexual harassment. Ever heard of it?"

The look on his face told me he did and understood the definition quite well. "What's that have to do with you disappearing with no explanations to anyone?"

"Plenty," I replied, hearing the bitterness in my voice. "You seem to have forgotten the ultimatum you gave me. I either slept with you, or I could forget any promotions or advancement. I even recall the afternoon I declined to have drinks with you when we left the office. You reminded me that you *chose* me for the position, and anytime you saw fit you could also terminate that position. I had a lot of other things going on in my life during that time. You only provided the additional stress that I didn't need."

For the first time since I had met Bryce, I saw he was momentarily at a loss for words. Then true to the Bryce style, his voice took on a tone of nastiness. "Oh, for Christ's sake, Maddie. You weren't some innocent schoolgirl. You knew the score. There's more sexual escapades in politics than a whorehouse. It goes with the territory. Besides, you're quite the attractive woman. Don't tell me there aren't plenty of guys who'd like to get you between the sheets."

I shook my head in disbelief. "So what you're telling me is that because you found me attractive and sexy, what *you* wanted was the paramount consideration. What is it with you guys? Do you think your looks, your power, and your intimidation automatically gains you entrance between a female's legs?" I was quickly beginning to understand that Bryce felt entitled to anything and everything he desired. The shocking realization was that he honestly couldn't understand, or didn't want to believe, that what he demanded was not only wrong, but against the law.

"Hey, most of the time the females love it as much as I do. Nothing wrong with a playful romp in bed."

I could feel my anger rising. "There's everything wrong with it when the female says *no*. You might not be aware, but we have the right to refuse. I don't know who the hell you think you are. But I do know you're one hell of a pompous, arrogant, smug bastard. You intimidate because it works in your favor. Many females are too frightened to lose that well-paying job and because of this, pricks like you end up getting what they want. It was worth it to me to lose everything to hold onto my self-respect. What I should have done was sue you for sexual harassment. It's still not too late."

I saw the color drain from his face. "You little bitch. Try it. You won't get very far. You have no evidence whatsoever. Besides, that was two years ago."

Finishing off the last of my cabernet, I glanced at my watch before speaking. Where the hell was Mark? It was now six thirty. "Don't be too sure of that, Mr. Senator. There's no statute of limitations on sexual harassment cases and don't look so smug about my lack of evidence. You have no idea how much evidence I might have." Standing, I felt my own smugness coursing through my body and it felt good. I walked a few steps away from the table, then turned around to face him. "If I were you, I'd be very careful who I hit on. You just might be facing her across a courtroom some day."

During the taxi ride to my apartment, I wasn't sure if I was angrier at Mark for not showing up or more elated about standing by my convictions.

CHAPTER 22

Ten sutures, with a bit of artistic effort, would keep scarring of the boys face to a minimum. I knew there were fractures in his mandibular bone as I touched his tender cheek.

Connie assisted me with x-rays; one of the realities of a free clinic being that doctors and nurses had to know how to do everything. We had no specialized x-ray technicians to make the job easier. Good old Connie never left me in the lurch; she was always available to work late, helping me through mini-crises.

I needed help on this case, especially because the boy had had enough pain to make anyone irritable. Despite strapping him to the table, he wouldn't be still. I ended up holding his face in my hands to achieve a useable x-ray. My heart went out to the poor kid, and for a while I forgot my throbbing headache.

The break was jagged and ugly. The boy required a specialist, and I wasn't qualified to do the work myself. The repair necessary was a very tricky job. Every time the boy moved his jaw the bones separated along the fracture. I called three hospitals before finding an oral surgeon who would perform maxillofacial surgery on the boy as a professional courtesy to me.

Connie and I pooled our cash to get taxi fare to carry mother and son to the hospital and back. As the taxi drove away, I looked toward my smiling nurse.

"Thanks, Connie, you come through every time. Sorry about the cash, I'll give it back to you in the morning. Don't carry much money around in my pockets—part of my street experience."

"Not necessary, Mark. I wanted to help, too. Are you all

right?" she asked, as she placed her fingers around the back of my neck. "God, you're bleeding."

Glancing at my watch, time dictated that I had to get to the hotel to be with Maddie, but my legs were so rubbery I needed to lean on Connie for an instant to keep my balance.

"What's wrong with your head? I've been wondering why you have that dressing." She reached toward my wound.

I moved my head away. "It's nothing." Clearly, I was being stupid and untrusting. The woman was keeping me upright.

"You'd better get inside to lie down for a few minutes. Let me look at your head."

"I'll be fine after a bit of rest."

"Your ass, doctor."

Connie helped me into a cubicle and positioned me for an examination of my head.

She intended to see to my wound, but I couldn't let another person know about my disappearing acts and the frying pan Maddie was forced to use to protect me from myself. I was feeling lousy and thinking worse. "Connie, call Dr. Stein, will you?"

She moved toward me again. "I'll just . . ."

"Please, I can't explain right now, but I need Stein. Just call him."

Turned down lips and narrowed eyes told me her feelings were hurt, but I had run out of diversions. Maddie would be alone with the two-faced senator. Smart Dr. Puccini was powerless to go there or accept the help of a trained nurse.

Despite the uncomfortable table in the examination area, the pain medication I had taken about four o'clock helped somewhat, but it also made me drowsy. When Dr. Stein arrived, my mind was in and out of dreams. He touched my shoulder, waking me with a start.

"Thanks for coming." I looked at Connie. "Sorry, but we need to talk alone."

"You don't need me Dr. Stein?" she asked, placing her hands on her rounded hips.

I shook my head and looked away from her.

"I think we'll be all right, Connie. Thanks for staying," Stein said.

As she was walking away, he had the dressing off. "This is a mess, Mark. I've never seen a blow to the head leave such irritation and maybe infection."

"I've been on an antibiotic, too."

"We need to assess the wound, so let's anesthetize the area." Stein went about his business to prepare my head. Intent, he was doing what he had been trained to do.

In a short while, I could feel the Lidocaine taking affect. Stein gently probed the base of my skull, as I tried to watch his expressions in the small mirror on the wall. Neither of us had a good guess what could be causing the problem.

"Jesus," Stein said.

"What?"

"There's something in here."

"Yeah, brains, I hope."

"It's a membrane of some sort. I've never seen such a procedure or read about one like it. Can you understand me?" His voice peaked in amazement at what he saw.

"Yes, I understand perfectly, but what's it for?"

"The material is covering, eh . . . protecting a hole or injury to your skull. When did you get this injury?"

"I don't know. Maybe as a child."

"Cutting the membrane is drastic since we don't know what's in there, if anything. An x-ray will help us."

"Cut it."

"No, Mark. We need an image to define this foreign object."

Again, I went to the x-ray room to receive another dose of routine radiation. Back in the small cubicle, he opened a package of sterilized instruments, removing a scalpel with a thin, short blade. Adjusting my head position, he looked at me, silently asking if he should continue. I nodded. He probed, seeming to be cutting superficially. A bit of soft material dropped into the aluminum dish. He worked for another ten minutes or so. "It's metal."

"What is?" My mind raced, searching for a reasonable function for a foreign object in my head.

"It's a metal object lying just below the epidermis. Christ, I don't believe this." Stein shook his head.

"Take it out." My words were pleading.

"I can't."

"Try again," I said in a non-doctorly tone.

Sweat formed on his forehead as he worked. Stein was mumbling to himself, often using the name of someone else's savior.

"Don't move," he said, leaving in the direction of his office.

I heard a dull sound on the asphalt tile floor. He returned with a small dark, metal object that smelled of alcohol.

"This is a magnet."

The situation suddenly seemed funny. My lips curled as I was laughing at the stupidity of it all, but it also hurt to laugh.

Stein continued to work. "I've got it."

The object was less than the diameter of a dime and twice as thick. A watch battery came to mind, but it was darker than the shine of most batteries. Stein wiped it with a clean piece of gauze and placed it in the dish. "Lay still, I need to close here."

Twenty minutes later, a substantial dressing covered the entire shaved section of the rear of my head, but my skull ached as the pain killer wore off. My thoughts were crazy, perhaps exactly like the thoughts of a patient enclosed in a padded room in a mental hospital. In an effort to change the flow of thoughts in my brain, I scoured the walls and ceilings, studying each imperfection in the plaster. The room needed a coat of paint. One section had mildew. Christ, what a clinic this was. I couldn't look Stein in the eye.

"Sit up," he said. "Tell me what's going on here."

Before I could think of any sane answer, the front door resonated with dull sounds. Then, a smashing noise. We were still looking at each other when two men came into the room.

"Who the hell are you?" I shouted, causing shooting pain all across my head.

Dr. Stein moved aggressively toward the closest man and

stopped. His eyes were as big as a circus clown's. The man waved an automatic pistol at us.

Stein had no intention of leaving me alone with the two unfashionably dressed characters, but there seemed little virtue in complicating his life. I nodded once, then again, but he didn't move.

"It's okay, Bruce, don't be concerned." I had called him by his first name only once before.

"Okay, my ass."

My attempt to keep him away from the threat of these strangers was wrong. He thought I didn't want him to be involved, but my motive was to protect him. Bruce's lips scrunched against each other as he experienced the hurt. Here was my mentor, the man who saved me from the streets. I cut him off. Getting him out of the clinic was the right thing to do though.

"Bruce, I'll be fine. These gentlemen are with the government. I'll see you tomorrow."

Stein didn't believe me. The two men watched, evaluating us, especially me. The good doctor took off his white smock, walking to the front door without looking back or inspecting the damage to the doorway.

"How'd you know we're federal agents?" a man with a strong New York accent asked.

"I didn't. Just wanted my friend to leave. Who are you?"

The older man held a wallet with an ID card and a badge in front of my face. The picture and the name was John Grundig, District Director, Investigations, INS.

I looked at the younger man.

He also showed his identification—Philip Corso.

"Immigration and Naturalization Service? You're kidding me. I don't believe you. You couldn't want *me* for doing something illegal. What're you doing here?"

"You have something we want," Grundig said.

At that instant, a pain screamed across my skull. I bowed my head to hide the hurt. Corso moved to my rear to inspect the dressing on my head.

"You've had some surgery?" Corso asked.

"No, I had an accident and the wound hasn't healed. Why have you guys been following me?"

"Not us," Grundig said.

"Don't try to shit me. I see your BMW all the time."

"Feds don't drive BMWs. The pugs in the BMW are your enemies. We've been following them and they led us to you."

"Who are they?"

"It's not important, Puccini," Grundig said. What had been an informal, friendly voice, now turned stern.

"It is to me. What do you want from me?"

"The metal object," Grundig said. He held out his hand.

"I don't know what you're talking about." Anger made me shout at him. I didn't know what was happening to me and they'd expect me to have a good explanation.

"The metal object that was planted in your head under the membrane." Grundig smirked, knowing he had the upper hand.

"You've got a surveillance mike in these offices, haven't you? What right do you have to spy on me?" Raising my voice again hurt my cranium. I held my forehead, lowering it to try to relieve the pain.

Grundig pressed closer with his hand near his holstered weapon. "I want it, now."

I knew the feds wouldn't shoot me. Bruce had dropped the object. My eyes focused on the aluminum dish, while the gaze of the two agents followed mine. Corso had the object in his hand in an instant and studied it, using his palm to estimate its weight.

"This is incredible. Almost no weight at all," Corso said, impressed with the object.

"Shut up," Grundig said. "Dr. Puccini, we can talk better at our office. You're not being arrested. We want your assistance."

* * *

They drove me to an old federal building not far from the familiar FBI headquarters. The discussion wasn't exactly an interrogation, more like a forced conversation in which events became clearer to me. The INS had followed Robbie, certain he had violated the law. By chance, an Intelligence agency intercepted a signal that was correlated to Robbie's whereabouts. Then, because of the Global Positioning System, the INS, or whatever organization Grundig belonged to, was able to keep track of Robbie. While tracking him, there was another signal that couldn't be interpreted that drew even more attention.

The men in the BMW had also followed Robbie, and by doing so, highlighted themselves to the feds. The feds found me by keeping tabs on the BMW, subsequently bugging the clinic. Being interrogated made me feel like a criminal. I asked for a lawyer, but they convinced me that wasn't necessary because I wasn't charged with a crime. Still, I wasn't comfortable talking about myself. Besides, how could I describe the disappearing incidents in my life when I had no idea why I walked away to do something I couldn't control? Immunity was a possibility. Knowing that was from television cop shows like *Law and Order*. Before I told them anything about myself, a prosecutor from INS granted me immunity from prosecution, dependent on my full cooperation.

The object that had been hidden in my head was taken for analysis with a promise to share the results of the testing with me. Within minutes of discussing immunity, it became clear that these men considered me to be a victim. The sole reason for that judgment was the implanted device. Obviously, they knew more about my circumstances than I did. I wasn't sure why I was a victim.

* * *

Because I was more than a little stressed and tired, Corso dropped me off at my apartment, but now I had to face Maddie at almost ten o'clock at night. Despite the hour, waking her was necessary and important. How did the senator treat her? Was she all right?

The bedroom door was ajar and Maddie was lying propped against two pillows with eyes wide open. She sat upright and seemed prepared to lecture me, but her eyes narrowed as her lips parted. My appearance must have shocked her.

"Where have you been? Is that blood on your collar—are you okay?" Questions tumbled out of her as she rose from the bed.

"I'm sorry for not coming to the hotel."

Maddie looked me over, cautious after another failure to help her. "Was it the music?"

"No. But tell me about Pope." I knew it was time to listen to her problems and felt guilty for shortchanging her.

"He was the same overbearing, miserable man he always was. Pope thinks he has a right to any woman he takes a fancy to and doesn't mind telling you to your face. I wish there was a way to make him pay for the abuse he's heaped on people over the years. I hate him." The word *hate* exploded from her mouth.

"Did he touch you? Physically?" I reached for her hand, but she stayed put.

"No, he didn't hurt me. That's over. What about you? Why are you so late and why is there blood on your clothes?"

"My head wound bothered me so much that I asked Bruce to look at it. He found something lodged in my skull. Something placed there surgically."

Maddie put her hand over her mouth to muffle the sound she involuntarily made. "What was it? Let me see your wound." She approached me, touching my face. Tears had formed in her eyes.

"None of us, the two guys from the Immigration and Naturalization Service, Stein, or me know what it is. A small metal object, but I'm sure it has everything to do with the music. The feds have it to test."

Maddie started to ask about the government men, but I cut her off, giving a detailed review of what had happened. As I spoke, tears filled her eyes again and she hugged me, tightly, as if I would go away.

"I haven't been a very good protector, Maddie. I failed you twice. That will never happen again."

"You haven't failed me; but if I'd known how serious your situation was, I might have helped you more. I'm sorry I hurt your head."

"You started the process that'll release me from my prison; a type of control I don't understand. Maddie, will you stick with me? Even if we find out I've been an instrument of ghastly acts? Maybe I'm evil, too."

Maddie nodded, reaching for my hand. "We're in this together. You must know I love you."

* * *

We woke up as we had gone to sleep, wrapped in each other's arms. Maddie was in a deep slumber, accented by tiny, feminine snores. Wiggling out of her grip, I slipped out of the room still dressed in yesterday's clothes, complete with dried blood.

The newspaper from the day before lay open on the table. Middle-sized print on the lower half of the front page caught my attention.

Politics Threatens Health Bill

Senator Bryce Pope, (D/Mass), is losing his grip on the Pope-Brigham Health Act, which he earlier seemed to stake his reputation on as the most effective health legislator in the Congress. Budget woes following the market downturn and the September 11th attack have driven most states and many Washington politicians away from extending health benefits at a time when job losses and unemployment compensation are taking a higher priority.

Pope faces the prospect of removing the bill from debate rather than face what appears to be a potential defeat and loss of face in an election year.

Observers speculate that there will be little interest in the health care broadening measure for another two years and a Presidential race. The bill breaks new ground with the government sanctioning and paying in-kind for volunteer medical services for the working poor and the indigent. It would also broaden existing programs without adding new bureaucracy and extend benefits to millions who are without health insurance.

Speaking off the record, a knowledgeable staffer said the risk isn't worth the gain this year, as neither Democrats nor Republicans can expect a sizeable political payoff for an extension approach to health care.

No Washington politician seems willing to take the risk and seem impotent at a time when the nation needs strong leadership.

Falling into the sofa, the events of the past twenty-four hours seemed to close in on me. Issues raced through my mind. Was I a half person, controlled by someone else? Could I regain my independence and humanity? Could I be the man that Maddie needs and deserves? Could the street doctor help the poor who need care this year?

Senator Pope had to stand up for this bill, even if we helped in ways that he wouldn't appreciate. Would the INS really help me?

CHAPTER 23

Living with Mark was beginning to feel like the movie version of a Tom Clancy novel—federal agents, foreign objects implanted in the scalp, good and evil. Turning over in bed, I stretched out my arm to reach for Mark, only to realize the bed was empty. Shit. Now what?

Opening the bedroom door, I saw him peacefully asleep on the sofa. Walking into the kitchen, I began preparing the coffeepot. I loved Wednesday—our day to relax and enjoy each other's company. Today was extra special. Our first visit to see Sylvia at Grace's Retreat. Her weekly phone calls for the past four weeks had been encouraging. She sounded happy despite a tough first few weeks going through withdrawal. I detected a much more relaxed tone in her voice. She bubbled over with excitement the night before when she called to confirm that Mark and I would be coming today. She also said she had a surprise for us.

"Good morning, Beautiful," Mark said, as I felt him nuzzling the back of my neck.

Turning around, I clasped my hands behind his head, gently touching his dressing. "How does that feel this morning? Still a lot of pain?"

Mark shook his head. "Not so bad. Much better than yesterday. Maybe I'll take some Tylenol though to stay on top of it."

"I'll get it," I said, heading for the bathroom medicine cabinet.

Mark was quiet as he took the white tablets, then he sat at the table with coffee.

I broke the silence. "Do you have any idea what that thing in your head was? Or who put it there?"

"Not really," he replied. "But I have no doubt it has something to do with Robbie and me in that orphanage. The feds have it now. They'll let me know. So, Good Looking, what are we doing today?"

I could tell Mark wanted to change the subject. "Sylvia called last night before you got home. Today's the day we can visit her, but I know you're not feeling that great. I can go by myself."

He reached across the table for my hand. "Not a chance. I'm fine. We're going together."

* * *

We arrived at Grace's Retreat promptly at eleven. The young girl at the desk contacted Grace to let her know we were there. According to protocol, we were to meet with Grace privately before visiting Sylvia.

"Hi, there," she said, walking toward us, extending her hand. "Let's go into my office."

I recalled four weeks before, sitting in the same leather chair, filled with apprehension and doubts as to Sylvia's future. Today looked much brighter.

Confirming this, Grace said, "Sylvia has done well here. She's managed to adapt to the program with no problems. Of course, an addict is always just one step away from maintaining their recovery, but I feel Sylvia is going to do better than most."

Relief washed over me. "Thank God. I've been worried sick about what would happen to her and the baby if this program didn't work."

Grace nodded. "There's one thing though. I'm assuming that you and Mr. Puccini were planning to have Sylvia return to your place in two weeks to reside with you?"

"Yeah, that's what we thought would happen. Why? Is there a problem?"

"No, not at all. It's just that we have what you might call

a step-down unit. It's a lovely home on the outskirts of Washington. We have two housemothers there. This home opened five years ago and we've been getting excellent results with it. Not all the girls that come to Grace's Retreat are candidates to reside there. Our staff has meetings throughout each girl's six-week stay. Then we vote as to which girls would benefit most and would be interested in staying there. Normally, the girls live there during the first year after giving birth. By then, they've acquired their education, secured some type of employment to keep them off welfare, and are better prepared to function on their own."

"That's great," I said, believing it. Then why was I experiencing such acute emptiness? "How does Sylvia feel about doing this? Has she chosen to go there?"

Grace nodded. "She was quite excited. The other girls consider it an honor if they're chosen, because of the extra opportunity for assistance. It's a major step forward for them to rebuild their life and make a better life for their child."

As if sensing how I felt, when *I* wasn't even sure what that was, Mark reached for my hand. "This is a tremendous program. It's almost like having a child get accepted to college, from the sound of it."

Grace laughed. "Well, college is certainly down the road for any of the girls who show an interest. One nice thing about living there is that the girls are looked after, but it's less stringent than residing here. That's another criterion that's considered. If the girl adjusted well here with rules and regulations, then chances are she'll succeed with a bit more freedom."

"Hmm, true," I said, wishing the damn ache inside me would go away. "I imagine this is the surprise she mentioned last night on the telephone?"

Grace smiled. "I believe this was part of it. She knew I'd be discussing it with you and Mark first. But she has another surprise for you, so I'll let her tell you that one. Come on, I'll take you into the sitting room. She's there waiting for you."

The first thing that struck me was the obvious fact she was now over four months pregnant. When Sylvia arrived here, she showed no physical indication. She was wearing one of the attractive maternity smocks I'd purchased for her. Small yellow flowers in the fabric created a glow on her cheeks. I had to admit— she looked terrific. Her long sandy color hair was secured back from her face with a yellow satin ribbon and the few pounds she'd gained did her justice.

She ran toward me with arms outstretched. "Oh God, Maddie, I've missed you so much!"

I could feel the small bulge between us as I hugged her, "Sylvia, you look wonderful. I'm so proud of you."

After a few moments, she released me, turning to Mark. He returned her warm hug, saying, "Hey, kiddo, we're both proud of you. You're going to make one terrific new mom."

Laughing with excitement, she took our hands, leading us to the sofa. "I guess Grace explained about my moving to the other home?"

When I only nodded, Mark said, "Yeah, and what great news. Sounds like a super start for you and the baby."

Sylvia bubbled over with enthusiasm. "I know, isn't it? I'm really fortunate to be chosen. Some of the other girls are jealous, but a few of them are returning home to their parents. I'm doing great in school and I'll have a chance to attend college now. They provide day care right at the house, transportation to college, everything. Oh, and I'll even get to see Ben. I'm allowed to go out on Friday and Saturday nights. We have a curfew to be back by midnight, but that won't be a problem. Wait till Ben finds out. He'll be happy about that. I think he's missed me."

I had to laugh at her schoolgirl exuberance. "Hey, wait a second here, kid. *I've* missed you. A lot. But all of this is great, Sylvia. I'm so happy for you. I really am."

Sitting between us, she reached for my hand and Mark's. "Okay. Now for the really big news. I had an ultrasound yesterday." She paused for a moment, before making her big announcement. "I'm having a girl! I wanted a girl so bad—well, I mean a boy would have been okay too, of course. But a *girl!* I'm so excited."

This news put me over the edge. I could feel the tears wetting my cheeks as I leaned over to hug her. "Oh, Sylvia, I'm so happy for you! A daughter."

"Congratulations," Mark said, joining our happiness.

Sylvia's face beamed with joy. "A couple more things," she said, as her hand rested on her stomach. "I've chosen her name. I'm going to call her Marlene. She'll have the first two letters of both your names."

"Marlene," he said, "a perfect name."

"Sylvia, I'm so touched. You mean we'll have a namesake?"

She nodded her head excitedly. "Yeah, you'll always be Aunt Maddie and Uncle Mark to her. And I hope you don't mind, but I'm giving your names and phone number to be contacted the moment I start my labor. Will that be okay?"

Mark laughed, answering for me. "Hey, we'd be insulted if you didn't. Just make sure you get to the hospital in time though. I haven't done any OB training in years."

"You can be sure of that. I can't have my daughter being born anywhere but in a hospital. I was born in a taxi, you know. Yup, my mother couldn't even get that right. No wonder my life's been so screwed up." Sylvia laughed in a way that indicated she knew it was events following her birth that caused the problems.

By the time we left Sylvia, I was feeling somewhat less rejected. Later that evening, Mark and I were relaxing with a glass of wine.

I was lying with my head in his lap as he traced the outline of my face with his fingertips. "Feeling better?" he asked.

"Hmm, I guess so. How'd you know I wasn't feeling so great?" It still amazed me that sometimes he understood me better than I understood myself.

Looking up, I saw a smile cross his handsome face. "Ah, Maddie, every now and again you're an open book. It's only natural you'd feel a bit sad that Sylvia's moving on. Similar to the empty nest syndrome."

I nodded. "Yeah. I'm thrilled she has this opportunity, but I guess I just assumed she'd be returning here with us."

His hand stroked my arm. "She'll be just fine. It's not so bad here with only the two of us, is it?"

Pulling his head down, I kissed his lips. "No, not in the least. I'm getting to like all this privacy we have."

"And you never know, Maddie. I've had a vasectomy, but they now have excellent results with reversal surgery."

I reached up to touch his face. In that moment, knowing that he would consider doing this for me, I loved him more than I thought possible. How could he know that was part of what had bothered me earlier in the day? I was losing Sylvia, but also the baby I thought would be living with us for a while.

"I love you, Mark," I whispered.

His hand moved to my breast. "I know we can't make a baby right now, but how about if we practice by making love?"

I smiled as I stood up and reached for his hand, leading him into our bedroom.

CHAPTER 24

Richard Witton sat staring out his office window on the fifty-sixth floor. His brow was furrowed; he was in deep and disturbing thought. Everything seemed to be going in the wrong direction after all his work aimed at making this world a better place. No one could blame him, but the mission demanded perfection, so leaders who didn't reach that level were soon gone from positions of authority. He had worked hard all his life—now this.

Lester had brought the news. Beethoven had been the worst situation ever experienced by the project. Mozart's suicide was bad enough, with the loss of enormous resources and training investment, but Beethoven's arrest could mean the total destruction of the program.

Witton had sent Lester to get answers to his questions, by picking the brains of the street men. Lousy reporting was another problem Witton had to deal with. He waited, tapping his fingers on the arm of his leather chair. The door opened without an announcement from the secretary.

"Well?" Witton asked.

"It was the INS, sir. The arrest came about seven in the evening."

"Where are they holding him?"

"In the same building."

"Do you know if there are holding cells there? Are you sure they arrested him?"

Lester felt the pressure of the interrogation. He breathed faster. "He didn't come out, so we assumed . . ."

"Dammit, man, we can't assume anything. Is the tracker operating?" Witton's hand smashed flat onto the desk.

"We tracked him to the INS building where he stayed. Then the signal stopped."

"God in heaven. The entire Omnibus system failed?" Holding his face in both hands, Witton sighed deeply. He was losing control and needed to regain his composure.

"Yes, sir. We think so."

"I want a technical man here tonight to explain to me all the potential situations that could have led to this failure and what we might expect now. Tonight. Understand?"

"I do, sir. He'll be here. Do we continue to follow Beethoven, if he's released?"

"No, it's too risky. We could alert the INS to something they don't see now. Lester, why the INS?" These words were consoling, almost conciliatory.

"They could be part of a secret undercover element posing as INS, but our people in the government—in the highest places—would have completely failed to not know it."

"All right, that's all. I don't think everyone could be failing like we are."

"But, sir, we couldn't . . ."

"We could be blamed and will be with the accompanying penalty for failure. Nothing must interfere with this mission."

* * *

Sylvia's good news provided pleasant relief from our stress. The girl had become an important element of our small family. Maddie was like a sister to Sylvia, but I was more at ease as a father figure. Worrying about Sylvia gave us another reason to be close, even though Sylvia seemed to be doing well on her own.

Waiting for the INS report on my foreign object was nerve racking, but Maddie and I managed to control our emotions with work at the clinic. I also had to decide about the issue of the health bill.

On the third day after my encounter with the INS, a call came at the clinic. Grundig and Corso wanted to meet that evening. Remembering spy movies I had seen, I told Grundig that I would only meet them in a public place. At that point I made a fateful decision, Maddie had to be there. As work wound down at the clinic, I approached her. "Want to go out for dinner with me tonight?"

"You think we should? Dinners out cost a lot of money and we aren't exactly rolling in it. I can make something just as nice, plus there's a good bottle of bardolino in the pantry."

"There's a catch. The INS guys want to meet me at seven. I don't want to see them alone. Christ, I'm having guilt pangs over what I might have done before being deprived of my personal music subscription. Whatever they want to talk about, I'd feel better with a witness. Could you go with me?" Besides being a witness, Maddie was also an advocate in a game where the feds controlled the odds.

"Yes, of course. I'm pleased you want me to be there. Mark, don't you understand I love you and want to help you? Where will we meet them?"

"The Library of Congress—a reserved room."

* * *

The room was reserved for Johnny Jones and Mark Puccini. Maddie and I sat a bit unnerved when twenty minutes past seven rolled by. As I contemplated leaving, Grundig, Corso and an older man came into the room. There were no greetings or introductions as they sat across the table from us.

"Sorry we're late. Didn't expect your visitor," Grundig said. He looked her over suspiciously at the same time he covered his butt with his superior.

"I need someone as a witness. Trust isn't my strong suit."

"Sorry, miss, but . . ." Grundig rose from the chair in an effort to escort her from the room.

"If Maddie goes, I go." We sat quietly waiting for their

decision.

"Maddie, I'm Johnny Jones, Director of Special Investigations for the INS. There's no danger to Dr. Puccini from us." Jones' gray hair provided a distinctive touch, but his inexpensive, wrinkled suit labeled him as a fed.

"I'm staying, sir." Maddie's teeth were clenched. She spoke strangely through them.

A smile broadened my face. What a woman.

Grundig entered the discussion again, while Jones and Corso leaned back in the wooden chairs looking weary from a long day. "We were surprised by the test results on the receiver. We need to know everything about you. Finding the persons who planted the device is critical, so we need your cooperation." Grundig's facial expression telegraphed a solemnity approaching mine.

"What is it?" I asked. God, he had my attention.

Grundig looked at Jones to get permission to continue. Jones nodded. "A very sophisticated GPS tracking system with location set and a satellite audio receiver. What sort of messages did you hear?"

"I didn't hear any messages."

"Puccini, let's save ourselves some time here," Jones said. He talked with his hands, as well, making his message more acceptable and less demanding. "Have you ever been hypnotized?"

"I don't think so. Where's my receiver? I want it back," I said, hoping to move the conversation along, not truly caring about where it went. These men were here for a reason and I wanted to understand it.

"The device can't be returned to you. It's evidence," Jones said in a tone that sounded final.

"That isn't what Grundig told me when he took it for testing. Is there a law against owning a GPS receiver? They're sold in marine shops and outdoor sports clubs." I sounded more angry than I was.

"That's part of what we want to talk to you about. The receiver—your receiver—was destroyed in the testing," Jones said

"Destructive testing?" My words came out slowly with

emphasis on each syllable. While I knew little about testing, I was aghast.

Maddie watched me as I countered the comments, not really understanding where I was going.

"We didn't intend to destroy the object, but it was exceedingly difficult to open. The case was completely sealed without a seam. We need another just like it," Grundig said.

"What was it made of?" I asked.

The three men looked at each other, but none of them answered.

Maddie touched my arm, wisely wanting me to listen, not let them off the hook.

"We can't discuss it, now," Jones said, finally taking charge. "Where's your friend Robert Mozart buried?"

"In Potter's Field."

"Which one?" Corso asked, apparently being the guy who had the task of finding Robbie's resting place.

"I don't say any more until I know what you want." Maddie patted my arm in approval.

"It's important to find Mozart's grave. We believe he also has a receiver implanted in his skull. Yours is beyond repair. After we find it, we want to re-insert the receiver in your skull cavity and hope your friends attempt to call you again," Jones said.

Maddie's mouth dropped open, but I just shook my head.

"They aren't my friends so why would you want me to be at their beck and call again?"

"The problem's new. We've not had this much information about Project 1947 before and want to capitalize on this opportunity. The receiver was beyond our technology—more than a GPS system. It used the GPS satellite, but added very sophisticated touches. The state of miniaturization of the components is amazing. An important question is who could have technology beyond our country's." Jones kept his eyes down as he spoke.

"What's Project 1947? I'm not cooperating unless you tell us more." I tried to be determined, but had little to support my demand.

"Immunity's a valuable commodity, given we've made you the number one suspect in several murders and believe there are more that we haven't discovered as yet. I personally believe you're a mere pawn in a deadly game, but if your hand committed the act, then immunity is precious to you," Jones said. "You've been used—against your will—but as I say, our amnesty will relieve you of proving your utter inability to control yourself. Dr. Puccini, we tailed Mozart and we know a lot about the operation."

"You know more than I do then."

"For your continued freedom from prosecution, we expect you to tell us where Mozart's buried and to agree to an operation to re-insert his device in your skull," Jones said. His hand thumped the table. The judge had ruled.

Maddie's emotion erupted with a reddening face and blazing eyes. "No. You don't know what it's like. Will you be with him twenty-four hours a day? Can you be certain you can protect Mark from *them*? No, you can't."

"We can," Grundig said. "They're enemies of all of us and it's your duty to cooperate."

"Who are *they*?" Maddie asked the critical question.

"If Puccini and you help us, we'll know the answer to that," Jones said.

"Back to my device," I said, "what was it made of?"

Jones looked at the other two men before he answered. "We don't know. The material of the case couldn't be identified in our lab or in the FBI lab."

"Just a second," I said, "are you saying you don't know the origin of the metal used for the case?"

Jones nodded.

* * *

The dark night was perfect for disinterring a body. The graveyard had no name written on an arch spanning the entrance, and there were no headstones. Metal markers were pushed into the soil. Former grassy areas had been overcome by weeds growing tall and spreading widely. Connection to any living person had been severed after the bodies were placed here, much as many of them had lived their life—disconnected and isolated.

I had remembered the grave number for one simple reason; it was my age repeated—4545. After scouring that number from my mental data bank, I expected the feds to do their work in a legal way without my help. Instead, there I was at a Potter's Field, under cover of darkness, without a court order to disturb the dead. Why was I there? They needed me to verify the body as Robbie's.

I smiled to myself as two men I hadn't met began to dig in the spot below marker 4545. They had no digging equipment, only shovels and hand labor—a scene from a Boris Karloff movie. Unreal, but serious with a threat to me because I had no choice in the matter. Cooperate or be arraigned as a murderer. Worse yet, I had no defense and couldn't even feel confident that I did none of what I would be accused of. Being an unwilling partner to this crime didn't absolve me from the punishment getting caught would have brought. A few times, I found myself praying these were genuine federal agents.

A dull thud told us they had arrived at the casket after an easy dig, because the original grave diggers hadn't bothered to go down the required depth. No extra effort had been given to those isolated in life.

The casket was bare wood with a solid lid that they pried off with a crow bar. The body was wrapped in a sheet-like cloth that Corso pulled away.

"Jesus Christ," Corso said as he twisted away in shock from the exposed half-face.

Robbie had shot himself in the face, probably trying to hit the back of his mouth, but had done a lousy job. A shudder went through my body.

"No one'll identify this stiff," Grundig said. "What a mess."

What we saw no longer resembled a face. The other doctor in the group stretched a pair of heavy rubber gloves on, then pulled hard to turn Robbie's body on its side. Standing with one foot out of the casket and one in, the man reached up for a drill.

Chills ran down my back and across my forehead. "What're you going to do?" I asked with obvious annoyance.

"Mind your own business, doctor. I'm the surgeon here."

Corso held the long flashlight focused on Robbie's head, trying to watch me as well.

The doctor asked for the electric shaver and clipped hair away from the area at the right base of the skull. Someone had told him where my device had been planted. He then was going to drill over the area near the tiny scar.

"No," I said. "Christ, he may be dead, but there's no need to mutilate him even more. You don't need a drill; a scalpel will do the job."

He ignored me and I couldn't stand by any longer. I dropped into the grave space, taking the spinning drill from his hand. All I had to say was *gloves* and the guy knew I wasn't going to stand for any bullshit. He put three clean gloves in my hand. I stretched two on my hands, letting the third fall into the grave. Grundig gave me a mask that helped with the stench a bit, but it was unpleasant. The drill doctor was snickering at me. A medical examiner, no doubt.

I carefully opened the skin above the old scar, then widened the open area. The tracker was sitting in the same position as mine was, just below the epidermis.

Grundig handed a long thin magnet to me. "Remember, we were listening to your conversation," he said. "The magnet was a good idea then and will work now."

With a little more nudging, the device popped onto the tip of the strong magnet. Grundig grabbed it before I could begin to climb out of the grave.

"Aren't you going to close, Dr. Puccini?"

"Fuck you, Dr. Jekyll," I said.

Grundig's face showed that he wasn't happy about our snipping at each other as I realized that the plan was to have Dr. Jekyll insert the device in my skull. No way. Now the whole idea was sounding very bad for me.

That night I had added to my list of crimes, only this time I knew what I had done. Opening a grave without authorization and violating a body was surely a felony. I wondered if the INS was recording the entire affair to accumulate further evidence against me.

All I wanted to do was go home to my Maddie.

CHAPTER 25

Sun filling our bedroom caused me to squint as I rolled over, snuggling deeper into Mark's chest. I could hear his easy, gentle breathing, which consumed me with love. Mark had arrived home after midnight. Now I recalled his graveyard story that added another bizarre situation to the list. One thing I knew for certain—I had no understanding of implanted receivers, but I knew Mark was incapable of intentionally hurting another human being. No matter what heinous acts may have been committed, it wasn't the Mark I knew that had carried them out. I stroked the side of his face with my fingertip, careful not to wake him as I kissed his cheek.

Engrossed with the Sunday paper and coffee, I was startled by the ringing telephone. The only calls Mark and I usually got were from the clinic. When I picked up, I heard Bryce's voice laced with anger.

"Listen, you bitch, don't get any thoughts about joining this witch hunt."

Confused and trying to hide my fear, my voice took on a quality of self-assurance. "I have no idea what you're talking about."

"No? Well, open up your paper to the Metro section. As I said, don't even think about joining this select group of pathetic females. None of you have a shred of evidence. Consider this a warning, Maddie."

The slamming of his phone echoed in my ear as I walked back to the table. Pulling out the Metro section, I saw the headline immediately, along with a flattering photo of Senator Bryce Pope and his attractive wife, Lila. *Sexual Harassment Charges Filed Against Senator Pope* was in bold print above the photo. Three females had filed suit against the senator. All three were employed on his administrative staff, two in Washington and one in his Boston office. Alison Taylor of Marblehead, Massachusetts, had recently been let go from her position. The two local women were still employed at the time of the interview. The article went on to say that Lila Pope was the former Lila Buchannan of Concord, Massachusetts and the daughter of the highly acclaimed Attorney, Adam Buchannan with the Boston law firm, Fitzpatrick and Buchannan. The article ended by saying an investigation was being held and Senator Pope was not available for comment.

My first thought was you reap what you sow, followed by wondering how I could obtain Alison Taylor's home phone number. There was no doubt that Bryce's power was now catching up with him—and not in a favorable way.

* * *

The Sunday paper sent an important message to Maddie, highlighting that we had a conflict of interest developing. She seemed intent on seeing justice done to the arrogant senator, but I wanted to see him popular enough to push the most important health bill in years through the congressional process.

He already had cold feet over the political atmosphere, as he seldom risked a political setback that would spoil his impeccable record of sponsoring successful legislation.

One thing was certain, Maddie had a just cause and whatever we did together, there was no good reason to deter her from pressing her issue. At the same time, my scruples stretched to achieving both ends by misrepresenting a thing or two to the senator and his staff. Perhaps I had a sick mind, but there were numerous scenarios flying through it. Using

Maddie as a counterbalance to the three accusing women could work, at least until the bill was passed. I wasn't ready to approach Maddie with my idea yet.

* * *

To my utter disbelief, the Wednesday morning paper had an article headlining the Metro Section: *Grave Robbers Mutilate Corpse*. Who would have imagined that a gravedigger, too lazy to dig a proper hole for a lonely slob, would have reported a disturbed gravesite to the police? The article revealed that a rubber glove had been found in the loose dirt. Chills leapt up my spine as I read. Christ, this wasn't my week or month—maybe not my whole life. When would luck follow me? Then I felt sheepish. Maddie represented all the luck any man needed.

Even with Maddie's support, there was a bad problem. My fingerprints could be on the single rubber glove casually dropped into the dirt that night—four days ago. Could anyone trace a print to me? My heart started beating faster and I felt flushed.

Connie stuck her head into my cubicle. "Mr. Romano is waiting for you in number two, doctor. Mark, are you all right? You look strange."

"I'll be right there."

I remembered the one time the cops arrested me for vagrancy. They fingerprinted me, keeping me all night, allowing me to escape the ugliness of the cold, damp night on a Washington park bench. I hadn't minded getting an arrest record at the time, but now shuddered at the thought. There was little time to waste in getting to see Senator Pope and a good chance that my so-called INS friends wouldn't even know me if I was arrested. Who would believe my story about INS agents screwing around with an American citizen and unknown substances used to make advanced systems that our best technologists couldn't sort out? I hardly believed it myself.

As soon as I treated Gino Romano, I took a taxi to the senator's office, using the plastic pass I had been given to enter the building. The woman who carried my script to me previously was her usual cold, Washington I-don't-give-a-shit self, telling me that seeing Senator Pope was impossible. She never did cotton to a street bum and that was all I could ever be to her.

Barton James was my next resort and he was his usual aloof self, too, but he spoke to me as he came from his office.

"Hey, Mark. Good job at the hearing. I was impressed."

I was going to ask why he didn't congratulate me at the hearing, but thought better of it. He wasn't about to lower himself to a street person in public and certainly not on C-Span. "I need to see the senator, Barton." I used my best professional tone.

"I can help, I'm sure. No need to bother the boss." Since he didn't invite me into his office, we continued to stand in the enclosed hallway.

"I don't think so."

"What's on your mind, anyway?"

"The bill. I want to see it passed. The papers say that Pope is considering tabling the bill because he thinks his support is waning."

"It's a political decision, Puccini, but you're not a politician and wouldn't understand. The point is Bryce wants to live to fight another day. Nothing will change his mind."

He turned away about to return to his office, but I latched onto his arm. Barton looked at me from the corner of his eye, but stopped.

"Give the big lobbies a full year to work the system and this bill will never pass in a form that'll do any good for the people who need it. It has to be pushed now. This bill has to go forward now," I said. "Can't you see the insurance industry figuring an angle that will line their pockets? I was a surprise, Barton. Volunteerism was a surprise. No one suspected we could have fresh ideas and pull them together in one session. But given time, the medical associations, the insurance mob, and everybody with a bone to pick will cut the heart out of it."

"You understand the lobbies, but there's no chance Bryce will change his mind."

"The news of his sexual harassment hobby could be an interesting turn."

"Piss off, Puccini. Senator Pope never harassed anyone for sex or any other reason. This man is a goddamned saint. We need ninety-nine other senators just like him and we'd make this country right again."

"Passing a health bill that benefited millions of needy people would go a long way toward silencing the press, and the public, about his sexual escapades. Hell, at least he isn't gay, that'll help. Some women will vote for him because he's a stud. You remember that . . ."

"Never mind, I don't need any reminders of political studs who have screwed their way into the hearts of female America."

"The bill could help him weather the storm, couldn't it?" I persisted with him.

"Possibly. What do you have in mind?" He motioned for me to follow him to his desk.

"What if another woman—a former employee who left under questionable circumstances —could cast strong doubt on the testimony of the three who are bringing the charges?"

"You know of such a person?" Barton toyed with a crystal paperweight as he considered my story.

"I might."

"Don't play fucking sophomore games with me, doctor." Throwing the paperweight against the wall, Barton displayed a violent temper.

"Tell the senator that I might be able to help him—for a price." I ignored the tantrum and continued pressing him.

"The price is?" He sat on the edge of his desk, showing me that he was under control again.

"Continuing to press for the Pope-Brigham bill."

"Christ, it's a choice of one political defeat or the other. You're stupid, Puccini."

"Talk to him. He may see it differently."

"Okay, but you take no steps of any kind until I get back to you. Got it?"

"Sure, Barton old boy."

* * *

Later the same day as I wrote in a patient's record, a tall man glowered around the clinic's portable screen. "Dr. Puccini?"

"Yeah, what can I do for you?"

A second man appeared.

"You're under arrest for grave robbery and mutilation of a corpse."

The tall man roughly jerked me around, pushing my face over the metal desk. Handcuffs clicked once, twice. He started to spiel off the Miranda advisory, which I knew by heart.

"You forgot a few words, copper," I said. "I want my full rights."

He used my arms as leverage to slam my head into the wall, bringing intense pain. My vision began to gray out. I had a sensation of falling and was sick to my stomach when the sorry cop grabbed me by the shoulders.

"Shut the fuck up, mister."

* * *

The interrogation was brutal and dumb. They really knew nothing about me, treating me like a lowlife, forgetting my professional education. If I had any tendency to talk to them, this was the wrong approach. I wasn't a bum anymore. My response was defiance, structured with foul language that they understood better than good English. The tall cop tilted my chair up on two rear legs. With the handcuffs gouging my wrists, my balance was entirely in his hands. I was still woozy from the pain and anxious about what was coming next. He pushed the chair over, slamming me to the vinyl floor. My head cracked against the chair on the way to the vinyl. The sharp pain was the last thing I remembered for a while.

The cell was cold. The bump on the left side of my head and

cheekbone ached. My eyes opened slowly as someone shook me.

"Dr. Puccini, can you sit up?"

He was well dressed and handsome. A senator-to-be was my first thought as I eased to a sitting position, feeling like shit.

"I'm Assistant District Attorney Pageant. Are you all right?"

"I don't know, yet."

"I'm sorry for your discomfort, sir." This man sounded truly concerned for me.

My eyes opened wider. Someone was sorry about all this shit?

"I've explained to the police that the evidence against you is circumstantial, at best. The glove that was found in the grave with your fingerprints could have been dropped there when you attended the funeral of Mr. Mozart, your friend. That is the case, I assume," Pageant said.

"Yes, I suspect that's so."

"Charges have been dropped. You're free to go."

"You sound like my defense lawyer. Are you a city D.A.?"

"I'm a federal attorney, sir."

I tried to stand up, but my legs were weak. My moans surprised me. "Jesus, I hurt."

The tall cop with the art of tipping chairs was standing behind Pageant watching my rescue. I hadn't seen him since I was revived. The local cops didn't trust the feds.

"Stand for a minute, Mr.—I mean Dr. Puccini." Pageant helped me to regain my balance. "Let's get out of here."

The urgency in the lawyer's voice told me that we had only a slight advantage over the cops. I suspected that the feds wanted me out of this cell before any other information was passed and the cops weren't happy about the deal. Their arrest had been superseded by a federal agency and the chief-of-police probably had been involved in my release. No cops liked that kind of inter-ference.

I didn't like being beat up and slammed to the ground with my hands cuffed.

I felt stronger; the weakness in my legs was gone and my head wasn't spinning. Walking toward the cell door, I moved in front of the tall cop, whirling around to slam my body against him. The sound of his head hitting the metal bars was music—almost as good as Beethoven.

"I must still be dizzy," I said, smiling.

"Yeah, you almost fell over," Pageant said. "Let's move."

With his eyes closed, the tall cop looked content lying in a heap on the floor.

Feeling much better, I followed Pageant down the concrete corridor. "You're with INS?"

"Right. I've arranged for a ride to your apartment. The police won't be bothering you anymore."

"Can I count on that?"

"Count on it. We've exercised our considerable influence. Don't go murdering anyone, though. There are limits even to our power. Say hello to Maddie for me. Tell her Glen Pageant sends his regards."

"You know Maddie?" I stopped to study his face with my mouth hanging open like an idiot.

"I used to be a staffer for Senator Pope. She's a neat lady."

CHAPTER 26

A phone call from Glen the week before wasn't quite the surprise it might have been. When Mark returned home from his ordeal in jail, he said that a Glen Pageant had been instrumental in helping him and passed on Glen's hello. *Glen Pageant* . . . I hadn't heard his name or thought of him in about three years. The year before I went into my self-imposed exile, Glen had left the senator's staff to take a position in Washington. I struggled with my umbrella, which seemed to have a mind of its own. Pouring rain and high winds were rendering the fabric protection useless. Just great, I thought, trudging along the street for my one o'clock lunch with Glen. He had made reservations for us at a trendy Italian restaurant near the Capital. Now I was going to arrive looking like a drowned rat.

Arriving fifteen minutes early allowed me time in the ladies room to attempt a repair of my hair and wet clothes. When I exited, I saw Glen waiting for me near the entrance. He hadn't changed much since I had last seen him—tall and slim, but I now could see the beginning of a receding hairline with a few wisps of gray along the edges of his brown hair. Glen was five years older than me, so I'd always considered him a brother. He was a pleasure to work with in Boston and had always been extremely kind.

As I approached him, a smile lit up his face. "Maddie," he said, hugging me to him. "God, it's great to see you! You look terrific."

"So do you, Glen. Washington must agree with you. It's so nice to see you again."

A hostess escorted us to a table in the rear of the restaurant. With the wine order given to the waitress, Glen placed his chin on his folded hands and smiled. "I've wondered what happened to you. I heard a rumor a couple years ago that you left Pope's staff and sort of disappeared into thin air."

I nodded. "There was nothing in Boston. I wanted a new start."

He was silent for a few minutes. "I always liked you, Maddie, as a friend. Besides wanting to see you again for old time's sake, I have some information that might be valuable to you. I could be way off base, but I think you have a right to know."

"Information for me?" I was more than a little surprised. "In relation to what?"

"Bryce Pope. I've seen the recent headlines about the sexual harassment charges against him. You might not realize it, but I saw and overheard a lot when I worked with you in the Boston office."

I waited till the waitress placed the glasses of cabernet in front of us before I spoke. "What exactly did you see and hear?"

"He was putting major pressure on you, wasn't he? For sexual favors. I saw how his hand lingered a bit too long on your shoulder or around your waist. I also remember an evening I was working late. I was about to knock on his office door, but heard a confrontation going on between you and him. He wanted you to have dinner and drinks with him. I waited to make sure you were okay before I returned to my office. Then I saw you leave the building alone, getting into your car. He's a scumbag, Maddie. If you join the others in these charges, I'll testify on your behalf."

All those times I needed somebody to confide in, to talk to, I had no idea that Glen was my advocate. His telling me now touched me and I smiled.

"I'm not really sure what I'll do, Glen. But no matter what I decide, I want you to know how much I appreciate your sharing this with me. I had no idea you knew. I'm sure he didn't either. He always tried to be so discreet. Just knowing that you were looking out for me means a lot."

Glen broke off a piece of the crusty Italian bread, dipping it into the olive oil and herbs. "There's more, Maddie. More that I think you need to know."

"More? About Bryce?"

He nodded. "Do you know a guy by the name of Garret Dawson?"

The look on my face betrayed me.

"You dated him for awhile, didn't you? And then testified against him in a drug case, right?"

"How do you know?"

"Boston news gets some space in the Washington papers. I read about it. I also read he was released from prison after only serving two years. He threatened you, didn't he? When he got out?"

My hand shook as I reached for the wineglass. The horror of that night had a way of insidiously creeping back into my mind. Like flipping through photos in an album, the pictures, although faded, jumped out at me—Garret losing control of his temper, shoving me onto the floor, the pain and humiliation of my body being violated and the shard of glass. The glass that sliced the side of my face, touching every nerve ending like a hot poker. I took a deep breath, not meeting Glen's eyes. His hand reached across the table, squeezing mine.

"It's okay, Maddie. It's okay. Maybe he got off easy the first time, but we're going to get that bastard this time around."

"This time around?" I looked up and saw the determination in his face.

"There's more to this Garret Dawson than you realize. I'll tell you what I know and it's not rumor, but don't ask me how I have this information, okay?"

I nodded and waited.

"You met Garret at a fundraiser in Boston, right?"

I nodded again.

"Didn't you think it was odd that although he wasn't involved in politics, represented no major corporation donating to the cause, and had no well-known clout in Boston circles, that he was in attendance?"

"Not at first, I didn't, no. He projected the image of an affluent businessman. He seemed to belong and didn't look out of place. It was only later, when I realized he was a drug dealer, that I wondered why he was really there."

"He was really there because of Lila Pope."

"What?" I gasped. "Lila? What does she have to do with Garret Dawson?"

"A lot. Garret is Lila Pope's personal drug dealer."

"You must be kidding," I said, incredulously.

"No, I'm afraid not and it gets better. Hubby Bryce is the one who makes her purchases."

Suddenly I was having difficulty comprehending what Glen was saying. None of this made sense. Lila a drug addict? Bryce purchasing drugs? This was sounding like a low budget film.

Glen continued. "I'm afraid our illustrious Senator is the antithesis of what our taxpayers might think. His bio isn't the glowing account he'd like everyone to believe. I'm sure you're aware of the alcohol problem Mrs. Pope had and the rehab she went through?"

I nodded, waiting for the next piece of startling information.

"Unfortunately, her rehab was short-lived. She transferred her addiction for alcohol to drugs—mostly cocaine. If this news got out, Bryce knew his career was over. Certain circles knew him for the womanizer he was and I'm sure he felt they'd blame him for his wife's problem. A nice Radcliff grad, daughter of a top attorney, extremely attractive. He was probably right. The public can be fickle and switch their allegiance in a heartbeat. He couldn't risk that. He also couldn't risk daddy finding out that his daughter's married life was less than desirable. After all, it was daddy that put the title *Senator* in front of his name."

"So what are you saying, Glen? That Bryce condoned Lila's drug addiction? That he lowered himself to meet with a street drug dealer, and that he actually enabled his wife's access to cocaine?"

"That's exactly what I'm saying, Maddie. I don't think it'll be much longer before our senator will be forced to pay the piper."

"All his power is falling down around him. He thought he was untouchable. Could take and have what he felt he deserved. Because he was Bryce Pope and he was entitled." I shook my head in disgust, but a million questions were racing through my head.

Was it because of Bryce that Garret had served such a short sentence? Did Bryce know about my rape and how Garret had threatened to kill me? After I disappeared, giving up everything in my life including my identity, did Bryce know the real reason? I was beginning to feel that *yes* might possibly be the answer to all these questions.

CHAPTER 27

Sleeping was difficult the night before my scheduled operation even though I knew it was a simple, if abnormal, procedure. Many hours were spent staring out the window and walking the floor. I didn't wake Maddie up, but I disturbed her sound sleep, which she traded for wakeful periods. Still I had no choice. Lying in bed with my eyes open was more than I could stand. Therefore it was good to see the sun come up.

The new light allowed me to study Maddie's face. She was beautiful. I had become accustomed to not noticing the scar on her face, but this morning it received my full attention. The ugly gash marked a period in her life where all she had accomplished was lost. Maddie had good reason to hate, but her feelings fell far short of hate, because she wanted justice. The justice she deserved should impact a senator and a drug dealer, not to mention a senator's wife plus countless others whose life was affected by them. While I wanted her yearning to right the balance to be quelled, I also had a goal of my own. Our goals were in conflict and I needed a way to make them compatible, but first, I needed Maddie in my arms.

I rose from my position on the floor beside the bed and lay down next to her. My eyes feasted on the long curve of her back, her derriere and the smooth, muscled thighs and calves. God, she was beautiful. Gently rolling her shoulder, I caused her to be on her back. Her breasts were magnificent. Small, but firm and pouting so that her nipples protruded from her nightgown. I wanted to kiss her breasts, but didn't want to disturb her slumber.

She loved me to kiss her breasts and welcomed my kisses every-where. Kissing was the erotic part of our preparation to make love and to lose ourselves in each other.

Her eyelids flickered. A smile formed that erased the damage of her scar. White teeth welcomed me. I kissed her lips, feeling her tongue meet mine.

"Good morning," I said.

"Good morning. What a great way to wake up. I've felt you staring at me for a while, but enjoyed your admiration too much to open my eyes." She snuggled into my chest and wrapped a leg over mine.

"You're beautiful. I'm so lucky to be here with you."

"Me too. You didn't sleep very well, did you? You'll be exhausted after the doctor finishes today. Is that why you didn't sleep? Are you anxious about the procedure?" Maddie raised herself on her elbow in anticipation of my answer.

"A bit. I've been thinking that I could become a puppet again at the whim of someone I don't know and don't want to know. Maybe controlled again, beyond my ability to resist. Perhaps, I shouldn't be letting them do this."

Sitting up straight, Maddie's breasts drew my eyes to them. "I'm against it. You know that. Don't do it, you don't owe them. You're a victim here."

"If I've done evil things, I could be prosecuted. Might never see you again. I can't forget about an organization that's taking control of minds, creating a sort of zombie human being . . . that's what I was. I know the surgery's the right thing to do, but need you to watch my back. Are you still up to it?"

"I'll watch your back and your front," she said smiling. "Kiss me."

The warmth, which hadn't been very far away as I enjoyed seeing her body, came back quickly. She made me feel wanted, loved like I'd never been before.

Maddie hugged me with both arms as we rolled our bodies until she was straddling me. She pulled her nightgown over her head as I rose to meet her breasts. The taste of her body drove my thoughts away from surgery. How I needed her. She was in control and the pleasure was incredible. Her whimpers made my passion deepen. Her movements quickened as she experienced the same passion I was. We both moaned, emitting almost animal sounds of joy. Total release and intense emotion from making love to the one we loved.

"I love you," she said. "You give me pleasure that's unmatched in my life. We were made for each other. You could never have done anything evil. I'm sure of that."

"When all this is over, the perfect ending would be that you're right. God, I hope you're right."

Over the next hour, we lay in each other's arms enjoying the warmth of the afterglow. We made love again; it was even better than the first time. How could it always be better? It was. Maddie lay without speaking for a long time before she said, "I was thinking about Lila. Instead of Bryce helping her get off drugs and counseling her to soberness, he's killing her a day at a time. I hate him, Mark."

"Do you really hate him?"

"Yes, I do and Garret Dawson is in the same class of scum. I'll see that they pay and do it within the law."

"Why do you think Glen spilled the beans to you? He could have kept it to himself as he has for years." I harbored a tiny jealous thought about Glen.

"He's my friend. He wants to see justice done, too. Just like me."

Unable to resist the need, I asked, "Was he ever more than a friend?"

"No, we're pals. There was never any romance. Only friends. Are you jealous?"

My face flushed enough that I felt the difference. She read me like a sale catalogue. "No, not exactly. After all, he's better looking than me and might be a better lover."

"But I love you. He isn't better looking than you. You're my handsome man. Stop searching for compliments—no one loves me as you do."

"Okay. The thought's gone. I'm not jealous, but I need to ask you something."

The serious tone I used caused Maddie concern. She turned to look at me. "What?"

"What do you intend to do with what Glen told you? Are you going to join the suit and verify the accusations made by those three women? Will you carry it further to finish off the senator and put Dawson in jail?"

"Whoa, one question at a time." She looked away from me for a moment, watching sun rays brighten the room. "Will you help me?"

"You're helping me in ways that make me indebted to you. Why wouldn't I help you?"

"I intend to testify against Pope during the trial. I didn't tell you before, but Bryce threatened me. He said I'd better not join the women. I'll need your support, but it could be dangerous. That's one reason why I won't join the suit. I don't want his money; I only want him to pay the piper."

"Please understand that I don't give a shit about Pope. He's not my vision of the ideal U.S. senator and I despise his decision not to press for the health bill, because he thinks his reputation as a winner is more important. He won't risk the possibility of the bill being defeated. He stinks. Having said that, I'd like to spare him for a while. We should blackmail him; not for money, but for his action to drive that health bill through congress. If he does, the President will sign it, I'm sure."

Maddie moved away from me and sat in a yoga position on the bed. She studied her hand for a moment while gathering her thoughts. Disappointed. "You mean let him off?"

"No, I mean lie to him until the bill becomes law, then kick his ass. Do just what we said we wouldn't. Sink him and Dawson together. Save Lila."

"But the bill might pass next session, Mark." For the first time since I met her, Maddie had a whiny quality to her voice. She was pleading.

"Who knows? Given the lobbies set against it, the bill may

never have a chance again. You can't underestimate the power of money in Washington. The lobbies will only grow more powerful. Time's on their side. The poor folks who need volunteer doctors, nurses, and health care insurance won't grow stronger. Of that, I'm positive. It's now or it'll never happen."

"How can you be so sure?"

"I *am* sure. I need your help, Maddie." Now I was pleading.

"You have a funny way to enjoy my afterglow," she said, smiling. "Did you make love to me to put me in the right mood? Are you a calculating man?" She reached over to bring her lips to mine. "Did you seduce me for your own ends?"

"Yes, to feel the exhilaration of your body over and under me. To feel your body wrapped around me. Are you going to help me?"

"You have a one-track mind."

"Will you?" I asked, praying that she could see it my way.

"I will. What's the plan? Pope doesn't deserve honesty anyway. He wouldn't know how to handle it."

We both laughed at the truth of the statement. Honesty had a double meaning in Washington.

"Thanks. I love you. Now we're co-conspirators."

"Do we have to get up yet?" she asked.

We made love again.

* * *

The site for the surgery was the Research Department of the National Institute of Health, in Maryland. Even though it was an outpatient procedure, I was in bed being prepared. Maddie held my hand, seeing me filled with second thoughts. Would it work? How could the INS protect me from myself?

Johnny Jones had some answers. He came into the room smiling like a cat that had just killed a bird and was bringing the kill to his master. "You look relaxed, Puccini," Jones said.

"You're a poor liar, Jones," I said. I knew he was needling me and nearly offered him a one-finger salute.

"Could you excuse us for a few minutes, miss?"

Maddie looked at me before answering, unsure if I wanted privacy.

"No, Maddie stays," I said and held my hand out for her to take. The scene was juvenile in retrospect, but my situation demanded a full partner completely in the know. Besides, calling her *miss* was a bit too much.

"It's sensitive. Maybe you don't need to know," Jones said to Maddie.

I could see from his face that he thought he had the trump hand.

"Does it have to do with me, the operation, or the thing you're re-inserting into me?"

"Yes. You're also a mind reader."

"Start talking, Jones, because if you don't I'm out of here."

"I'm trying to give you some confidence in us, doctor. You're worried about being susceptible to whoever implanted the thing in the first place. Right?"

He continued before I could answer, but I would have said *yes*.

"Of course, any right-minded man would be. We know you're a good guy. We followed your testimony in the congressional hearings. All of us are impressed." Jones walked around the bed, perhaps thinking he shouldn't tell me and Maddie what was on his mind. "We've added some hardware of our own to the device. It fits behind it. The hardware prevents you from being at risk."

"I thought the device was carefully and exactly emplaced," I said. "If you added to the size, how can it be reset?"

Jones paused, shifting his eyes away from us. "We'll have to cut a bit deeper."

"Cut deeper? How thick do you think my scalp is?"

"Our doctors say that it won't matter if your skull is penetrated."

"What about the added risk of infection if I have a hole in my skull?"

"Our doctors . . ."

"Don't know what the hell they're talking about," I shouted.

"No soap. Let it protrude. I'll wear a dressing. It won't be there for long anyway. I don't *want* it in there for a long period. Do you understand?" I wanted to scream that it matters to me if I have another hole in my head, but the *juvenile scene thought* made me hold my tongue.

Grundig entered the room. He must have heard the raised voices.

"John, get the surgeon. I want to see the surgeon and the anesthetist—now," I said.

He looked at Jones. "It didn't go well, I take it."

"Get them. Let him talk to them," Jones said.

Over the next half hour, I discussed the procedure and made it plain, with repeated oaths, that I wasn't submitting to deeper placement of the device. The two men understood my professional issues and personal wishes. My gurney was pushed into the surgery with their promise that my demands would be followed to the letter.

CHAPTER 28

I felt better than the procedure should have allowed. My skull had been hit with a frying pan, gouged and re-gouged, but the only side effect of the unnamed surgeon replacing the electronic device was a mild headache. *Mr. Lucky* was the name for myself two days later.

Back at work in the clinic, life was almost normal. I had called Barton James, arranging for the earliest possible meeting with Senator Pope, which was one week later. Even that was only achievable because I mentioned Maddie. James must have known of her issue with the senator.

Dr. Stein was most interested in my new dressing. Without being obnoxious, Bruce insisted on seeing the spot where he had probed. Why had I replaced it? Was I mad? What the hell was this thing anyway? After the questions I truly deserved, Stein told me that the sutures evenly spaced in a circle around synthetic skin-like material were expertly performed. When he asked me who did the work, I had to tell him I didn't know the doctor—not even his name. Then came the tirade with the shaking finger. Had I no concern for my life? Let a government doctor operate and not know his name?

I tried to stay away from the reasons for having the device re-inserted, but felt obliged to tell my learned doctor friend that I was cooperating with a government agency that was important. That's as far as I could go, but he seemed satisfied, telling me at the same time that I was nuts. He was right.

Maddie was always at my side. Her presence completed my life.

I had gone from a street bum to a reasonably respected doctor again, because I had met her, fell in love, and got my life in line. A strange turn of events. Yes, I felt like Mr. Lucky.

I wanted to go out with her, so after the last patient left, I asked her to accompany me to a music store. We hadn't had a lot of music in our lives and I missed it. She accepted my invitation, with the added enticement of dinner at a French restaurant near the Smithsonian.

"My budget will allow buying a modest CD player," I said.

"We have the tape player and the turntable, Mark, do we need to splurge now?" Maddie asked.

"Yes, and I want to get some new Mozart CDs."

She looked at me with slits for eyes and a knotted brow. I was annoyed at her reluctance to assist me in an innocent and inexpensive purchase. I deserved to be ashamed at my burbling anger, but I wasn't.

* * *

We took a taxi to a chain electronics store where I bought a small CD player that plugged into our existing stereo system and was inexpensive. I carried the package to the music store down the street relishing the prospect of new music.

Flipping through a stack of Mozart compositions in the CD rack, I gathered six.

"What's going on here? You told me that Mozart wasn't your favorite composer. Wrong time period, you said. Now you like him enough to buy all those CDs?"

"I don't think I said that. He's my favorite composer." Why was Maddie being so contrary about a few CDs?

"Mark Puccini, I don't believe you. Beethoven's your favorite composer, bar none. You said that twenty times if you told me once."

She was mistaken, making me annoyed now. She was building a big deal out of an inconsequential purchase. Why? "I liked Mozart and never enjoyed Beethoven. Can we leave this subject, please?"

"Are you feeling all right?" Maddie pulled my elbow, drawing me to her. "Do you hear Beethoven again? Or Mozart?"

I was staring at her, but somehow lost the context of the discussion.

"Mark, stop it. You're frightening me. Let's go home." She tried to pull me by the arm.

"No, I want to buy these." I pulled away, marching to the checkout counter with the new recordings.

"We have to carry that merchandise now? What about going to dinner?"

Her words suddenly had meaning to me again. "You're right. We have to walk back home to drop these things off. Then we'll take a taxi to Le Domaine."

The walk seemed too silent. Maddie kept looking at me, as if I might walk away from her. She took my arm, which made carrying the CD player much more difficult, but I didn't complain. I had the distinct feeling that I had been unreasonable, but wasn't sure why.

At home, I began to un-box the machine and connect it to the stereo. Hearing the robust music was the most important thing on my mind.

Maddie watched me. She made me uncomfortable, but she smiled at me and the tension seemed to go away.

"How about a pizza? Let's order one," Maddie said.

"Great idea, I'm starving." Le Domaine was wiped from my memory.

* * *

I went to bed early that night with Mozart playing much too loud; the stress must have gotten to me. Falling asleep without Maddie in bed seemed all right. My mind focused on other things. The dreams that started immediately were of my childhood. The last dream, just before dawn, left me screaming, soaked with sweat as Maddie held me in her arms. The doctors were cutting me.

They went to my scrotum—it hurt. Not knowing what the surgeons were doing was the most frightening. My mind passed through all the evil things these monsters might do. Screaming was all that was possible.

* * *

The sun had set and shadows took over the city. New York was the finest night city in the world. Witton observed the traffic below his office window, allowing his mind to race to other days and better times when he was in control of smaller operations. He had never screwed up. The sharp sound of a door needing oil drew his attention. He turned to see Charles Lester approaching with a broad smile on his flattish face.

"Get that door seen to, will you, Charles?"

"Yes, sir." He paused. "The news is good, very good. The connection is definitely to Mozart's apparatus, but it's in Beethoven's head and it's been modified. All the sensitive cerebral responses are there. It must be implanted."

"Someone, maybe the INS, thinks they can monitor us or him. How laughable. They're so ignorant," Witton said.

"It's basically a crude scanner that steps down the frequency and retransmits the signal to another receiver. Unfortunately for them, we can either jam the step-down frequency or insert a message or signal that we wish them to hear. We have them in our palms."

"The control mechanism is working?"

"The hypnotic sequence is underway. Dr. Second is sure the conversion time will be short because the program differences are rather small. Mozart and Beethoven were in the same group. They were destined for the same type of operation."

"I'm relieved, Charles. Why don't we have a cognac from the bar. Will you do the honors?"

Charles Lester carefully poured two fingers of the heavy brown liquid. Then he dropped two tablets in each glass, rotating the cognac until the tablets dissolved. He gave a glass to Witton.

"To success, sir."

"To our reprieve and final success." He drank the contents in successive gulps. "It's too bad we have to adjust this wonderful drink. Some day I'd like to take the risk and see what it means to be drunk."

"You're braver than I am, sir."

* * *

The next days were better. Maddie told me that I was in a good mood and patients seemed to be happy with my services. Of course, poor patients weren't in a position to complain a lot. Without actually knowing at the time, I had been a bear to get along with. Whatever the problem was, I was feeling better and Maddie kept me on my toes at home.

"Glad you're over your period, doctor," she said.

"Oh, boy, here it comes. So, it was my time of the month? I don't do it every month," I said, relieved that she brought my strangeness up.

"Maybe it's male menopause." Maddie was laughing at me.

"Okay, I'm sorry for not being nice. I don't know what the hell was bothering me, but I feel great now."

"You don't need to be. I think the operation and the headaches took their toll on you. That's all. Do you hear the music any more, Mark? I mean since they re-implanted the thing in your head." She grimaced just thinking about it.

"No. I haven't. Only the dreams, they came at me in an inferno for a few nights, but they're gone, too. Must have had memories that came back whether I wanted them or not."

"Do I need to follow you? If you seem to go away without a good reason? You know what I'm saying," she said.

"Yes, I do, and no you don't need to follow me. The boys—Grundig and Corso—are doing that. They've told me that they fixed the device and now they can interpret any signals. No kidding. It was a relief. My worry was being under control again, but now I can relax."

"How can you be certain?" She held my arm and her worried brow told me she was concerned.

"Maddie, we're talking about the government of the most advanced and technically superior country on earth. I can trust them and so can you. Don't worry, I'm all right now."

She hugged me so tightly that we needed to search for a breath. I laughed at her and kissed her lips. The hug aroused the best thoughts I had had all day. "God, I love you, Maddie. It's going to be all right, honest."

"Okay. Where's the wine you promised me at the clinic?"

"On the way. I'm looking forward to a night on the couch. Maybe we can listen to some good music."

"How about Frank? Or Tony Bennett?"

"Sure, as long as you let me play a Mozart piece that I really love—Alleluja. Sarah Brightman sings it."

Maddie's lips registered disappointment at both ends. Shaking her head slowly, she seemed to be considering my musical taste. I thought I saw a hint of tears, but must have been wrong. We made love on the living room floor. Like young kids, we enjoyed our love with abandon. I truly was lucky.

CHAPTER 29

A week following Mark's procedure, he still exhibited signs of anxiety with occasional agitation. Not quite as intense as the day in the music shop, but enough that my concern failed to diminish.

Normally easy going and pleasant, it was surprising to see this other Mark emerge. I'm not sure he recalled the episodes when he became short-tempered with me, but I saw no reason to dwell on it. If it continued, I planned to discuss it with Dr. Stein. I was finishing up the breakfast dishes when the telephone rang. Hearing Glen's voice, I smiled. "How are you, Glen? I'm afraid Mark isn't here. He's out doing some errands."

"No problem. Actually, I called to talk to you. Have you given any more thought to testifying against our illustrious senator?"

I shook my head. "No, I really haven't. I've been busy with other things. Besides, I'm not sure I want to get involved in all of that."

Glen was silent for a few moments. "You might find it interesting that I had a dinner date with Rebecca Sanford last night."

The name meant nothing to me. "Rebecca Sanford?"

"She's one of the two women bringing charges against Bryce."

I was quickly catching on. "And you want me to speak to her, right?"

His laugh had a trace of embarrassment. "Well, let's say I was hoping you would. Rebecca asked if I'd get in touch with you to see if you'd at least call her. The whole deal could be falling apart. It seems this Alison Taylor is possibly changing her mind about testifying."

I was surprised to hear this and the line was silent. "Okay, Glen. I'm not promising anything, but give me Rebecca's phone number."

"Hey, Maddie, I really appreciate it," he said, proceeding to give me her office, cell phone and home telephone numbers.

Jotting them down, I laughed. "Any preference which one I should use? That is, *if* I decide to call her."

"She leaves the office around five. After that, if there's no answer on her home phone, try the cell. And Maddie, thanks again. You won't be sorry if you call her."

* * *

Later that afternoon, I placed the call to Rebecca's office and Glen was right. I liked the tone of her voice immediately. She sounded like a sincere and kind person.

"Maddie, thank you so much for agreeing to speak with me. I do wish you'd consider testifying with Jenna and me, but that isn't the main reason I wanted to talk with you."

I waited for her to continue, with my curiosity aroused.

"I'm sure you read in the paper that three of us are bringing suit against the senator. I got a phone call from Alison the other day and it seems she's backing out. She won't give me any details. It doesn't make sense because she was the one that contacted Jenna and me to initiate the action."

I nodded. "Yeah, that does seem a bit odd. Do you think ole Bryce got to her? Offered her money or something to keep her mouth shut?"

"I don't think so," Rebecca said. "I don't know Alison all that well—only from her work-related visits to Washington—but she seemed like a person with integrity. I'd be quite surprised if this was the reason. I was wondering if perhaps you could phone her? Maybe she'd be willing to tell you why and between the three of us we might get her to reconsider. I know you're from the Boston area, so she might be more willing to talk to you."

I was relieved that Rebecca hadn't planned to badger me into testifying, but I also wasn't thrilled to phone a stranger with an attempt to get details of this sort. "She doesn't even know me, Rebecca. I doubt she'd tell me more than she's shared with you. Besides, that's a difficult conversation via telephone."

"True. That's why I'm so grateful you phoned me as soon as Glen told you. Alison's in town 'till tomorrow evening. She flew down here yesterday to get some things sorted out with bridging her health benefits to a new position she has." Rebecca paused, allowing me to absorb the information. "Maddie, she's staying at the Capital Hilton. Can I give you her number there?"

* * *

Once again I found myself in a taxi heading to the Capital Hilton during rush-hour traffic. I reached Alison in her room and was more than a little surprised at how agreeable she was to meet me. After I explained who I was, she said, "This is about Bryce, isn't it? Can you meet me here in the lounge around five thirty?"

Walking into the semi-crowded lounge, I spotted her immediately from the description she'd given me. She appeared to be in her mid-thirties, exceptionally attractive with very short, stylish, blonde hair that accentuated her striking features. We made eye contact as I walked toward her. When she stood up, I saw she was tall, slim and wearing a fashionable two-piece chocolate brown suit that contrasted nicely with her hair color. She definitely fit the profile as one of Bryce's female employees.

"I'm Alison," she said, extending her hand. "You can call me Ally."

"And I'm Madeline. But you can call me Maddie," I said, returning her handshake as we both burst out laughing at the similarity of our nicknames.

We ordered cabernet and I liked her. She was one of those

people that had a pleasant demeanor and it was easy to see how Bryce took advantage of her.

She got right to the point. "Rebecca wants you to get me to reconsider about testifying, doesn't she?"

I smiled and respected her candidness. "Yeah, she does. I think more than anything she's confused as to why you changed your mind."

Taking a sip of her wine, she nodded, but remained silent for a few moments. "I can understand that since I was the one that approached her and Jenna about bringing suit. Initially, it was anger at Bryce and forcing him to pay. Not to say that the anger has disappeared. It hasn't. There's just more to my story than anyone realizes, so I'm not sure I want it to become public knowledge."

"I can understand that. Unfortunately, this is what happens in rape and sexual harassment cases. It can all get turned around with the victim ending up looking like the culprit. The bad guy goes free and the woman's reputation is less than desirable."

"Exactly. And I have a lot at stake here. I'm beginning to wonder if making Bryce accountable is worth the price I might have to pay."

When I remained silent, she said, "Are you testifying?"

"I'm not quite sure, Ally. I've given it a lot of thought, but I'm still not sure. So believe me, without even knowing your whole story—I do understand."

"Did you sleep with Bryce?" she questioned bluntly.

The bluntness of her question surprised me. This woman had no qualms about being up-front. I shook my head, and replied, "No, I kept refusing—he kept trying. But it never happened."

"Well, it did for me," she said quietly. "I gave in and had sex with Bryce. Numerous times, actually."

"I see," was all I could manage to say.

"Sordid, isn't it?" she replied, and then continued. "I guess I should start at the beginning. I have a twelve-year-old daughter. Aubrey was born with a neurological disease. The first two years of her life were spent mostly in and out of hospitals and rehab facilities. The medical costs were enormous, but my husband had excellent health coverage with his job. Right before Aubrey turned three, Brad couldn't take it anymore. He said he couldn't face the rest of his life with a handicapped daughter and our marriage was falling apart because of it. Brad packed his bags and was gone."

I shook my head. "Helluva nice guy, wasn't he?"

Ally shrugged her shoulders. "Guess we all make our choices in life. Brad made his. Aubrey is the light of my life and I was determined to do everything I could to make her life as great as possible. I was thankful for my degree in political science. Applying for the position with Bryce, I naively thought *this* was what got me such a high paying job with excellent health benefits. It was my looks and body he was interested in and not my intelligence."

"Yeah, I'm afraid most of the females he's hired have been naïve about this. So you weren't alone."

"I had Aubrey in a wonderful day program which enabled me to work and know she was safe. Safe, but also being worked with to reach her full potential. Aubrey learned to speak—well enough that we can communicate verbally. Unfortunately, she's still unable to walk and has to use a wheelchair. Her last testing showed her mental ability probably won't go much beyond a ten year old.

"About three years ago, her school lost the funding needed to keep it going. They gave us six months to make arrangements and place our children in other programs. Needless to say, I was distraught. I've always been terrified that somebody would take advantage of Aubrey in a sexual way. Reports about abuse in day-care centers only frightened me more."

The waitress approached our table and we each ordered another glass of wine. I glanced at my watch—half past six. I knew Mark would be wondering where I had disappeared to and regretted not leaving a note for him.

Ally continued. "Surprisingly, Bryce was the one that came up with the perfect solution—but there was a catch. He suggested that I keep Aubrey at home, hiring a private nurse and physical therapist to be with her during the day while I was at work or traveling for business. Yeah, perfect solution. Except health insurance doesn't cover this when there are outpatient facilities available. Bryce offered to pay for both the nurse and therapist."

He had manipulated her right into a corner. "And all you had to do was keep him supplied with sexual favors, right?"

Her eyes were shiny with tears as she nodded. "Yeah, just like a prostitute. In protecting my daughter, I guess I prostituted myself."

Reaching across the table, I squeezed her hand. "In all honesty, that bastard didn't give you much of an option."

"But it wasn't right. I know that now."

"Who's to say what's right, Ally? None of us are so pious that we have room to judge."

"Well, for two years we had this little agreement. He wrote the checks to the nurse and the therapist, and I had sex with him in hotel rooms. Aubrey got to stay in her own home with people she came to love and trust, and she thrived. I got her a puppy, we took trips to Cape Cod and Disneyworld, and I felt very fortunate. But last year, Bryce began making more and more demands on my time outside work. To the point where it was beginning to take away my time with Aubrey. I refused to allow that, finally forcing myself to look at the situation and figure out where I was headed. The arrangement we had could be ended anytime he chose. He always held the trump card and I finally woke up." Ally took a sip of her wine. "That bastard says he fired me. It's a lie. I gave him my resignation." I heard anger creep into her voice.

"You did?" I asked, in surprise.

"Yeah, I did, but it's his word against mine. In the end, he tried to ruin me any way he could. But you know, sometimes life can be very kind. I had no idea what I was going to do, but I knew the time had come to grab what strength I had and change things. I was honest with Cath, Aubrey's nurse, and I told her I had to leave my position. That it would be financially impossible to keep her any longer. She was devastated and said that Aubrey and I had become family to her. Cath is in her mid-forties, divorced with no children. She made me an offer I couldn't refuse. If she could move in with us and take the guest bedroom, it would decrease her expenses enormously. Therefore, she'd be able to accept whatever I could afford to pay her."

I shook my head in astonishment. Life really can be good sometimes when you encounter the right people. "God, that's great, Ally. What a blessing that was."

"You have no idea. And three times a week, Cath takes Aubrey in her van for outpatient physical therapy and waits for her. She's a godsend. I don't know what I'd do without her. Despite Bryce badmouthing me, I was able to get a well-paying job in Boston at the State House. I get the feeling that many people know the real Bryce Pope."

"What an incredible story with a wonderful ending. But Ally, after what Bryce put you through, I would think you'd have all the more reason to push the suit against him."

"That's what I originally thought, but then I found out that neither Rebecca nor Jenna gave in and had sex with Bryce. I'm the only one that did. The more I thought about it, the more I felt I had been just as wrong. No matter the reason. I know if I testify, this will all come out. I'm not sure I can sit in a courtroom and tell the public."

I reached across the table and squeezed Ally's hand once again. "Your fear is justified, but grab on to that strength you showed when you confronted Bryce and got away from him. Focus on the strength you have, not the fear. Let a jury decide. I don't think they'll be judging you on morals—but they will judge Bryce for the wrong he committed against you."

CHAPTER 30

The Brass Pitcher had been a bright spot in New York for a long time. In days gone by, one could see Joe DiMaggio there, later Mickey Mantle, along with other slugging Yankees. Because of its star attraction, the Brass Pitcher was also a good place not to be seen. No one paid attention to millionaires or politicians. Men in the public eye could bring their latest sweetheart without fear of being discovered by the press. Important men and New York's crime families rubbed shoulders over a bottle of wine or a draft beer brewed on location.

Ronald Owens relaxed every time he came to the Brass Pitcher, regardless of the reason for a meeting. He was anonymous as the number two man in the United Nations organization. Owens loved the cold, dark, almost sweet draft ale they served. He was drinking his third glass when Richard Witton approached the table.

"Sorry I'm late, sir."

"Richard, I hope we can dispense with formalities for the evening. We don't have many opportunities to talk for social pleasure. My friends call me Ron."

"Oh, yes . . . Ron, I'm happy to relax with you. I have a lot to say."

"Don't you find the bar lighting to be a minor wonder of this world? The light and the pinkish mirrors cast a glow throughout the club. It's hypnotic; and I should know about hypnotic." Owens laughed easily. "These people have a certain touch with lighting."

Witton had never seen him so relaxed. He stared at the glass half-full of ale.

"Ready for a cold drink?" Owens asked.

"Yes, I'm prepared." Witton took a small pill case from his pocket, picking out two tiny capsules. He dropped the tablets into his Manhattan glass as soon as the waiter served him.

Owens stared for a moment at a big man who came in the door with a loud laugh. The maître'd rushed to greet him, shaking his hand.

"That's David Wells, a great pitcher. Have you been to the stadium this year?"

"No, I haven't. Been awfully busy. Actually, I've never been stimulated by baseball."

"Wells is a good example of why I like these people. A free spirit, yet there's a discipline during the game that many lack. A lot of our people lack these qualities."

Witton straightened his posture and seemed to bristle at the criticism. "I'm not aware of any of us being short on discipline. It's our trump card." Witton realized he had contradicted his boss. "I mean, I haven't met anyone myself, sir."

"I know what you mean." Owens smiled at his serious underling. "Thank you for coming tonight. We need a long talk. You've been under a great deal of pressure."

"The project is back on track." Witton was defensive and touchy as he rushed his speech out. "Beethoven is under control again and the INS has foolishly given him back to us. They're so ignorant of our technology that it's funny." Witton tilted his head jauntily as he did when he was instructing his inferiors.

"Don't underrate them."

"I don't intend to. We'll eliminate each of the agents who have gained knowledge of any aspect of the project. I've already made the assignments."

"Why do you frown?" Owens asked.

"The duality of it all is a concern for me. My task is to do what'll be best for the world as a whole, but elimination is contrary to how I've been indoctrinated. It's the right thing to do, but . . ." Witton, and Owens for that matter, seldom gestured with their hands in the way of Italians or other Mediterraneans, but he rocked his hand as he said *duality*.

"To save hundreds or millions, you take a few lives. That's a tradeoff we must make. Especially when we have to use the skills of these people. They are so limited. The days of having our man in control are constrained. The newest treaty brings restrictions— unless we can make a good case as we did with President Benton. There was a man. The goal was to end the Cold War. He did it— one of our own. Such a shame that it was necessary to take his mind, but he became too connected to these people. It was one of our best operations. We saved many millions to be sure, which is not a small feat for mere *Visitors*."

"I know you're right, but you see my dilemma?"

"Yes, but remind yourself that everything is permitted in the name of control."

Witton was being reprimanded again, gently, but without doubt. He needed to change the subject. "I thought you might have instructions for me that you wanted to deliver in person."

"Only that the few INS operatives who know of us must be dealt with swiftly. There's no time to lose. Use Beethoven if you must, then deal with him as well."

"Will other INS agents be read into the work?"

"No. Access has been curtailed so we may eliminate all vestiges of knowledge. No one will be read in. I have the word of the highest authority." Owens smiled knowingly.

"I'll get on with it, sir."

"Good. There will be relief coming, but you and I won't see it. The scheme will take many more generations. We've always known that, but it's good to see traces of the kind of thinking that'll make it easier. Have you been following the discussions coming out of MIT about the inflationary universe?"

"Not closely, sir."

"One brilliant physicist said that an advanced race could harness the drivers of inflation of the universe to create a cosmos from scratch. That this universe could be such a creation.

Quantum theory holds that things can materialize out of a vacuum. Doesn't that sound like the voice of one of our own? Now we're getting to the core of our evolution—undermining the belief that there is a cosmic purpose for the existence of man. The losers are, of course, the religious teachers of the world. So, Witton, my good man, take heart and enjoy the changes that we have planned for centuries. They're coming to pass. Soon even religions can be discarded when control comes our way—through the intellect."

Witton didn't speak, but knew from Owens' relaxed state that he was correct and the plan was on track. He also realized that his role was important, possibly critical.

"Now let's have a few brews and watch the characters enjoy themselves. They always amuse me." Owens laughed at his own amusement. He cast his eyes around the room, not speaking again until they departed an hour later.

* * *

Maddie's call to Alison drove my thinking about the passage of the healthcare legislation. I had begun to consider the potential law as mine despite my very small role in its drafting. The fact was that the key change—recognition of volunteer work with federal dollars—represented a major shift in thinking, allowing a change in health care for the country.

With Senator Pope opting for the safe road rather than the revolutionary one, he surrendered to the death of the bill. He realized that the strengthening lobby opposition doomed any chance of passage in the next session of congress, yet could only consider his political reputation. I thought he had aspirations to be president, believing that too could play into our hands.

My call to Barton Lane was maddening. He controlled the senator's appointments by approving each potential visitor before the secretary could schedule a meeting. Lane refused an appointment for Maddie and me.

"Barton, it's clear the decision's been made, but there's time if the situation is as I see it," I said.

"Look, doc, since when has political maneuvering been your forte?"

"Since I found some incriminating evidence about good old Bryce."

"Bullshit."

"Can you afford to take the risk? Will you? Without allowing Bryce to have a say in the decision about seeing me? I've nothing to lose. Christ, I was a street person, but he has a career to squander. I have no qualms about doing whatever it takes to make my case. With the ear of the press due to my public stance on the health bill, there's an audience for me." I imagined Lane squirming at his desk. Worried about his boss because of me.

"All right. I can fit you in about ten days from now."

"Two days. No longer."

"No way, Puccini." Lane was shouting into the phone.

"Two days from now, I talk to Pope or to the media. Your choice." The idea was to wait for his decision, however long it took.

"You're a bastard."

"Could be true; I was an orphan." The smile's effect on my voice must have been obvious to him.

"You win. Tuesday afternoon at four in the senator's office."

"The senator will thank you for this."

* * *

My first task was to convince Maddie that Bryce could be blackmailed and that the senator wasn't going to get off. I intended to make him face the political and civil music after I got his support for the legislation. Maddie had integrity, but she also was a realist. She agreed, but with some hesitation. Now I had to keep my promises, realizing that lying was immoral, but part of the Washington game of dealing in exchange for a higher goal. I too was fooling myself by rationalizing away my sins.

Taking the state boards was tough on my nerves, but waiting for the four o'clock meeting with Pope was worse. After arriving, we were kept in the outer office for forty minutes past our appointment time. Finally, with a flair, Lane opened the door, ushering us into the senator's office.

Senator Pope proceeded as if he didn't know what the meeting was about. He was very warm in his greeting and offered us a drink. Pope seemed to have had a few already, so I declined the offer, needing all my senses at peak performance. Maddie followed my lead.

Barton Lane surely had briefed him and prepared a defense of sorts, but he took a seat behind us, quite out of the conversation. He couldn't be trusted; neither could I.

"I appreciate your support for my bill, Dr. Puccini. I hope I've expressed my thanks sufficiently before today."

I nodded, then watched his social performance.

"It's always so nice to see you, Maddie. You get more stunning with each year. How do you do it?"

"Good genes, senator."

"Please, not so formal. We were very close," he said.

"We were never close. I worked for you, that's all," Maddie said. A chill descended on the room. She had drawn a line in the sand.

"Senator, you've tabled the bill. I know why you would do that, however, you must also know that it's this year or never. There are too many enemies of our ideas; time is on their side, not ours. We're here to ask you to change your mind."

Pope seemed relaxed again, sipping his bourbon and leaning back—in control. "Barton said you would threaten me. Is that your intent?"

"No, sir, but direct talk *is* in order," I said.

"Talk." The master politician barely looked at us and he knew nothing I would say could change anything.

Pope and I had the floor.

"I ask you to reconsider."

"The decision's made. We can't allow a Republican advantage

in the senate. Strength is a matter of sustaining one's position—never losing."

I worked to make my voice sound lower and more serious. "There are other kinds of loses. Personal loses that harm your position for the long term."

"Such as?" Pope was cool as he smirked at me.

"You expect Maddie to refrain from joining the civil sexual harassment suit against you. The threatening phone call you made to her tells me you fear such an event. Maybe four voices raised against you are much worse than three. But I don't know Washington politics like you do; you may be correct."

The senator moved back to the small bar. With a fresh drink in his hand, the lecture began. "Civil suits in sexual harassment cases seldom win. It's my word against each of them. Loose women at that, present company excluded, of course." Pope smiled.

"Is that also true for associating with a rapist? Your friend Garret's a liability especially since he raped one of the women who may testify against you. Birds of a feather and all of that stuff. Maddie's testimony will come with a double whammy. Your sexual harassment that ruined her promising career and your pal's rape. His attack may not be admissible in court, but in the press it's dynamite."

"Rape?" Pope asked, with the first hint of fear in his voice. "What the hell are you talking about? You expect me to believe this shit? I don't know a thing about a rape and I'd bet my Mercedes that you don't either." His arms moved rapidly as his temper took hold.

Maddie leaned forward in her chair, extending her hand, palm up. "Really, Bryce? Then perhaps you'd better hand those car keys over now. *I* was the one Garret Dawson raped, and I have the scar to prove it," Maddie said, turning her head so he could get a better look at the damage to her face camouflaged with make-up. "He threatened to kill me after the rape. I hope you haven't flattered yourself into thinking I left Boston only because of you. I left Boston because I was terrified of Dawson.

He only served two years for narcotics dealing and I knew it was only a matter of time until he found me and followed through on his threat. You probably helped in his release."

Pope was quiet for a few minutes, trying to comprehend what Maddie was telling him. The stunned look on his face told us he had no prior knowledge of what Dawson had done to Maddie, but he quickly regained his composure along with his arrogance.

"You aren't listening, Puccini. I don't expect to lose any civil proceeding. I hold the upper hand." He stood nearer us and looked down to emphasize his point. I felt like a prisoner on the sofa.

"Your reputation will suffer. Could you win re-election?"

"Amateurs. That's what you two are. Amateurs." The senator laughed. He left his chair to refill his glass again with a hell-of-a-lot of bourbon.

"There's another connection with good old Garret."

"Such as?"

"He's your drug dealer," I said.

Pope threw his heavy glass across the desk and bourbon soaked the papers scattered about.

Barton Lane came out of his chair and grabbed my jacket collar. Tearing me apart seemed well within his capability, even if he was a short shit.

"Sit the hell down, Barton," Pope shouted. For the first time, he looked directly into my eyes. Pope sat down, too.

"Why didn't you get help for your wife?" I asked. "Counseling would have been better than feeding her drugs— for your reputation and her health. You can't survive that accusation. Never mind a trial."

"I don't know what you're talking about. How dare you impugn my wife's reputation? Any other talk like that and I'll win a civil suit against you, Puccini. There's absolutely no truth to that accusation. I demand an apology."

Something had changed in Pope's demeanor. Even his anger seemed false.

"There'll be no apology. Garret Dawson supplies you regularly. I have times, places and witnesses who will testify against you. Not just for political reasons—for motives of right and justice."

"This is outrageous. Get out, you bastard."

"If I get out now, I'll call a press conference before the day is through," I said, not knowing why I chose those words. Hell, I didn't know how to call a press conference. "Senator, why put yourself through this? You don't have to prove anything to me, but you know I'm right about your wife and no matter what you do, the truth will come out if we pursue it. Why do this? All we ask is that you try to get our bill passed. Maddie has agreed not to testify and we won't press any of our knowledge. You can continue being Mr. Good Guy and maybe Mr. President."

The man was still for a long time. My thoughts played the scenario where Pope was tired of the whole mess with Dawson and expected that sooner or later he'd be caught.

"I'll try." The Senator sat with his eyes gazing down. All of a sudden he looked tired—too tired to fight any longer.

"Senator . . ." Lane said.

"Enough, Barton, I've made a deal. These people have no conscience. My wife's too sick to have to deal with the likes of a street bum. It's Lila I'm thinking about." Pope stood, returning to his desk where he sat with his elbows in bourbon.

Maddie and I left without confirming our agreement or ending the conversation.

Maybe it was the stress or perhaps the physical strain of the meeting, but my skull ached as we walked toward the taxi. Hearing the first strains of a Mozart concerto, the music stopped as suddenly as it had started. God, where were Grundig and Corso?

* * *

That same evening, my pain became more severe than my

worst hangover. Maddie put a wet cloth on my head and massaged my shoulders with a strong touch. She made the discomfort ease before we slept in each other's arms for hours.

A blaring car horn awakened me, causing the hair on my neck to stand up. Easing Maddie away from me, I walked to the window, to see a car parked across from the house. One man was sitting in the car, but I couldn't tell which agent it was. Seeing him was comforting.

Then the music started again. I began to dress, but had no idea why.

* * *

I raised my head from the hard concrete. There must have been a spot worn where my head had been touching the coldness. This was home—in front of our house, but why was I lying on the sidewalk?

My fingers were sore. In the darkness, I could see the red marks across the inside of them. A little more irritation and they'd be bleeding. What the hell was I doing out here? Going upstairs, I knew I had been away again, but where? Could I slip into bed without Maddie hearing me? The answer came soon.

She opened the door for me, stepping aside. Tears were gathered about to rush out. "Do you know where you were?" she asked. Maddie kept a broad distance between us as if she intended to separate herself from any misdeeds I might have committed.

"No."

"So where were Grundig and Corso? The agreement was that you'd be watched and protected. Where was the protection?" Emotion surged across her face as her lips drew tight across her teeth and tears flooded her cheeks.

"I don't know, Maddie."

She took my hand, but I grimaced. "Ow, it's sore."

Through tears she tried to nurse me. "It's a mess. You've pulled something strong like a wire or sharp metal. It's cut into your fingers. Come in here, I'll bathe it for you. You're going to have terrible swelling if it's not treated."

"Cold water," I said. "God, I'm beat. I need to get some rest."

"In a few minutes, Mark. Why don't you sleep in? I'll make your excuses at the clinic."

* * *

The buzzer rang over and over before either of us woke up. Maddie said she'd get it and put her robe on while walking down to the door. I heard talking and jumped up. Grundig looked terrible.

"Early for a visit," I said.

"It's been a long night. Got any coffee, Maddie?"

We sat in the kitchen drinking strong coffee before Grundig let us in on the reason for a dawn visit.

"We're making progress. Your transmitter's been active and we've pinpointed the source of the originating signals—the command signals—to a square block in New York. Manhattan, to be more precise."

Maddie looked at me and I could see the fear in her eyes. She reached for the coffee pot to cover her uneasiness.

"That's great. So what's next?" I asked.

"We keep working the intercepts until we have a smaller triangle to achieve a more accurate position."

"Why are you here now? In the middle of the damn night."

"We've had a mishap. Did you see Corso last night—watching?" John was tense. He drank coffee and avoided our eyes.

"Someone was in the car, but I couldn't say it was Corso."

"We found his car in a Jersey dump. It was rigged with tracking devices or we'd still be looking. He's dead, garroted. Some bastard damn near cut his head off with a thin wire."

I felt sick. Nausea came over me as I lurched for the bathroom. With little food to bring up, the dry heaves burned my throat and stomach. Part of my cleaning up was to wipe the Vaseline from my hands.

Grundig was standing alone in the kitchen when I came back. "You all right, Mark?"

"Sure, must have eaten something that didn't agree with me."

Maddie came from the bedroom to my side, putting her arm around me. God, she felt good, but she had been crying and I knew she was crying for me—not Corso.

"That's all. Just wondering if you could provide any clues, but you slept through it all."

"Sorry about your partner. He was a nice guy. Can I help in any way?"

"No, just keep your eyes open. Either Jones or myself will be with you from now on."

"Great," I said, "I feel better about that."

I didn't offer to shake his hand as we often did. We skipped the Washington formality, and watched him go down the stairs. Maddie was crying. "Mark, what do we do now?"

"Go to the clinic. We have a job to do."

"We can't go on like this."

"It's almost over." I pulled her into my arms, needing the warmth of her support.

CHAPTER 31

There was no question in my mind that I had killed Phil Corso. On previous occasions, there had been reasonable doubt about the control someone had over me, but now with the controlling device re-inserted in my head, I had been directed to kill an innocent government worker.

Maddie and I decided, after a long, painful talk, that the instrument must be removed, regardless of the urgency assessed by the bureaucracy. Nothing could justify my taking life as I was sure I had. How could I live with myself and be a caring mate to the woman I loved? She knew that I could be brutal. Could Maddie trust me? Not wanting to know the answer, I called John Grundig to set up a meeting.

* * *

We sat in Lafayette Park with the sun beaming down on us and the humidity causing our pores to open. I hadn't been to the park since working at the clinic. The experience brought back memories, most of them bad.

"John, I want the device removed."

"Is it becoming painful? Perhaps we can give you some drug for relief."

"Not physical pain, it's knowing what's happened."

He squinted to get a clearer view of me in the sun. "Sorry, I don't follow you."

"You got very good info the same night Phil was murdered.

Right?"

"Yeah, there must have been numerous transmissions. Great results. Our guys really did some great work." His face beamed with pride.

"I suspect most of the transmissions were to me."

"So what? That's what we expected," he said with a sweep of his hand.

"Did you expect me to kill Corso?"

"What?" Grundig twisted toward me, eyes wide despite the direct sunlight.

"Corso was watching me—protecting me. He didn't contact anyone when I approached him, because he knew me. We were on the same team."

"You remember that?" Grundig's words flashed with anger.

I shook my head. "No, I'm surmising."

"Hell, you could be dead wrong."

His reaction was normal. Knowing me, almost as a friend, he didn't see me as a killer. "Look at my hands. Phil was garroted."

"You don't know how your hands got those marks?"

This sounded like an excuse. Had he been incompetent? "Only a guess, but I'd bet my life on this guess."

"If you were directed by Project 1947 to kill Corso, then they know what we're doing. They know who's read into the project and where we are. Not possible." His hand pushed downward, ending the discussion.

"I'm going to turn myself into the local police."

"No. You can't. We're too close now to let them slip away. The President's briefed every day about this work. The importance is beyond critical." John wasn't advising me—these were orders.

"But people are dying and no one's being punished. I can't be a party to it any longer."

"Jones and I were told this morning that Corso won't be replaced. They can't risk having a new guy briefed into the case letting some information slip out."

"So it's not so important." I thought I'd won the debate. It wasn't so important after all.

"Only three of us know the reasons for what we're doing. The President, Jones, and me. The sensitivity is so deep that the risk of other people knowing is overriding."

"What about the people who brief the President? They know."

"Jones briefs the President. Have you wondered why INS is handling this investigation? Why not the FBI or CIA who have far greater resources? The reason is that no one will suspect that we're on to them if the INS does it."

"This isn't making any sense." How else could I convince the government that I didn't want to be a tool of an evil clan?

"The sense is this, Mark. If it slips out that we know about Project 1947 and don't stop them, the damage will be horrendous. Our life as we live it in every country will change. The impact will be irreconcilable."

"So, I'm to go on killing anyone that they tell me to kill? You want to make me a fucking serial killer." I shouted at him, aware that my fists were white.

"No. We'll do a better job of tracking you to prevent murder before it happens. As soon as we make a final location, the device comes out, then you go on with your life."

"If there are only three of you in the know, what happens if one of you dies? If *they* knew Corso was on the program, why don't they know about you and Jones? Is the President going to run the program after you get knocked off?"

"There are things I don't know about, so I can't answer you, but you've got to have faith in your government."

"You're shitting me, right? The most important project in government is being run by three people. You can't get replacements for men being killed in the line of duty and I'm supposed to have faith in this system?" My uneasy laugh mocked him and the entire program.

"Hang in with me, Mark. You're doing what's morally right, even if you don't think so now. You won't be prosecuted; I promise you." He pleaded with me and I knew he wanted to tell me more, but couldn't.

"Why doesn't that make me feel better? Having a license to

kill isn't something to feel good about."

"Maybe the whole world will thank you."

I stared at Grundig for a few moments to be sure he wasn't going to burst out laughing. He didn't. I had never seen a man who was more serious.

* * *

Still being upset over the turn of events, Maddie and I made a pact. She wouldn't be separated from me. She would follow me if I went away mentally or physically. Despite the new danger this agreement might have been bringing to Maddie, we believed it was the only solution my conscience could live with.

Chapter 32

I glanced at the clock over the kitchen table—six pm. Mark had been missing for two hours. I wasn't sure which emotion was stronger—fear or anger.

Mark had seemed fine when I left the clinic at four, heading to the post office to pick up mail for Dr. Stein. Today was my birthday and earlier in the day Dr. Stein, Connie and Mark had surprised me with a cake followed by a rousing rendition of *Happy Birthday*. Dr. Stein gave me the latest Barbara Taylor Bradford novel and Connie gave me a lovely set of bath products. Mark said his gift was a surprise for later in the evening over dinner. My choice had been to have Chinese food at home and spend a quiet Friday evening together.

When I returned to the clinic, Mark had already left. Connie assured me everything was fine and I should return home as Mark would be along shortly. But she didn't know about Mark's ability to suddenly disappear or about the pact we had made not to be separated. I poured myself a glass of wine, took a sip and said, "Happy Birthday, Maddie," hearing the sarcasm in my voice. As much as I loved Mark, I was beginning to have some doubts as to what I was getting involved in. Although it was difficult to believe that Mark was capable of killing another human being, it was obvious he had no control of his actions when he was instructed via the transmitter. My fear was escalating. What if he was instructed to hurt me? What would prevent him from doing so if he had no control? I knew he would never intentionally hurt me, but there were times Mark was not the person that I had come to know and love. Shivering, I walked to the living room window.

Glancing up and down the street, there was no sign of Mark. I heard the clock strike six thirty. Damn him! He promised we wouldn't be separated. The deal was that I would follow him. Yeah, right—I had no clue where the hell he was. Anger overtook my concern for him as I headed to the kitchen to refill my wineglass. I heard his key in the lock.

Mark walked into the living room with a huge smile on his face carrying a bouquet of yellow roses and a shopping bag filled with Chinese food in one hand—and red leash attached to a medium size, black and white, furry canine in his other. I stood there trying to take in the scene and wasn't sure whether to laugh or throw something at him. The dog, sensing the tension, edged back, looking from Mark to me.

"I'm sorry I was running late. It took a bit longer at the pound than I counted on. Adopting a dog is serious business." Walking toward me and attempting to give me the leash, he said, "Happy birthday, Maddie. I hope you'll like your present."

What was he, nuts? Our life was total chaos and he brings a dog into it? Just what we needed. Responsibility for a four-legged creature.

When I stood there mute, he passed me the bouquet of flowers. "These are part of your gift. I already stopped to pick up the Chinese food." He quickly realized not only was I not speaking, I was making no attempt to have any contact with the dog. Holding the leash, he walked into the kitchen, placing the bag of food on the table before turning to me. "You don't like her, do you? It was a mistake to get the dog for you, wasn't it?"

All of a sudden, the past months with Mark began to hit me. Transmitters implanted in his head, murders, the INS, being followed, constant fear of what was coming next, and Mark's vacil-lating behavior. "Mistake?" I said. "Maybe the mistake is you and me. You have me make a pact with you—to follow you constantly like some detective—then you nonchalantly take off from the clinic with no information for me about where the hell you're going." I could hear my voice rising and I saw the dog edging further behind Mark's legs, but I didn't care. "How dare you suck me in and get me involved in this danger. Then you don't even care enough to tell me where you're going or even that you *are* going somewhere. I return to the clinic and you're *gone*! What the hell am I supposed to think?" I swiped the tears streaming down my face.

In one motion, Mark dropped the dog's leash and pulled me into his arms. "You're right and it was inconsiderate of me. I'm so sorry, Maddie. I was just excited about surprising you with the dog. I was wrong and should have mentioned something to you."

Despite the warmth and tenderness of his arms, I pulled away. Taking a deep breath, I shook my head. "I don't know what we're going to do, Mark. I hate living like this. I'm beginning to think it was better being on the street." Although it was what I felt at the moment, I saw the crushed look on his face.

"God, Maddie, don't say that. Please. I know this hasn't been easy for you, but it'll be over soon. I promise. Please don't back away from me. I love you so much."

I wiped the tears that refused to stop falling. "I'm scared, Mark, and I'm not sure even love can take away my fear."

"I understand your fears, believe me, but we're being protected by Jones and Grundig."

"They can't protect me from you," I said. The look on Mark's face told me he understood exactly what I was saying.

He nodded slowly. "You're right, they can't. And I have no right asking you to trust me, but, Maddie, I'd never hurt you. There's no way I could ever hurt you. Please believe me."

I felt my anger beginning to slip away. "Mark, I know you wouldn't intentionally. But while you have that transmitter implanted, you can't be responsible for anything you do."

He pulled me into his arms again and this time I didn't pull away. I felt his lips on my neck as he whispered, "Please bear with me, Maddie. Just a little while longer."

"Okay," I whispered back. "A little while longer." During our entire confrontation the dog sat on the kitchen floor, listening and watching. "Did she come with food?" I asked. "And does she have a name?"

Mark grinned. "I thought we'd take her for a walk later and stock up on her food. And I thought since she's your dog, you should name her."

For the first time, I took a good look at the dog. She was adorable and difficult to resist. She had shaggy fur indicating some terrier in her heritage, with soft brown eyes that looked at me waiting for any indication that I was interested in her.

Kneeling down on the floor, I reached my hand out toward her. "Come here, sweetie. If you're my birthday present, we need to get acquainted."

Hesitantly, she walked toward me sniffing, with her tail wagging. I stroked the soft fur between her ears. She licked my face, forgiving me for my previous lack of interest. I looked up at Mark, seeing his look of happiness. "What should we call her?" I asked.

"You name her. Whatever you'd like."

Thinking about it for a moment, I continued patting her. "Didn't she have a name at the pound?"

"They had Emma written on her cage," Mark replied.

At the sound of the name, her tail wagged harder. She looked up at Mark, her face filled with expectation.

I laughed. "Then Emma it is. Welcome to our home, Emma."

"I saw her there a week ago," Mark said. "She was found wandering the streets and her time was running out. They told me if nobody claimed her by yesterday, they'd have to put her down. When I paid for her last week, telling them she was a birthday present for today, they promised to hold her for me."

A pang of sorrow went through me. A lovely dog like this? They were going to destroy? I put my arms around her neck, burying my face in her fur. She pushed her shaggy body closer to me, licking my ear. During that moment of affection, Emma and I bonded.

Standing, I put my arms around Mark's neck. "Thank you. I love her and she's the best present you could have given me." I kissed his cheek, then held his face between my hands as I looked into his eyes. "I love you, Mark. No matter what, I will always love you."

Emma edged closer to my leg and whined. "Maybe she's hungry," I said.

"Let's have a glass of wine and dig into that Chinese food. I think we can entice Emma with an egg roll till we get to the store for dog food."

"Good idea. You pour the wine and we'll eat after I get these gorgeous roses into water."

* * *

A week later it was difficult to think that Emma hadn't always been with us, because she easily settled into our routine. Mr. and Mrs. Kaminski fell in love with Emma the moment they met her. They were extremely fond of dogs, but felt they were getting too old for the responsibility. Therefore, Emma became their surrogate pet. They saved ham bones for her and half of the toys in her basket were from them. Washington was into its third day of a brutal heat wave—ninety-eight degrees and steamy. Mark and I had been able to pick up a couple of fans trying to find some relief for sleeping. But all it did was blow the hot air around the apartment. Both of us had tossed and turned all night trying to find a cool spot on the bed. Mark was still sleeping and even Emma was moving slowly this morning.

As I refilled her water bowl with ice, the doorbell rang, followed by Emma's bark. "It's okay, girl," I said, patting her head, and then went downstairs to see who could be at our door at nine in the morning.

I opened the door to see two delivery men on the porch with a large Sears truck behind them in the street. "Maddie Chappelle?" the taller one questioned.

I nodded my head and waited.

"We have a delivery of two air conditioners," he said. "Where do you want them?"

"Air conditioners?" I replied, sounding stupid.

"Yeah, you know. To keep ya cool from this heat."

Thinking there must be some mistake, but acknowledging we could straighten it out later, I said, "Upstairs, this way," and proceeded to lead them into the living room. I held Emma by her collar as she growled at them, demonstrating her abilities as an excellent watchdog. They placed two large boxes on the floor, asked me to sign that I had accepted delivery, and left.

Emma and I stood looking at each other. Then she cautiously walked over and began sniffing the boxes. Mark opened the bedroom door, rubbing his eyes and stretching. "Christmas come early?" he asked.

"Air conditioners," I said. "Did you purchase them?"

He laughed. "No, I'm afraid not. I wish I had. Are you sure they're for us?"

I looked at the paper I had signed and nodded. "Yeah, it says Maddie Chapelle with the correct address. Who would have done this?"

"I have no idea," Mark said, heading to the kitchen to get a knife to uncrate the boxes.

Summer would be over before we'd find out our mysterious benefactors were the Kaminskis, who considered Mark, Emma, and me their family.

By putting one in our bedroom, one in the living room window and closing off the second bedroom, we were able to cool the entire apartment, getting blessed relief from the sweltering heat outside.

That evening, when we returned from Emma's walk, Mark and I soaked up the delicious coolness of the living room, enjoying a glass of wine, and listening to music. The phone rang and I heard Sylvia's excited voice.

"I'd say within the next two weeks, you're going to officially be Auntie Maddie," she said.

I laughed. "What's the latest update from today's visit?"

"The doctor says I'm dilated two centimeters and Marlene has turned. Her head is in the birth canal and she's in perfect position."

"That's great, Sylvia. I bet you'll be glad to have her in

your arms. It must be miserable being eight-and-a-half months pregnant during this heat wave."

"It's not so bad. We have air conditioning here at the home and Ben is a sweetheart. He's always taking me out for ice cream and even got me a small fan for my room. I'm just so anxious for her to be born though, so I can hold her."

I wished her luck, making her promise to call me with the first contraction, then joined Mark on the sofa to relay the latest baby update.

He put his book down, pulling me close to him as he kissed my cheek. "I love you, Maddie. I'm glad our paths crossed that day in the park."

Returning his kiss, I nodded while looking around the cozy living room—Emma sleeping soundly at our feet, candles flickering on the table, and Frank Sinatra's mellow voice filling the room.

"I am too," I said. "As crazy as our life has been, being here with you like this, we almost seem to be a normal couple in love without a care in the world."

CHAPTER 33

Dinner was special. Maddie never claimed to be a good cook, but her French dishes were better than gourmet. They came with quantity and panache. *Steak Diane* was tender with large mushrooms in a white wine sauce, served with brown rice and my favorite French-cut green beans. The bread was Italian with thick hard crust and an abundance of air holes.

My contribution to dinner was to open a bottle of French table wine we had bought on sale. I didn't feel like a former street bum as I ate, drank, and watched my beautiful woman across the table.

A walk in the early evening cool air was Emma's idea. She jumped around us until we realized that a walk was in order. Strolling along the city streets made a perfect ending to a good day. Upon returning, I heard the telephone ringing and hustled through the doorway leaving Maddie and Emma behind.

Barton Lane was insistent. "Puccini, you've got to come now, they're meeting in thirty minutes. You owe it to the senator to see for yourself what he thinks of Dawson."

"Why would it matter?" I asked, truly meaning the question.

"It matters because you're pressing him in ways that aren't fair. You've no right to make his life worse than it is. Give him a hearing at least. Look, Puccini, Bryce has brought Lila down to Washington. From now on, her permanent home isn't Boston, but here where her husband is. This isn't a visit for a party. This is a new life."

"But he'll see me and . . ."

"Look different and stay far away from his table. No one will recognize you, if you're careful. Will you come?"

"Yeah. I'm on my way."

"Where?" Maddie asked, as she listened to the last bits of the conversation.

"Begonia Café in Southeast. Pretty rough section. Pope's meeting with Dawson, and Lane intends for me to see the *real senator.*"

"He'll recognize me for sure, but I'm going. I'll find some place to stay while you listen or watch," Maddie said.

She held my arm, pressing it in her hands. That gesture told me she was with me all the way. "Thanks. You're terrific."

I found an old T-shirt and a Yankee baseball cap that wasn't too disreputable. Maddie changed into a pair of dark slacks and an old, light jacket. Finding old clothes was easy for us. I called a cab and we waited outside the apartment.

Across the street and down fifty yards, Grundig sat in the car that had tailed us all day. I waved. He blinked his lights at us, then followed the cab.

The street was messy with vehicles doubled parked along the curb. Groups of young men hung out in doorways eyeing us as we drove by.

"Maddie, I can't let you stand around this café alone. That'd be asking for trouble in this neighborhood. My guess is that half the kids here are dealers or gang members. We're out of place. Christ, I don't see any white faces."

"I can't go in with you. Driver, how much further to the café?" Maddie asked.

"Twenty yards on the right. That'll be fourteen bucks."

While paying the cabbie, I noticed a beauty salon across the street. "How about there? They'll let you sit for a minute if you ask nice."

"Yeah, good idea. I can see you and Pope won't see me."

Maddie crossed the street, going into the salon. After a minute, her beautiful face peeped out the window.

The café was brightly lit and crowded with people taking

advantage of a cheap meal. There was an overpowering odor of burnt coffee and rancid cooking oil. French fries must have been a core staple.

Pope and Dawson sat in a corner of the room. Pulling my cap down over my eyes, I found a table to sit with my back to them. I looked out of place, but not as much as Pope in his striped suit and tie. At least, I looked like a redneck. My table was only eight feet away and the mirrors on two adjoining walls allowed a clear view of the men's side faces.

This didn't seem like a social meeting. Unfortunately, it was sordid business. Dawson passed two books to the senator, Bryce put them in a small brown bag and handed him an envelope. A drug transfer and payoff were made in public.

Pope drank some coffee and seemed to start a new conversation. Dawson shook his head.

"No, I don't want to," Dawson said.

Pope pointed a finger at his partner and said Maddie's name at the beginning of a sentence. The finger pounded the air as if there was a drum invisible to the rest of us. The senator was speaking with theatrical emphasis.

"It's true," Pope said.

"Bullshit."

Words were flying between the men now.

"Assaulted . . ."

"Never."

". . . truth."

Dawson's hands started a regimen of protection against the senator's finger. His hands flew as he talked and his voice became louder. "The bitch deserved it."

Pope's hand slammed to the table and customers stared. The two men were silent for a brief period.

"She'll pay and I'm going to do the collecting," Dawson said, in loud, punctuated words.

"Don't you dare," Pope said with words blasting across the café crowd.

"Stop me, boss," Dawson said as he stood, knocking the chair backwards into a customer's table.

Dawson threw a ten-dollar bill down and spilled his coffee on Pope's side of the table. He looked around the place and bent his head to deliver the parting words in lower tones.

I strained to read his lips, but my ears were enough.

"Maddie dies."

Pope waited until Dawson was out of sight and rushed to the door. Standing on the curb, he raised his hand and a black Chevrolet turned toward him and popped up on the sidewalk. Pope threw his body inside as tires screeched, zooming down the street.

I ran out to see Maddie appear at the salon door, then run across the street.

"Are you all right?" she asked. "Did they see you?"

"No."

"Well . . . what was it all about?"

"You. I believe they talked about you. Pope didn't know about the rape. They argued and Dawson swore an oath that he would . . . kill you."

"Garret would have done that a long time ago if he had found me, but now we know he's going to be looking again." Tears welled in her eyes.

I wrapped her in my arms to let her know I'd protect her. "Don't worry, Maddie, I'll take care of you. I can be aggressive if I have to be."

"I know. That's something that bothers me."

* * *

Grundig was close to us until we got to the apartment, then he dropped back to park. I had some questions for him and this seemed to be a good time. I took Maddie by the hand, walking his way.

The engine started and he began to pull away.

I held up my arm to signal to him before he pulled into another parking space and waited.

"Hey, John, I need to ask you some questions."

"Mark, we can't talk here. No one else can be around."

"I'll wait on the steps. Go ahead, men," Maddie said, as she politely walked away.

"Is it clear that you can't tell her anything?" John asked. Grundig's voice conveyed his irritation at having the burden of protecting the secrets.

"Shit, I don't know anything. I'm not read-in, as you say, so how could I give anything away?

Shaking his head in exasperation, he said, "You know a lot. You have a responsibility."

"According to Tom Clancy and Jack Ryan, I don't have an obligation until I get cleared—is that the correct terminology?"

"Right. What questions do you have?"

His resignation to this discussion caused me to smile. "First, do you work all night? Who relieves you if there are only three people clued into whatever it is?"

"No, I'll be relieved by an INS guy who has no idea why you're being protected or watched. His guidance is to follow you and help you. We do say that he has to stop any criminal activity he detects. So it works fine."

"Who does the signal analysis? Are they cleared for your secret stuff?"

He considered my question and how to answer without violating the law. "We have a lot of support from intelligence agencies who do routine kinds of work and report without knowing the details of who they're tracking."

"So many more government guys are assisting you? Maddie's helping you, too. She goes everywhere I go. Of course we sleep together, also. Never out of sight. That's for your protection, too."

Grundig smiled. "My protection?"

"Right. What if I'm commanded to take you out? Tonight you didn't have your hand on your weapon as you watched me approach. There could have been a weapon in my pocket," I said, trying to make him think.

"I suppose you're right." He had a you'll-never-take-me-out grin. "I'll be more careful. Thanks."

"That's all I ask. Maddie's helping me, but you need to be aware, not only for yourself, but for me as well. I don't want you to shoot me, in a trance or any other condition I might be in."

"You don't have the killer instinct, Mark."

"Don't be so god-damned stupid. I don't know what I do sometimes or how or why. We need to help each other here. And how long will this go on? The implant makes me someone I don't want to be. Understand?"

"The search area is down to a single building in Manhattan. Lots of floors, but we have equipment in the building. From our perspective, as soon as you get a command, we could end this shit."

"One more?" I couldn't believe my ears. Exhilaration made me laugh.

"Maybe a couple of events, not more than a few for sure. Mark, the program's worth it." He leaned closer to the open window. "You're doing what no one else could have done."

"Okay, that's what I really needed to know. I just can't go on indefinitely. See you later. Keep your hand on your piece."

Walking across the street, I was relieved for the first time in weeks. There was an end in sight. I wasn't sure how long Maddie could keep up with the crap, but I admired her. I also loved her more everyday.

CHAPTER 34

All of it now seemed meaningless. I left my home, everything I owned, my entire identity. For what? Only to be found by Garret more than two years later? I wanted to believe Mark and know he would protect me and keep me safe. But I also knew how ruthless Garret could be. Damn, life wasn't fair. Now I had Mark . . . the man I loved more than I thought possible. He was everything to me and I felt secure in his love. We had enough complications with the INS and now we had the additional threat of Garret. The way I saw it, I had two options. I could flee once again, consumed with fear, allowing him to win. Or I could continue living a life I created with Mark, being cautious, yet *living* rather than merely existing. No, life was definitely not fair. And then I chuckled. "Who the hell said it was supposed to be fair?" I asked out loud, knowing which option I'd take this time. Emma was curled beside me on the sofa, looking up at the sound of my voice. I smiled at her as I stroked her silky coat and resumed looking through the latest issue of *Better Homes & Gardens*.

"This chicken dish looks good, Emma. I bet Mark would like it. Move your head, sweetie and I'll get the scissors to clip it out." Reluctantly, Emma allowed me to get up and then repositioned herself on the sofa. I was taping the recipe to the fridge when the phone rang and I heard Sylvia's excited voice on the other end.

"Maddie? It's me. My water broke a few hours ago and I'm at the hospital. Ben is here with me. We're so excited. Can you and Mark come?"

I laughed. "So you think this might be it?" I recalled her two previous false alarm trips in the past two weeks.

"Yeah, it is. Really. I'm getting some pretty strong contractions now."

"Okay. Mark went into the clinic for a couple hours. I'll call him and we'll be there as soon as we can. You do a good job. I love you, Sylvia."

"I love you too, Maddie," she said, then her voice trailed off as I could hear Ben in the background instructing her to breathe. He had attended all the birthing classes with Sylvia, taking his position as her coach seriously. "See you soon," I said, smiling as I hung up the phone.

I dialed the clinic and waited while Connie told Mark he had a call.

"Dr. Puccini here," he said, sounding very professional.

"Maddie Chapelle here," I replied in my best business-like voice, "but about to become Aunt Maddie as we speak."

Mark laughed. "No kidding? You think this is the real thing this time?"

"Yeah, I believe it might be. Her water broke and she's having pretty strong contractions. Ben's at the hospital with her, but she wants us to come."

"Okay, no problem. But I have three more patients waiting to see me. First babies are notorious for taking their time. I'm sure it'll be a few more hours. Why don't you come down here, Maddie? Then we can take a taxi to the hospital together."

"Sounds good. I'll be there within an hour."

"And Maddie? Please be careful walking over here, okay?"

"I will. Promise. I love you."

* * *

Opening the front door, I stepped out on the porch with a glance up and down the street. No strange cars parked with someone waiting inside. No Garret. Over the past two years, I had forgotten what it was like to know fear. To always be looking over my shoulder. Now it became my constant companion. I took a deep breath, firmly convinced that living in hiding wasn't the answer.

A block from the house, I noticed a late model Buick slowly pass by at less than the thirty mile speed limit. Pulling the wide-brimmed straw hat further down to conceal my face, I increased my stride. Approaching the clinic, once again I saw the same car go slowly past and this time I glanced toward it. I couldn't be certain, but there was a lone male driver. Jogging up the few steps to the clinic, I could feel my heart rate increase and quickly closed the door behind me.

"Are you okay?" Connie asked with concern.

I nodded as I caught my breath. "Yeah, fine. I must have walked too fast."

Connie smiled. "How exciting. Mark said Sylvia's in labor? She's a little early, isn't she?"

"Yes, about two weeks, but the doctor said everything was fine. Poor Sylvia is so impatient for this baby to be born, I'm glad she's early instead of late."

Connie laughed. "I have to agree with that. Mark is with the last patient. He shouldn't be too much longer, Maddie. I have fresh coffee in the break room. Want a cup?"

I shook my head. "No, thanks anyway. I'll just sit here and wait for Mark."

A half-hour later, Mark emerged from the examining room, while removing his white lab coat. He saw me and smiled. "All set to welcome Sylvia's baby into the world?" he asked, as he pulled me into his arms for a tight hug.

I kissed his cheek. "More than ready. Any chance we could pick up a bottle of champagne to take to the hospital?"

"Absolutely. I had the same idea." He turned around to Connie. "The next time you see me, I'll have a goddaughter."

Connie smiled. "Be sure to tell Sylvia I wish her all the best and congratulations."

* * *

Walking into the hospital, I became lightheaded and reached

for Mark's arm. I wasn't sure if it was caused by the earlier fear of Garret or the antiseptic odors that floated around me. "Are you okay?" Mark asked, as he steadied me with his arm.

I nodded. "Yeah, just excited I guess." I had decided to postpone telling Mark that I suspected Garret might be looking for me.

We approached the nurse's station in the maternity wing and I noticed large colorful posters of babies on the walls. All of them smiling, healthy looking, and irresistible. Briefly, I felt an emptiness inside. The perky, blonde nurse looked up from the chart she was writing in as Mark inquired about Sylvia.

"Oh, she's doing terrific. She really did her homework on the birthing classes. She's now dilated eight centimeters and I'd say she'll deliver within an hour. Would you like to see her?"

Mark looked at me. "No, Ben is in there with her. Could you just tell her that Maddie and Mark are here?"

The nurse stood up and smiled. "Of course. We have a lovely waiting room just down that corridor. Coffee, cold drinks, and pastry. Help yourself and I'll send Ben out as soon as she delivers."

The waiting room was empty, with a cozy, warm feeling to it. Cushy sofas and chairs, shelves of books, and magazines on glass tables. We settled ourselves on the sofa and he reached for my hand. "Are you okay?" he asked. "You seem a little quiet."

"Yeah, I'm fine. Would you think I'm terrible if I said I was a little envious of Sylvia?"

Mark squeezed my hand. "Because of the baby?"

I nodded. "I'm happy for her. Really I am. I guess I just got a momentary wave of maternal feelings." My eyes stung as I prayed the tears wouldn't squeeze through. "Hell, I'd probably be a terrible mother anyway. You know, do all the wrong things and end up with a neurotic child." I laughed to cover my emotions. "I think I saw Garret today," I said, wanting to change the subject.

"Oh God. Where?"

"I can't be certain, but walking to the clinic there was a Buick driving slowly down the street. I saw it twice, but couldn't make out the driver. Just a lone male."

"Shit," Mark said, as he got up and began pacing the room. "I never should have let you walk to the clinic alone."

"Mark, it's not your fault. You can't be with me every single second." I got up and walked toward him, putting my arms around his neck. "Besides, I'm not giving in this time. I refuse to allow him to disrupt my life again, so I plan to be careful."

"I love you so much, Maddie. I'd die if anything happened to you."

"It won't," I said, and felt his lips on mine. We turned around to see a triumphant Ben walk into the room, garbed in blue scrubs, paper hat, booties, and a mask dangling around his neck.

"It's a girl." His voice was filled with pride. "Eight pounds, eight ounces, twenty one inches long. Marlene Benita entered the world ten minutes ago."

I could feel the laughter and excitement bubbling up in me as I hugged him tightly. "Congratulations," I said. "How's Sylvia?"

Mark shook Ben's hand and clapped him on the shoulder.

"She's fine," he said. "She did so well, I can't believe it. It was pretty intense at the end, but she hung right in there and kept breathing and focusing. They're cleaning up the baby and making Sylvia comfortable. We'll be able to see them in about twenty minutes."

Walking into Sylvia's room with Mark beside me and Ben leading the way, it wasn't the baby in her arms that my eyes were drawn to—it was the incredible glow on Sylvia's face. She was bathed in light that seemed to radiate from deep inside her. The sadness and melancholy I had felt earlier were now replaced with a mixture of pride and love for this young woman who had come from the depths of hell to embrace life with determination and strength. With Mark's arm around me, I walked toward the bed for my first glimpse of Sylvia's daughter. "Oh, Sylvia," I whispered, "she's absolutely gorgeous. She looks just like you." The shape of her face, her nose, and skin color was a replica of Sylvia in miniature.

The new mother beamed with pride. "That's what the nurses said." She gently reached for the baby's hand. "Marlene Benita, this is your Aunt Maddie and Uncle Mark." I let the tears of happiness flow as Mark popped the cork on the champagne. The four of us clinked glasses, and he proposed the toast. "To the birth of your daughter," Mark said. "To many years of love and happiness for both of you."

"To life," I added. "To the precious gift of life."

CHAPTER 35

Not wanting to spoil Sylvia's moment of triumph, I didn't mention to anyone that Ben didn't truly toast the baby or the precious gift of life. He had raised his champagne, but didn't drink. Bringing the glass to his lips, he didn't open his mouth nor did he swallow the wine. At that moment, I felt that Ben was different. Why would a young man fail to toast his love? I knew he wasn't a tee-totaller. I wondered if he was the right man for our Sylvia.

Her maternity took the edge off our joint concerns, but not for long. Maddie was terrified knowing that Garret was lurking about in her life again, but she remained strong in her decision to live each day without fear controlling her every movement. I constantly thought about being commanded and out of control. While we promised each other that we would be together all the time for mutual protection, sometimes it wasn't possible and those times were scary for me. For Maddie, it might have been worse.

A brilliant idea came to me the night after the baby was born. Why not enlist the help of John Grundig to protect Maddie? I waited, knowing John would be in the car during a mid-shift watch. Maddie watched from the window as I walked to the black car. The passenger door opened when I was twenty steps away.

"That meant welcome, Mark."

"Thanks, John. That's what I thought."

"What's up or did you just come over to talk?"

"Maddie has a problem. Someone's after her; the same guy who raped her a couple years ago.

"She should talk to the police."

"What would she say? He hasn't been stalking her until recently. There's no witness to the threat he made to her." Then it hit me. "I take that back. There is a witness. Senator Pope."

"The senator you're working with to get health legislation passed knows a rapist who's threatening Maddie?" He frowned, certainly not believing me.

Too late, I realized I was talking to myself—out loud, blurting words. God, what a jerk I felt like.

"Is that true?" Grundig asked.

"Well, it's more complicated than that, but we need your help. This guy's after Maddie and I'm not sure I can protect her. I don't even have a gun."

He got out of the car, perhaps to emphasize his message. "Go to the police. Don't be stupid."

"No, but you can warn us and prevent a murder. Hell, you could go after him."

"I have no jurisdiction over him. I can't help." He waved me off with his hand and turned toward the open car door.

I grabbed his arm. "John, are you interested in keeping me alive?"

"You know damned well I am. You're the most valuable man in the country."

"How's this for a scenario? Garret Dawson comes after Maddie. He and I get into a struggle, and since I have no weapon, he kills me. Then there's no transmission to me and you don't catch the bastards who are killing people and doing whatever else they do." Watching Grundig's face, I knew my argument sunk in.

"Look, Mark, stay away from that guy."

"No way. I'll protect Maddie if I die trying." This wasn't boasting or overstating my feelings.

Grundig watched me for a few seconds. I could almost see the anger rising in his body. "Damn. What's this guy look like?"

Giving him a description of Dawson was a pleasure. And the limp—it was perfect, just like a B-movie. I had the INS by the balls and wasn't going to be letting go easily. As a final Hollywood play, I shook John's hand and thanked him, smiling.

"You're a bastard, Puccini. This better not cost me my retirement," he said with a bitterness he seldom revealed.

"Not if you're better than Dawson. Thanks." This time I meant it.

* * *

Maybe it was a sixth sense, or perhaps I was lucky, but the timing of my conversation with Grundig couldn't have been better. Maddie and I ate in the kitchen that evening and we were relaxing by listening to some standards from the forties and fifties on the tape player. A loud horn blast got my attention.

Looking from the second floor, I could see the man walking with a limp toward our building.

"Christ, Maddie, douse that light. Dawson's fifty feet away from our house."

She ran to grab my arm and clutched it with the strength of sudden fear.

"He acts as if he knows where we live," I said. "Since he knew about the clinic, it was only a matter of time before he ended up here."

"I know. What are we going to do?" Maddie asked in a harsh whisper.

"For the moment, let's watch what happens." I felt pressure of her tense hand on my arm. I patted her hand, then stoked her forearm.

Grundig got out of the car, beginning to close the distance between himself and Dawson. Whatever Grundig said spooked him. Dawson turned and began to run, dragging one leg.

"Whew, that was close," Maddie said. Her eyes were filled with tears.

"It still is. He knows we're here. We've got to get out now. He'll be back. Tonight, probably." My fast-paced words revealed my own fears. Maddie slipped her hand away and captured my attention with piercing eyes.

"Where do we go?"

"Out the back and to a hotel until we can get our act together. We need to get the cops involved, too. Take Emma, but don't bother with clothes. I don't think time's on our side."

In three minutes, we were running down the back stairs. Climbing on a potting stand next to our landlord's greenhouse, I helped Maddie over the wooden fence. Emma didn't care for our routing, but she moved despite her whimpers.

Through the dark yard of our unknown neighbors, we ran until we were about two hundred yards away. Maddie was out of breath. We leaned against an ancient soda machine with a giant padlock securing it.

"I need to rest," Maddie said, puffing out the words.

"Okay . . ." I was going to say it was all right, then I saw the shadow of a man with a limp. "Shit. We've got to find some place to hide. Here, back here—get down. Hold Emma and don't let her bark," I said, leaving no doubt what I wanted.

"Right. How the hell am I supposed to do that? Any idea how to stop her if she becomes surprised or afraid?"

"Sorry, Maddie. You don't need orders. Hang here until he passes. Then, we'll try to hail a taxi." I could see she felt better with even an incomplete plan.

The three or four minutes we waited seemed like forever. Dawson walked past our hideout, continuing toward the rear of our building.

"Okay, let's go. Quietly," I said. "Come on Emma, it's all right."

After three blocks of fast walking, we slowed. Emma saw a cat and began to bark. She wouldn't stop. I picked her up, looking behind us. I didn't see anyone, but couldn't be positive Dawson didn't hear the barking. There were no cabs in sight.

Then, I was gone. The music began.

* * *

Maddie was terrified. As she related my actions to me later at the post office, I could see the impact on her. I thought I saw chills race over her body. Holding her close, I asked her to go on. "What did I do?"

"You left us mentally and physically. I didn't know until I saw your eyes. They were blank. You didn't seem to recognize me; hell, you didn't know anyone. You walked away from Emma and me. What could I do but follow you? Mark, you walked so fast, we couldn't keep up. I fell back about twenty steps and began to cry."

"What was I doing?"

"Walking away from me. Leaving me to fend for myself with Garret."

"Christ, I'm sorry. Then what?"

"Thank God, you went into the post office. The building was well lighted and there were other people around. You didn't appear to see them. We followed; you moved to a large postal box and turned the dial as if you'd been doing it all your life. It opened on the first try. Emma and I were right behind you, but I don't think you saw us. I couldn't see at first, but then came around your side and watched you open an envelope and put a pistol in your pants pocket. You read a note that was in the box—it was a letter, I guess. You stared at it. When you closed the box and went to the telephone, I was stunned. You read a number from the letter, dialed, and listened."

"What did I say? Who did I talk to?"

"You listened for a long time—like two minutes before you tore up the letter and put it in a trash bin. Like you were doing what you had been told. Then, he came in."

"Dawson was alone? Grundig wasn't nearby?"

"No Grundig. Garret looked right at me. I thought he didn't see you at first, but he drew a gun and aimed it at you. He put it away as he noticed a man dropping letters in the out-of-town box. He just stood there. I was petrified standing there, holding my breath. I was so scared that I dropped Emma's chain and she ran at him. Emma started barking at Garret. The last man in the post office passed, saying goodnight to all of us, in general, and laughed at Emma who was now right in front of you, barking for dear life. At that moment, you were different. Your eyes became . . . open or aware—yes, aware. You saw us for the first time. God, you heard and then saw Emma."

"But . . . how did I shoot him?"

"Garret took his gun out when the last man left the post office. He aimed it at me and came toward me. He said he was going to put a bullet right in the middle of my face. I screamed. You fired."

"Holy God. I remember firing. That's the first thing I recall since we were hiding in the alley. That was close. You could have been killed or hurt. Maddie, I'm sorry." She wrapped her arms around me and her warmth told me it was okay.

* * *

At the other end of the post office lobby, Grundig had been talking to one of the policemen. The conversation seemed to stop the other cops from arresting me or us. John approached us, smiling. "Good shot, Puccini. He was dead seconds after you burst his heart."

"What now?" I asked.

"Sit here and help Maddie. Both of you stay calm; the situation's under control."

"Aren't they going to question us?" I asked, not sure everything was under control.

"Yes, but not now. We're waiting for Pageant, the federal D.A."

"Did I overhear you tell that detective that you saw the whole thing?" Maddie asked.

"You did."

"But I didn't see you, John," she said, persisting for an answer.

"I wasn't here." Grundig smiled.

"But . . ."

"Maddie, Garret got what he deserved, right?"

She nodded.

"Mark did the right thing?" Grundig asked, phrasing the

argument to make it straightforward and simple. "And we don't want too much snooping from the local cops. So, I'm confirming your story."

"But, you don't know since you weren't here."

"That's why you're going to tell your story first. Mark sure can't tell them. I said Mark killed him in defense of you." His easy smile told me things were under federal control.

Twenty minutes later, Glen Pageant rushed into the building. He waved at Maddie, then went directly to the police detective. Pageant showed identification, shook hands, and did all the talking.

The detective asked Maddie to describe the events as they occurred. When he asked me, I dittoed what Maddie said, but used slightly different words. The investigation was complete when Grundig confirmed Maddie's description.

* * *

The whole affair in the post office lasted an hour and a half. Maddie and I were exhausted and looked it. Emma, who had saved me and the day, acted ready for another walk. Nevertheless, Grundig drove us home. On the way, he answered a radio call. "Go ahead, Mr. Jones."

"Triple win on the pole today at Belmont."

"Roger. Ten-four."

Grundig touched my arm as we arrived at the apartment to allow Maddie to get a few steps ahead. "We've traced the source of the signals. Good work, Dr. Puccini."

"Not me. You guys did the work. When do I get the device removed?"

"Soon."

CHAPTER 36

The moment I opened my eyes I knew something was different. I could sense it. For the first time in well over two years, I was relieved. Since I met Mark, my fear had diminished, but it always hovered just below the surface. Although able to get on with my life and go forward, I was aware of the fear that never vanished. Being killed by Garret was always a possibility. Now it was over. I felt Mark's leg wrap around mine as he turned toward me in sleep. Glancing at his face, I smiled, feeling the warmth of his body and his love. Placing my hand on his hip, I was filled with a completeness that defied words. Closing my eyes, once again the post office scene flashed through my mind. All of it happened so quickly there had been no time to comprehend my emotions. But after we returned home, I fell apart. The enormity of what could have happened hit me and I couldn't stop shaking. But once again, Mark calmed my fears. We sipped cognac and he allowed me to release the terror that had consumed me. Over the past week, the sound of the gunshot, the sight of the blood, Garret collapsing to the floor—the confusion and chaos were slowly beginning to fade. Pushing it out of my mind, I snuggled deeper into Mark's shoulder and felt his hand slide up to my breast. "Good morning, beautiful," he said, his voice husky with sleep and desire.

"It is a good morning," I agreed, with the first stirrings of passion.

I felt alive, energized, and most of all, grateful. Grateful that Mark had come into my life at a time when I was certain that happiness and love were emotions I'd never experience again. I had no idea where I was headed before Mark, but despair and anger were the only sensations I'd been capable of. When I allowed myself to look back, recalling the anguish of drugs, alcohol, and prostitution, none of it seemed real. Like recalling snippets of a movie, the leading character wasn't anyone that I knew personally. Mark nibbled my ear while his hand continued to stroke my breast. "I love you, Maddie," he whispered, "more than I ever thought possible."

I heard myself moaning at his touch. "I love how you love me," I whispered back. As his tongue slid over my body, once again I was astonished at the synchronism of our passion and the ecstasy of love that we shared.

* * *

"Maddie, we're going to have to replace that strip of carpet if you don't stop pacing."

I felt Mark's arms go around me and smiled. "I know, but Sylvia said one o'clock. It's one fifteen. You don't think something happened, do you?"

"Marlene probably spit up on their way out the door and required a change. They'll be here. Relax. Nothing happened," he said, kissing my lips.

I nodded my head. "You're right. I'm being silly. I'm just anxious to see them." Emma's bark coincided with the doorbell. "See, here they are," Mark said, heading downstairs to open the door.

Sylvia walked in carrying a pink canvas tote bag filled with baby essentials. Ben was behind her carrying Marlene while Mark assisted with the port-a-crib.

Like the main character in my blurred movie, this girl possessed no resemblance to the drug- addicted street person of two years ago. In her place was a confident and self-assured young woman. Looking very chic in black Capri pants with matching black and white blouse and her thick honey colored hair styled into a French braid, Sylvia exuded happiness. Ben instantly placed Marlene in my waiting arms. With her delicate features, pink dress edged with lace and tiny pink satin shoes, she was the epitome of feminine. I felt the warmth of her against me and stared down into her deep brown eyes. "It's your Aunt Maddie," I cooed to her. I looked at Sylvia, smiling. "You've got one gorgeous daughter here." Sylvia's pride was obvious. "She's now sleeping through the night, Maddie. Just four weeks old. Can you imagine?"

I heard Emma whimpering by my leg. "Oh, poor girl. You want to meet Marlene, don't you?" Carefully bending down, I allowed Emma to sniff the baby. The wagging tail confirmed her excitement. "I think she approves," I said and laughed as Emma ran around in excited little circles. Dinner was a success and Ben raved about my scalloped potatoes. Marlene slept, allowing us to enjoy each other's company and conversation. While we had coffee and cheesecake, I glanced around the living room, marveling at how four strangers had become family. I recalled living in Boston and despite the prestigious career, lovely home and elegant lifestyle, something was always missing. There had been a nagging ache inside me I had never quite been able to define. Now I knew . . . love had been missing. That simple, yet most powerful of all emotions. What I found even stranger was how each one of us had come to find it in our lives. Listening to Ben and Sylvia talk about their plans for the future, I was struck by how two unlikely individuals had been brought together. In the same way that Mark and I had been. Totally unexpected and yet so right. No matter the circumstances, if we're lucky, we meet that one special person in our lifetime. That one person that is unlike any other . . . we feel the chemistry, we connect, and we know that what we share is the true definition of love.

"So I think we both agree the best thing to do is go slow," I heard Sylvia say.

Ben nodded. "I'll wait forever for Sylvia. I think she needs to take the next two years to complete her education. She's allowed me to become an important part of her life and share Marlene. I can't ask for more than that."

Mark's glance connected with mine and we both smiled.

"Sounds like a wise decision to me," he said, not taking his eyes from my face.

* * *

I gently kissed Mark's cheek, careful not to wake him. Throwing on a pair of shorts and sweatshirt, I whispered to Emma, "Come on, girl. Let's walk down to the corner and get the Sunday paper."

Stepping out on the porch, I could smell autumn in the air. The trees lining the sidewalk confirmed it. Yellow, gold and vivid red leaves reminded me of my childhood in New Hampshire. I loved spring, but there was something about autumn that filled me with warm, cozy feelings. This time of year brought to mind roaring fireplaces, hot chocolate, red wine, burning leaves, and long walks in the woods. I noticed even Emma seemed to have more of a zip in her pace as we walked to the corner shop.

"Hey there, Maddie," Charlie said. "Bit of a nip in the air this morning, huh? We'll be getting that first snowfall before we know it."

"I think you could be right," I replied, and paid him for the paper. "Any muffins left or am I too late?"

"I think you're in luck. Sophie baked extra last night," he said, checking the glassed-in counter. "We have blueberry and cranberry."

"One of each, please."

Charlie handed me the bag and then bent down to Emma, who had been patiently sitting beside my leg. "Here ya go, girl," he said, passing her a peanut butter cookie.

As was her habit, she looked up at me for confirmation. I nodded and said, "It's okay. You can have it."

She never deviated from her routine. Rather than eat the cookie in the shop, Emma proudly carried it in her mouth for the walk back home. Walking into the living room, she went to the scatter rug, lay down and happily ate the cookie.

I prepared the coffee and took the front page of the paper

into the living room. Emma curled up beside me on the sofa.

"I'll be damned," I said. Emma looked up at me. "I never would have believed it."

The headline jumped out at me in large, bold print. *Senator Settles in Sexual Harassment Suit . . . Wife in Rehab.*

The story stated that the testimony of Alison Taylor gave the jury more than enough evidence. Her emotional testimony swayed any jurors that may have had doubts and convinced them that the senator had used his influence and power to satisfy his wants and needs at the expense of a woman forced to make difficult choices. It went on to say that an undisclosed settlement to all three women had been agreed upon by both sides. Complicating the senator's life further was the fact that his wife, Lila Pope, had been placed in a drug rehab facility in Connecticut. "Apparently, Mrs. Pope has had a severe drug addiction for years, which she was able to keep hidden." I read out loud. "It is unknown how she was able to discreetly purchase these drugs. Senator Pope admitted to suspecting his wife's problem, although he had no knowledge about how she acquired them. A spokesperson for the senator stated that it was a mutual agreement of both the Senator and Mrs. Pope that she seek help for recovery of her addiction. Mrs. Pope's father, noted Boston attorney Adam Bucchanan, had no comment."

I shook my head as I put the paper down. "I'll be damned," I said again. "Sounds to me like the suave and pompous Bryce Pope got what he deserved and justice prevailed."

It was difficult not to luxuriate in the smug feeling that washed over me.

CHAPTER 37

The newspaper article about Senator Pope was shocking. The man must have made a lot of enemies in his career judging by the speed with which the lawsuit came to trial. The TV newscasters made a joke about the timing, especially those of a more conservative bent. Overall, it could have been worse for him, but his tactic had been to admit some wrongdoing early in his testimony, thereby taking the steam and newsworthiness out of the trial early on.

The parallel admittance of Lila Pope's dependence on drugs was a masterstroke of strategy. My money was on Barton Lane as the author of the plan to defuse the potential nightmare. Dawson's death also provided an opportunity for Pope to come partially clean without fear of his supplier copping a plea or further implicating him.

Lila, as always, was the loyal wife. After years of neglect, she faced the shrill beat of the press and the scalding light of public criticism without divulging the role her husband played in accommodating her habits and facilitating her addiction. She spared his career as she had done for years before at the cost of her own independence and self-respect. The wronged woman overlooked his sexual wanderings for many years, openly defending and forgiving him in the light of public focus. What a woman; he didn't deserve her.

Politicos argued about the possibilities of Senator Pope winning re-election in two years, but I believed the master of political deception would return to Washington a winner.

The Pope-Brigham Health Bill was another story. Pope kept his word by reintroducing the bill in committee and obtaining two-party sponsorship in the House. There was some hope, despite a general lobbying effort against it by the same opponents, but the sexual harassment scandal and the drug abuse admission ended any chance for passage in that session. The support shrunk from any connection with an admitted weak man who couldn't control his own family. If the world only knew the whole story.

Disappointment for me was both personal and humanitarian. My fifteen minutes of fame had come and gone. What more could I ask? I was off the streets of Washington and in love with Maddie. At that point nothing else mattered. At least that's what I thought.

* * *

The INS, with help from the Central Intelligence Agency, raided the International Holding Company just after five in the afternoon. Richard Witton, Charles Lester and seven office administrators were arrested without a shot being fired. The shock of finding Ronald Esterward Owens in the office generated an immediate decision to keep the raid under heavy wraps. All of the detainees were flown to Washington on an Air Force Special Forces helicopter. Those arrested were taken to the INS building near Constitution Avenue. None were charged pending instructions from a higher authority.

* * *

"We've pieced together a case that'll support charges of at least four murders in the United States. God knows where else they've operated," Grundig said. "So why aren't they being charged?"

"John, we need to be patient," Jones said. "The President is speaking with the Secretary General now, I was told. Hell, put yourself in his place. What could you tell the boss of the most insecure organization in the world? They can't keep a little secret, certainly not our secret."

"How about the others? They're American citizens. What's the excuse for them? I smell cover up."

"It isn't a matter of excuses; it's the impact if there should be a leak in any area. Don't be foolish. The President supported the program at every step, why would he want to cover up now?"

"I don't know, but I won't be a party to it," Grundig said. "I'll blow the cover rather than see this swept under the rug."

"Go get some coffee, John. Everything's under control."

As Grundig walked down the hallway muttering to himself, Jones picked up the secure phone and punched in a well-known number. "We have a problem."

"I've had enough problems for one day. What?" a deep, northern-sounding voice said.

"Grundig will revolt if he doesn't see an arraignment real soon," Jones said.

"You're his boss, why can't you instruct him otherwise?"

"I've tried to reason with him, but he won't stand for any hanky panky."

"When Pageant arrives, they'll release all parties. The President has signed a new treaty. One of the terms is release of Owens, Witton and the others. They'll be flown to Europe on an Air Force aircraft. No one will ever know."

"Grundig knows." Jones' voice was deeper than usual, reflecting concern about his colleague.

"Then do something about it."

"But . . ." He dropped the earpiece away from his ear.

"Jones, we have no choice. I'll brief the President tonight and he'll expect the solution to Grundig's stupidity at your brief in the morning. Are you listening to me?"

"I understand. The treaty has been signed?"

"Yes. Get with it, Jones."

"I'll see to him."

John Grundig didn't stay for the coffee. He left the building as soon as the area was clear.

* * *

The last man I expected to see at four in the morning was Grundig. He pounded on our door until I opened it. "Let me in," he said, as he pushed his way past me.

"Who is it, Mark?" Maddie called from the bedroom.

"John Grundig. Come out here, Maddie."

She came into the room blurry-eyed and grouchy. The frown on her face told the whole story of her view of a late-night caller. In minutes, we were both sitting opposite John waiting for an explanation.

"I listened at the door of Jones' office."

Maddie looked at me for some understanding.

"What the hell did you overhear that brings you to our place at this hour?" I asked.

"We arrested the crew in Manhattan. The people who have been directing you and others to commit assassinations. We have them dead-to-rights."

"Great," I said, "so what's bad about that?"

"I think they're going to let them go."

"Why on earth would anyone do that?" Maddie asked. "Look what they've done to Mark for example."

"I think Jones is going to try to kill me for saying I wouldn't tolerate a cover up."

My head felt like it was spinning. Here was a man who was my protector, the big government investigator and he was trembling in front of me. I searched for some words to calm him. "Maybe you're just mistaken. You heard wrong. Christ, John, these are your friends and co-workers that you're running from. How could that be?"

"The secret's more important than any one person's life."

"What's the secret?" We both urged him to get on with the meat of the story.

"I can't say any more about it, it's classified."

"They're going to kill you and you think keeping their secret's important?" Maddie said in exasperation.

"It's the world's secret."

"If you didn't intend to tell somebody about what you know, you wouldn't have come here," I said, realizing for the first time the truth of the situation. The INS team had disregarded Phil Corso's life that I probably took. They would have risked other lives until they located the source of the command signals. Death and killing didn't matter. John had good reason to be shaken. "Am I right? You want to tell us, don't you? If only to ensure that something's done about the problem."

"Mark, do you know what the problem is? Who's in jail and who wants to kill John?" Maddie asked. "God, I'm so confused."

"The problem is the Visitors. I know there's an agreement with them, but Jones said that they renewed the treaty," John explained.

"The visitors? Who are the *visitors*? Who renewed the treaty?" I asked not understanding any of this.

"The President."

"Then, it'll be submitted to the senate for approval," I said, still confident that the legal system worked.

"Don't you understand? We're so far behind the rest of them that we'd be a slave planet if we joined the rest. A source of labor— bodies for drudgery."

There was no logic to what was being said. I didn't understand him and my face must have displayed my ignorance.

"Mark, the Visitors are here. They agreed to certain stipulations to be able to operate freely otherwise."

"Why would any government agree to submit to someone who wasn't a citizen? Is the United States the only signing party?"

"Yes. There hasn't been any other power with the capability to affect the future."

The question remained, who are the visitors? What country did they come from and why did we fear them enough to let them go after murdering in this country? "Are there a lot of visitors here?"

Without understanding why, the question was difficult for me to phrase.

"Too many. They've been here for centuries, helping us."

"What nationality? I admit not understanding any of this," I said.

"They take an active hand when they believe we're going in the wrong direction."

"Active meaning, killing the offenders?" I asked.

"Whatever's needed."

"If they're so powerful and knowing, why don't they take over our country?"

"You mean the world."

"Do I?" I asked, not knowing what I meant, but seeing that bit-by-bit the story was being revealed.

"It's because we aren't ready. I told you we're so far behind."

"Behind what? Christ, I don't understand and you're going to tell me what this is all about. Visitors are aliens? Is that it?"

"They're born here. Right here among us, but they're affiliated to other parts of the universe. Visitors are different; we just can't differentiate them anymore."

"What can we do, John?"

Maddie took a deep breath as he looked at us with a stark, bewildered expression.

"You must tell the world that we're cavorting with them. Someone must know. Who's to say that our President's smart enough to make the judgments that'll affect all of us?"

Maddie's brow was furled. "Are you saying these visitors come from some other place? Another planet?"

"That's what happened eons ago."

"How do we tell what we know? Is there some documentation that we can use to power our position?" I asked.

Grundig took a small sheaf of letter-size pages from his breast pocket. He opened the package displaying dark red words across the top of the page—*Eyes Only-Moral Passage*.

Maddie leaned over my arm as we read the four pages that summarized the situation beginning in 3500 B.C. The estimate of current Visitors and the treaty-limited allowable number of participants brought chills to my body. So many things made sense to me now. I shook my head recalling items in the news that had no meaning to me earlier. Maddie looked at me in an attempt to ensure this was truly happening. We weren't dreaming.

"Take care of that paper. If something happens to me, you must take action."

"Honestly, I may not know where to take this."

"Mark, listen to me. Safeguard the paper and deal from its contents. See the President."

"But . . ."

"I've got to go or I'll put both of you at risk."

"We haven't done anything," I said.

"Where will you go?" Maddie asked.

"I'll be all right." Grundig started for the door. "Don't let us all down."

We didn't sleep the rest of the night. While the details were still fresh in our mind, we developed a plan we would attempt if anything happened to Grundig. Secretly, I was praying that John would do all he asked us to do on his own.

* * *

Three days later, John Grundig was shot at the gates of the White House as he attempted entry. The news reports said he forced himself past the first security guard after failing to present proper identification. John was identified only as an intruder. Secret Service agents firing from the roof responded to an alert INS agent warning, putting six bullets into his body. From inside the White House, the President heard a commotion, but was unharmed.

CHAPTER 38

Sleeping was impossible after John's visit, so the next day at the clinic was rough. The lack of sleep brought back memories of my medical residency. I knew that being overtired was never efficient and my day proved it again. Besides the lack of sleep, the issue was what could we do now that we had knowledge of a secret that could shake the world from its comfortable self-sufficiency. Making the day go faster would have gotten me closer to Maddie so we could decide on a plan. Time put a measurement on my anxiety.

Dinner was rushed as Maddie cooked hamburgers. I intended to ask her if she was afraid to be too involved in cooking to escape from something or someone. However, I knew what she might say, so I didn't ask. She was afraid and undecided.

"Want an after dinner drink?" I asked.

"No, I want a clear mind. My head tells me not to relax."

"Maddie, it's only a matter of time before the INS figures out that classified pages are missing. I noticed that each sheet John gave us has a control number written in ink. They'll know some have been taken. It won't be long before they look for us. Cleared parties know I was involved as a guinea pig, so to speak. They'll put two and two together even if they didn't follow John to our apartment. The questions are what do we do now and is there anyone we can trust?"

"Not Jones. We can't go to the President. Who is there?" Maddie sounded frantic. What were the options?

"How *well* do you know Glen Pageant?" I asked.

"We met in Boston while working together on fund raising and other projects. I know he's always been a gentleman to me, but not much else." She shrugged.

"He's been in or near everything I've done with the INS. My money says he's in the know even if Grundig wasn't aware of it." I was contradicting the INS and on unsure ground.

"But John said there were only a few with the clearances."

I began to pace as I searched for government logic. "Maybe he didn't know about the others. It makes sense to me that there are some things so sensitive that they don't know who has the clearances. That way you wouldn't talk among the others and the secrets stay safer. So maybe Glen is knowledgeable of the Visitors. Are you willing to allow the bastards to let the killers off without even a slap on the hand? Should we just forget all we know and have fun at our clinic, try to get better health care next year, and help poor people who need medical care? Anyway, would Glen help us if we asked him?"

"Not sure. If they let us forget about all of this, can we go back to our old life? Can we just forget?" Maddie asked. Her face looked blank for a moment.

"I'm not sure. The truth is they can't leave us alone. When they figure out that we have part of a document, we're in trouble. I believe we have to be proactive. For our survival."

"I'm afraid, Mark. I didn't want to know all of this stuff, nor do I want to second-guess the President. He must be doing the correct thing." She wanted out of the entire affair, but it was much too late.

"Is it right for killers to be able to continue to murder people based on some code we don't understand?"

"Of course not."

"Then we have to do something." Smiling, I took her hand. "Maddie, if we don't take the offensive, we aren't going to be able to defend ourselves."

"You sound like an NFL football coach talking before a big game."

"I didn't know you liked pro football. Hell, we have to

survive so we can watch the games together for the rest of our lives." This was a moment without fear. Somehow, we reverted to our personal lives.

Maddie laughed. My words seemed to have begun a chain reaction in her mind. "Do you think we'll be living together for a long time?"

"That depends on whether you'll marry me."

"Are you proposing, Mark?"

In an instant, I was inside her loving arms. "Can I answer that question after our battle's over?"

"I didn't intend to trap you." She touched my cheek with a light, long touch.

"You aren't trapping me. We need to get on with this problem and keep our heads clear that's all," I said, knowing that what we shared was one of the strong factors that might help us survive.

"Let's take a chance and talk to Glen."

"Right, my girl." I called the INS and through their voice mail identification system, got his extension and asked for an appointment the following afternoon.

* * *

Glen returned my call at the clinic first thing in the morning. When he said they had been wondering what happened to me, my skin crawled. I wondered if I had made a very bad mistake by calling him; however, it was done now.

"Glen, I was hoping we could talk to you—Maddie and I."

"Sounds great. You know I've always had a soft spot for Maddie. Oh, but I'm no threat to you." Glen laughed, trying to take the words back with his joviality.

"Not threatened. Maddie told me there was never any romance between you."

"Good. Maybe we can get together for dinner. Rotini's is a . . ."

"No, Glen, I'd like to meet in a place where we could talk openly about a sensitive subject."

"How about my office?"

"How about on the steps of the Lincoln Memorial?"

"Sure. Later this afternoon's okay with me."

"Five o'clock is good for us," I said. "The corner of the steps farthest from the statue on the south side. If there's a homeless person on it, we'll violate his rights and throw him off."

"Spoken like a true former street person. See you at five."

* * *

Maddie thought the meeting place was good. If they were going to kill us for what we knew, they'd have to do it in public. At least we wouldn't make it easy for them.

Leaving the clinic early was difficult since Dr. Stein wasn't feeling well, but there was little choice. Connie promised she would close the clinic doors if Stein became overwhelmed. In a way, we were pushing street people aside.

The long walk from the clinic to Lincoln's statue gave us time to consider our approach to Pageant. Maddie and I were full partners in this affair so we needed to combine our thoughts.

In the distance, I saw Glen seated on the steps. "Shit, he's waiting. That may not be good. If he prepared a welcoming party, they'd have to be in place before we arrived. Maddie, I ought to meet him alone. You . . ."

"No. I'm coming."

"But, if . . ."

"Mark, I'm with you and I don't want to hide in the rear."

Glen waved when we were a hundred yards away. Maybe the wave was a signal to the assassins. They were waiting for us. No weapons on either of us and we're playing with the big boys here. I felt stupid for getting us in a defenseless position. Glen walked toward us with a broad smile. If I hadn't known better, I'd have said he really was happy to see us.

Trying to think ahead of a potential ambush, I suggested that we sit on a bench placed alone on the grass still a distance from the meeting place. Glen agreed.

Maddie smiled at me, as she must have read my thoughts. Her smile was short of a laugh, but not by much. I couldn't resist an urge to laugh at myself and I did.

"Must be a funny subject," Glen said.

"No, a private joke. Maddie thinks I'm too cautious. She's laughing at me."

"You don't trust me, Mark?" He understood our private joke. Christ, he must have considered us sophomoric.

"The guys I trusted are dead—Grundig and Corso. Remember them?"

"I'm not an unfeeling bureaucrat yet."

I studied his face, but couldn't sense any emotions to go along with his professional feelings. "That was uncalled for. I'm sorry."

"What's the big secret we're going to discuss?"

"Please understand that we trust you, Glen. You're my friend. I'm sure of that, but so many unsettling things have happened that it's necessary to be cautious," Maddie said, helping to relax all of us.

"Mind if I smoke?" he asked.

Still concerned about a signal, I asked, "Can you hold off for a few minutes?"

"Right. Let's get right to it then before I have a nicotine fit. Grundig's death has you nervous?"

"We're angry about the release of murderers," I said. "Grundig expected them to get away."

"How did you know they were released? Actually, they were ejected." Glen lit a cigarette and I attributed his impatience to nicotine, not a signaling plan.

"I didn't know for sure, but you've confirmed it," I said. "These same people directed my actions to murder others, I'm certain."

"Yes and your friend Robbie, as well."

He was unemotional, even matter of fact, until I got angry. "Then why would *our* country cover this up?"

"Cover up murder? Haven't you heard of plea bargains?"

"Never mind. We know," Maddie said, "the papers John gave

us summarized the entire situation."

Glen didn't know about John giving us the information until then. He looked shocked. "Probably good he died, because he'd spend a lot of time in jail for releasing that data to uncleared people."

"But he did and we know. There has to be an accounting. My life and who knows how many other orphans' lives were destroyed by those monsters. What evil have they perpetuated?" I asked.

"I can't give you any answers because the explanation isn't up to me. I believe in what we're doing, but someone else made the decisions," Glen said.

"Who?" Maddie asked, sounding tired of half-answers.

"Each generation, a small number of Americans are read into the program. That's the only way to keep the secret. If it got out, everything would change—for the worse."

"*Who?*" Maddie repeated. She had never spoken so harshly to her old friend.

"I can arrange for the President to see you. If you don't understand after that, someone else needs to figure a solution." Glen leaned back as if he could offer no other explanation.

"Because you couldn't sentence us to death. It's not in you, is it Glen?" Maddie asked.

"No. The rationale is a strong one, but saving billions of lives still doesn't give me personally the right to commit murder. If we were at war, I'd be a draft dodger or a conscientious objector."

Somehow, despite my fear of anyone trying to control our world, I believed him. "Set it up," I said. "Do it quickly before one of your co-conspirators who doesn't have your scruples tries to take us out."

Glen smiled. "You have nothing if you don't have self confidence, Dr. Puccini. We're talking about the world's most accomplished assassins and you think all they would do is *try* to kill you? No wonder you survived the streets and the role of a controlled killer. You have guts."

* * *

Two days later, on Sunday, Maddie and I dressed in our best clothes and took a taxi to the White House. Those days were the strangest in my life, a life that had previously boasted too many unusual events. I looked over my shoulder constantly, sleeping little. Maddie was the only one I could trust. Making love was the only time either of us had a reprieve from the tension.

Since we had no picture identification, it looked as if we wouldn't get to the Oval Office. We didn't work for the government, had no driver's license, and never used credit cards. Neither of us had a picture to prove we were Chapelle and Puccini. After a long wait, Pageant came to the guard gate, vouched for us, and signed a release. Nevertheless, the guard at the door used a wand to check us for metal objects and performed a complete pat down.

Next, we waited for the President in his outer office. Few people working—normal for a Sunday, I supposed. When I turned, Glen was gone.

The secretary said good day to the Secretary of State as he entered the Oval Office without glancing at us. He smiled at her, but uttered no words. Ten more minutes passed.

An electronic tone rang. "You may go in to see the President," the woman said.

Everyone had signals.

Maddie was shaking as I touched her hand, easing her through the doorway with my arm at her waist.

"Thank you for coming, Dr. Puccini, Ms. Chapelle. Please have a seat on the sofa. It's very comfortable. My wife picked it out for reading in the late hours." The President shook our hands. "Secretary Close will also remain for our discussion."

The tall, staid Secretary of State shook our hands, but didn't address us.

"I'll come right to the point," President Webb said. "You've come upon some information you shouldn't have and now are in a quandary. Being good people you wonder about my morality that I would condone the release of a group of men with a scandalous record."

Maddie nodded, watching the man she had never voted for.

"The Visitors have been with us for a very long while. They

are far beyond our technical skills and consider us to be primitive, despite considerable aid they have given us for a very long time. They say we're slow starters. Their ability to annihilate us as a planet is a given. Since the end of the Second World War, we have had a treaty with the Visitors. Knowing that we would be slaves to other aliens if we weren't totally destroyed, the treaty was the only rational response."

"Sir, what does the treaty do for us?" I asked.

Secretary Close answered. "They've agreed to limit the operations they engage in. We have also secured a limit on the number of Visitors, but frankly aren't able to confirm their conformance to the terms since they are also born on earth. In any case, we aren't much use to them in our present social state."

My brow knotted.

"By that I mean, we're uncontrolled, a civilization without discipline by their standards. Their operations are designed to bring a certain order out of the chaos. Elements that control our people are considered positive, so religious organizations and legal institutions are monitored by the Visitors and given support on occasion."

"Dr. Puccini, it's a small price to pay to keep this beautiful blue planet pristine," President Webb said.

"How long will the treaty last?" Maddie asked.

"One more generation, twenty-five years, then it'll be re-negotiated. The negotiations will certainly allow greater numbers of Visitors.

"If we're treaty partners, so to speak," I asked, "why do you have a program to keep track of them? Don't you trust them?"

The President smiled. "We fear them. We honestly don't know how many Visitors are here and have no idea how many times they intervene in our society. By following you and Robert Mozart, we learned that our citizens are being controlled for their purposes. How many other homes for boys are used to train and change our youth, we don't know. What we know is this is better than the alternatives to signing treaties and accepting certain acts contrary to our morals and ethics. We'll continue to be a very near-free society in most countries. We will have control over our lives."

"Why did you tell us this, sir?" I asked.

"There's been quite a background check done on both of you. You're both very intelligent and brave. You've taken on a senator, a drug dealer, a rapist and the Visitors who implanted your head. We were sure you would understand and agree with us," Secretary Close said.

"I wouldn't have been able to be so frank with you, Dr. Puccini, if I didn't want your talent on my team."

"Your team?"

"The National Security Council. I want a medical doctor who knows about the Visitors and will understand the details of factors you don't have at your disposal at the moment," President Webb said.

"My job would be to . . ."

"Analyze the activity of the Visitors. No one else on the council would have the clearance, *Moral Passage*. Despite normal political rules and customs, the position would be established by National Security Memorandum and could not be abolished. I hope you accept my offer. There is much at stake."

"What about the access *I* have had, sir?" Maddie asked.

"You would be debriefed and sign an agreement that you'll never pass the information to anyone, under pain of legal prosecution."

"Can we have some time to decide, sir?" I asked.

"We can give you three days. By Wednesday, go to Secretary Close's office and give us your answer."

* * *

Maddie and I didn't discuss the visit with the President that night. An overwhelming heaviness of thought raced through my head. We made love; there were no visions of

Visitors in my dreams. The possibilities of some future day were far from my mind for a few hours.

CHAPTER 39

Riding to my appointment with Secretary Close, I was ill at ease. Part of my feelings was the result of Maddie's attitude about this meeting. She wouldn't be pinned down about what she thought of my job offer. I knew I could do the work, probably better than current members of the National Security staff. Brains, education, experience, and objectivity were my strengths and I knew my capabilities. My hesitation had to do with the woman I wanted to spend my life with. An opinion was all I wanted. I'm my own man and would have made my decision by balancing her viewpoint, but a lack of response didn't seem fair to me.

No response could mean she felt so strongly against getting further involved that her words would have derailed my preference. Maybe she did know how much I loved her and tried to make it easier for me.

Arriving early at Foggy Bottom, I saw an area near the entrance where State Department employees seemed to be gathered. I found a soft chair and sat to wait for my appointment time.

This journey had been incredible. Who would believe it, if I could tell the world? The control device was still in my head, but Glen Pageant had made arrangements for surgical removal next week. He had moved into the liaison position as far as I was concerned and I trusted him, mostly because Maddie held him in such high regard.

Glen also had a viewpoint that he had tried to lend to me. He believed that the Visitors had provided very positive and beneficial support to the world. Held in line, they could be tools of progress. The questions were could they be held accountable and could they be stopped if necessary? Could I make those judgments as a member of the NSC? Hell, did I want to?

At five to ten, I walked to the security desk to announce myself. The woman referred to an appointment book, asking for identification. Showing her my business card was the only option. She smiled, showing her patience with the inexperienced.

"Oh, yes, Dr, Puccini, I recognize you from the stories about you in the paper. Too bad your bill didn't make it. Maybe next time," she said, smiling at me as if she really knew me.

The news in Washington and its suburbs was national news. Newspaper readers in the area knew more about national issues than almost any one else in the country. The woman was proud of her knowledge and therefore seemed happy to meet me. In an instant, I felt some of the exhilaration that Washington politicians and bureaucrats must feel.

She gave me directions and a visitor's pass. The plastic card with a clip to fasten to my jacket had the word *Visitor* in bold letters. She had no idea why I was smiling about the pass. Ironic really.

A beautiful forty-something woman in slacks and white blouse met me at the security station and ushered me into Secretary Close's office. Her smile warmed me and I knew she must have been a very valuable member of the staff.

"Come in, Dr. Puccini. Find a chair you like," Secretary Close said.

I picked an overstuffed armchair and he seated himself across from me. This man wasn't an ordinary Washington bureaucrat.

"May I offer you a drink or coffee, tea?"

"No, sir," I said, trying to find the right tone for this man who would be my boss, if I accepted the job. "Thanks."

"Before you give me your decision, Dr. . . . ."

"Sir, please call me Mark."

He didn't ask me to call him Bly. Bly Close had a blue blood family and education. Yale shone from every move he made. His language was precise and unhurried and he carried himself as if he was from old money. Definitely an eastern establishment man.

"First, we do need your talents here at State. Whatever happens at the NSC, you'll always be a State Department man. As such, you'll report directly to me and my successors."

"How can I be sure about who I work for after you leave your position?"

"Your position is established in a Top Secret NSC Memorandum that President Webb has promulgated. This particular memorandum is in a class of actions that require special attention from future presidents. Trust me, Mark, we don't take our obligations lightly."

I didn't respond. Did I trust him? "Mr. Secretary," I said, watching his reaction. He was very comfortable with that address. "If my position is so important and special, why is there only one of me—I mean one position. Why not a complete staff that watches these critically important subjects?"

"Who told you there's only one position with duties relating to the Visitors?"

"No one. Just an assumption."

"Sir, you assumed wrong," he said. "Other persons have duties relating to yours, but they also report to me. And as Harry said, the buck stops here."

"Will I know them and work with them?"

"Not usually. You'll have your job and they'll have theirs. It's that simple. My special staff will bring the inputs together. This approach makes a much more secure operation. Do you have a problem with that arrangement?" He paused to allow me to think about his question.

"No, sir. I can live with those rules. Actually, I don't know what the job entails."

"You'll have primary responsibility to detect and warn about threats related to health. You'll also be the point of contact on health issues impacting national security. That means attending meetings and knowing counterparts in other organizations and agencies. Your undercover role will be to know all you can about the Visitors and pass the information to me."

"I'll know things by reading reports and . . . what else?"

"The reports won't be obvious. Your job requires recognition of out-of-the-norm events. You'll have to detect and analyze Visitor activity that they prefer to keep sub rosa. The treaty will give you valuable insights, as will the previously collected information about them."

"When will I read the treaty?"

"Today, before you leave. Mark, we'll be in a period of mutual restraint. The new agreement directs that the Visitors not conduct operations like those that involved you for twenty-five years."

"I don't understand why we just don't stop it permanently."

"You'll understand much more after a full indoctrination to the situation. When conditions are as now, with better control of our direction, we have more negotiating power."

"Then what am I going to be watching for?"

"They won't keep their agreement completely. It's the job of State to monitor the treaty violations."

"We're in a treaty with people who don't keep agreements? What am I missing here, Mr. Secretary?"

"We have no choice, but also it's true about all treaties. Without verification no treaty can be valid based purely on trust." He smiled, perhaps seeing that I knew almost nothing about international relations.

"Verification? Meaning our intelligence organizations have to determine whether they are doing what they agreed to do?"

"Exactly. Dr. Puccini, you will be part of the intelligence structure that determines how trustworthy the Visitors are behaving."

"Besides knowing more than I was supposed to know, what are my qualifications for this work, Mr. Secretary?"

He nodded, maybe thinking this was a good question. "Your medical training and scientific knowledge make you valuable. Visitors are different from us."

My stomach felt queasy all of a sudden. This man meant we had no choice because we didn't have sufficient power. Treaties gave us time to improve our position and check on our treaty partner. I rose from the chair to walk around the room looking at pictures and paintings on the walls. He seemed to know what I was thinking.

"Would you like a drink?" he asked.

"Too early for me."

"Me, too, but this is a special occasion. An eventful decision will be made in the next few minutes."

I nodded as he walked to the liquor cabinet stored behind a set of mirrors he moved with an electric switch. At first I continued to browse his memorabilia, but he caught my attention. Without turning completely, I watched him open a small case, a pillbox similar to one my orphanage counselor owned. He dropped two tablets into the glass in his left hand. Close turned to see if I was watching while I continued my perusal.

He gave me the glass in his right hand. "Here's to your decision," he said.

"I thought you were going to give me a Mickey Finn."

"No." He laughed; then seemed to be lost for words for a second. "It's my medication which I usually take with water." The Yale man's flushing face showed his embarrassment.

Did I catch him at something? "Sorry," I said, "just joking."

"So, are you going to be employed at the NSC?" This was the moment to decide. His stare told me it was up to me, without further explanation.

"Yes, sir. I want to do this work." As I said the words, I wondered what would have happened if I had declined.

"I'm very pleased. I'll have the paperwork to you in less than a week. In the meantime, enjoy your time off. You'll be working very hard from now on."

"Most doctors work hard as a way of life."

He smiled, but didn't seem to agree. "Now about an assistant. Miss Chapelle had an outstanding work record for Senator Pope."

The government had investigated Maddie and me. "You want both of us, don't you? We know enough that you can't afford to have us be very far away."

"I know talent, that's all. Please ask her if she'll join you." His tone didn't sound like a request.

"I'll ask, but don't be too disappointed if Maddie says no." I was speaking for Maddie and felt less constrained to be formal and polite.

He sensed my changed attitude and paused while he decided to tolerate it. "The President and I would be very disappointed if either of you decided to turn down the challenge being offered."

I understood exactly where I stood and liked the view from my position. This was the single, unique way in which I would ever learn more about the Visitors.

* * *

After the meeting with Secretary Close, I went to the clinic where Dr. Stein was jammed with patients. The shift was the longest five hours of my life. Ready to move, I prayed that Maddie would move on with me, but when I returned home that evening, I found a note she left me. After the shock and hurt, I realized she needed to get away to make her own life decisions. I thought I'd never see her again.

CHAPTER 40

As the 737 made its final approach into Logan, I could see the Boston skyline in the distance. A mixture of excitement and apprehension occupied my mind. None of it had changed in the almost three years I'd been gone. Glancing at my watch, I knew it would be a few more hours before Mark returned from the clinic to find my note on the kitchen table. The aircraft taxied to the terminal, and I felt a twinge of guilt. Today was the day Mark was to give his answer about the National Security Council . . . and I preferred not to be there for his decision. As of last night, he was still undecided and despite his persistence, I refused to give him my input. I wasn't about to be responsible if he made the wrong choice, as I honestly had no idea what the correct one was. Hell, I was having a hard enough time trying to decide what I should do with the rest of *my* life, never mind his.

Telephoning Alison Taylor turned out to be a blessing in disguise. I mentioned I was at loose ends about my future. Over the past week, I became aware that I was no longer living my life in fear or in hiding. Justice had been done with both Garret and Bryce Pope. For the first time in almost three years, I was free to go and do as I chose. But in the process of my survival, I realized the price I had paid in the loss of my identity. Mark was being offered a chance for a new position, an opportunity to become a productive member of society. Here I was with nothing on my horizon and I was frightened. All of a sudden, I was in limbo. The fear I had lived with for so long had been replaced by uncertainty about many things.

Walking through the terminal, I saw Alison in the crowd of people waving to me. When she offered me her place in Marblehead to spend some time sorting things out, I was hesitant—unsure of taking such a bold move. She explained that her daughter was at Disney World with the nurse and she would be leaving on Thursday to join them for a week. Without thinking further about it, I accepted her invitation.

"Hi, Maddie," Alison said, giving me a hug. "Did you have a good flight?"

I nodded, shifting the strap of my tote bag on my shoulder. "Yeah, it was fine. It seems strange to be back here again."

"I'm sure not too much has changed. One of the benefits of New England, I guess," she replied, as we walked toward the baggage claim.

On the drive to Marblehead, Alison chatted about Aubrey and how excited her daughter was to see Mickey Mouse and Donald Duck again. "I guess I can thank Bryce for that," she said. "I never could have afforded for the three of us to return there if I hadn't gotten that settlement."

"Maybe it's true what they say. Nothing is ever all bad. Some good is always to be found."

Alison rented a charming cottage in Old Town. The owner was a distant relative and now resided in a nursing home. She was happy to let Alison and her daughter live there and care for it at a reduced price.

"This is lovely," I said, as we parked in front of a blue two-story house.

"It has a lot of charm, but the parking can be tricky in the winter on these narrow one way streets."

We stepped into a small foyer with hardwood floor and a highly polished mahogany table. A vase of white gladiolas was surrounded by various size picture frames. I followed Alison to the left and into a small sitting room.

"Leave your luggage here," she said, "I'll give you the tour of the downstairs first. We use this as the main living room." My glance took in the chintz-covered sofa and cushy chairs arranged in front of an old fireplace. Brass lamps on cherry wood tables and a television in the corner completed the room. Despite the simpleness of the furnishings, coziness pervaded. A dog-eared magazine on the end table, an empty coffee cup beside it, a pink velour stuffed rabbit left behind on the sofa—all items that added a live-in quality.

"I was fortunate that Aunt Carrie left the place furnished," she said, walking into a room at the back of the house. "This is the kitchen and I'll show you where everything is later. I want you to feel at home here."

A medium-size kitchen overlooked a patio and small garden. I followed her into a hallway off the kitchen.

"These rooms are for Aubrey and Cath," Alison said, as she opened the doors to adjoining bedrooms. "And here's where Aubrey works with Cath." The room was filled with a mat table, wheelchair and various pieces of exercise equipment.

I followed her upstairs and she opened the first door on the left. "This is the guestroom. I hope you'll be comfortable here."

Walking into the room, I had a sensation of stepping back in time. The dormer ceiling provided a quaintness with a twin bed beneath it. Yellow and blue flowers dominated the wallpaper, comforter and curtains. An antique desk in the corner and an overstuffed chair added to the coziness of the room.

"This is lovely, Alison. I can't thank you enough for allowing me to stay here for a few days."

"Your adjoining bathroom is right here," she said, opening a door into a small, but adequate room. "And you can stay here as long as you like. Let's go downstairs and I'll make us some coffee before you unpack."

* * *

Following dinner of fish chowder, salad and French bread, Alison and I relaxed on her patio with a glass of wine.

"You have a lovely garden," I said, enjoying the bright yellow and orange marigolds. Other flowerbeds bloomed with the colors of autumn.

"Thanks. I enjoy gardening. I find it allows me quiet time for myself, and the finished product is enjoyable to look at."

I recalled my childhood in New Hampshire with the beautifully tended garden my mother had created and wondered if I would ever have my own soil or would I always be drifting through life, never quite certain where I belonged.

By ten P.M. both Alison and I retired. She had an early flight the next morning to Orlando and I discovered I was drained. Despite the fatigue in my body, my mind wouldn't allow me to settle enough to sleep. I missed Mark. I missed falling asleep beside him, curled up in his arms. I also felt guilty for taking my share of our household money to purchase my airline ticket. I knew it was an irresponsible thing to do, but I also knew I had to get away for a while.

* * *

Just as my last thoughts the evening before had been of Mark, my first thoughts upon awakening were also of him. Turning over in bed, I felt empty. I stretched my hand across the sheet, then closed my eyes. Almost a year since I had met Mark. I loved him more than I thought possible to love another person. That wasn't the problem. *I* was the problem.

During two years of being in hiding, I seldom gave a thought to my future, because there didn't seem to be one. Each day had meshed into the next. Everything was changed now and I had no idea what I wanted from the future that suddenly opened for me. Did I want to marry? Did I want to have children? I knew if Mark and I were to marry, children were not a possibility. How important was that to me? There were no answers because the future I had in front of me was blurred. Distorted like a window splattered with dirt. Not only could I not see through it . . . I had no way of knowing how to make it clean and bright.

Walking into the kitchen, I found Alison's note on the table. *Maddie,* she had written in large bold script, *Please help yourself to whatever you need. If there's an emergency, you have the number at my hotel. Relax, chill out and find your answers. Stay as long as necessary. ~ Alison.*

Pouring myself a cup of coffee, I marveled at how warm a person could be to another human being. Alison didn't know me that well, yet she opened her home to me. I also marveled at her strength. Life had really thrown her some curves, but she didn't wallow in it. She picked herself up and went forward. That's how I used to be. What happened to that woman? How did I become so unsure of myself and my destination?

Sipping coffee on the patio, I glanced at my watch . . . nine o'clock. I was grateful Mark was honoring my request by not calling me. The note explained that I needed to get away to think about many things. I didn't elaborate, but hoped he would understand.

After showering and dressing, I decided to walk downtown. I had always loved Marblehead, situated right beside the Atlantic with all the boats in the harbor. Walking down State Street, I could see the brightly colored sails blowing in the gentle October breeze. I headed over to the small park on a bluff overlooking the ocean. Sitting on the grass, arms wrapped around my knees, I wondered what it would be like to have a normal life again. One with routine and order. Since being with Mark, I had partially experienced this. But even the unspoken commitment we had was not total or complete. Was that what I wanted? What was it I was seeking? One thing I knew for sure was that I was not cut out to work as a Gal Friday in a clinic. The position had certainly accomplished what I needed a year ago. Now things had changed, and I wanted more.

Glancing to my right, I saw an elderly woman had set up an easel a few feet away. She had a demeanor about her that I couldn't quite define. Strands of white hair had escaped from the knot on top of her head, blowing across her face. Paying no attention, she proceeded to open a large box of paints, then placed a canvas on the easel. She sat on a small plastic stool with paintbrush in hand, while momentarily pausing to stare out at the ocean. Resolute . . . that's how she appeared. Determined, like somebody who had a purpose.

I watched for a few minutes as she began making strokes on the canvas. Curious, I got up and walked toward her. She glanced over at me and smiled.

"Hi there," I said, "mind if I watch you for a few minutes?"

"Not at all," she said, chuckling. "I enjoy an audience."

Standing slightly in back of her, I watched as she began to add color that was the identical shade of the ocean. Before long she added the horizon and sky. Obviously, this woman had a gift for painting. "I'm no expert," I said, "but you're a superb artist. Have you been doing this a long time?"

She shrugged her shoulders and made a disgusted sound. "I'm afraid not nearly long enough. Unfortunately, I ignored my talent when I was younger. Didn't allow myself to listen. Paid more attention to what everyone else thought I should do. It's easy to do that, you know?"

I liked this woman. She had an energy about her with a peacefulness that I admired; perhaps even craved.

I nodded. "I suppose it is. But how does one ever know exactly what they want and what's best for them?"

She looked up at me and I saw the deep lines in her tanned face, but it was her eyes that fixed my stare. They were blue, appearing to hold years of wisdom. "Oh, everyone knows," she replied. "All of us know, but still, we don't listen. We let other things get in the way. People, careers, day-to-day problems. But if we're lucky, one day we do listen, then find we've been given another chance to make it right." She pointed to the middle of her chest. "It's all in here, you know. All the answers and solutions. We just need to block out everything else and listen."

Sitting down on the grass beside her easel, I extended my hand. "I'm Maddie," I said, "and I'm pleased to meet you."

Her grasp was solid and strong as she returned my handshake and said, "I'm Felicia, but the pleasure is all mine."

In the course of our conversation, I found out that she resided on the next street to Alison, where she had lived since age sixteen. The house had belonged to her parents. She never married, therefore had never moved. She asked no questions, but was very open about sharing part of her life with me. Felicia had worked as a librarian up until ten years ago when she retired to finally pursue her love of painting.

An hour later, when I felt guilty for intruding on her time and got up to leave, she surprised me by inviting me over for afternoon tea. I accepted.

* * *

Opening the wooden gate to the brown clapboard cottage, I admired the small meticulous garden behind the sidewalk. Bright orange and yellow flowers provided a nice contrast to the brown of the house. Using the brass knocker in the shape of a sailboat, I heard Felicia holler come in.

Three cats greeted me as I stepped inside the foyer, meowing and rubbing against my leg. I had an acute pang of loneliness for Emma, wondering if she missed me. Bending down to pat each one, I saw Felicia walking toward me from the back of the house.

"Ah, I see Renoir, Monet and Van Gogh have properly greeted you. They are my constant companions and enjoy what little company I have."

"They're beautiful," I said, admiring their thick coats with fluffy tails.

"I thought we'd have tea in the sitting room. We have a bit of an east wind this afternoon which plays havoc with my arthritis."

I followed her into an old-fashioned, but charming room. The furniture was outdated and qualified as antique. An overstuffed sofa and two club chairs surrounded by small footstools with a tapestry covering, small mahogany end tables and a roll-top desk gave the feeling of the late 1800s.

"I think you'll be comfortable in the dark brown chair,"

Felicia said, as she sat down in the one opposite.

A book with tasseled bookmarker, eyeglasses, and a letter opener lay before her on the table. A stunning silver teapot and fragile flowered teacups were arranged on the table between us.

"I hope you like Earl Gray tea," she said, as she began pouring. "Help yourself to the sugar, cream and lemon."

After a brief discussion on the weather, Felicia asked what had brought me to Marblehead. I found myself telling this complete stranger bits and pieces of my background. I shared with her how I had lived in Boston, my position with Senator Pope, my need to escape, and reside in Washington. Although I didn't go into great detail about how I survived, I had a feeling she was able to fill in the blanks. I finished by telling her about Mark and my uncertainty as to where my life was now taking me.

She nodded, remaining silent for a few moments. "We never know for sure where our paths will lead us, do we? But I will tell you, one thing I learned for sure over many years is that love is the motivating factor in everything we do. Or it should be. Life has a way of making us forget this. In my case, I allowed obligations to come before love. Many people feel sorry for me that I never married and live alone. But they shouldn't. Because I once had the true love of my life. Not everyone does, you know—not everyone is that fortunate. Edward was that person for me. We had fifteen good years together. No, not as husband and wife. But maybe even closer than many married couples."

Felicia paused as she added another teaspoon of sugar to her tea.

"My parents were ill for many years and as the dutiful daughter, I stayed here to care for them. Edward was a patient man and felt we would be together some day. But life intervened and time was not kind to us. A sudden, unexpected heart attack took him from me. I grieved for many years. Once the anger subsided, for the first time in my life I began to listen to my heart. Instead of feeling cheated that Edward was taken from me, I began to feel grateful for all the wonderful moments we had spent

together. This enabled me to finally pursue my other love . . .
painting. It fulfills me, but also allows me to enjoy what I do
have in my life. One must always enjoy what has been given to
them. The most important thing is to be open and willing to
permit life's treasures to touch you. By closing ourselves off, we
miss all that our life has to offer."

This woman was not about to let life pass her by. Despite
sorrow and disappointment, she had not allowed an uncertain
future without Edward to hold her back. Felicia had jumped
in and welcomed whatever was ahead.

* * *

During the next few days, I replayed in my head everything
that Felicia had shared with me. I was still no closer to an answer
on the fifth day of my stay in Marblehead. Reaching for the
telephone in Alison's kitchen to dial the number, I was now at
least willing to take a major step toward my future . . . whatever
that future might be. Surprisingly, I felt myself welcoming it.

Hearing Mark's voice at the other end of the line, excitement
and passion in his voice . . . I also knew Felicia had given me a
valuable secret. Without a doubt, I knew in my heart that love
was indeed a strong motivating factor in all that we do.

"I'm coming back, Mark," I whispered into the telephone,
"and I love you."

CHAPTER 41

"Welcome to Washington and Ronald Reagan National Airport," the lively voice said on the PA system as the 737 taxied to the terminal. I smiled. Call it what you want, it would always be National Airport to me.

Reaching into the overhead for my tote bag, Mark's face flashed before my eyes. The five days away from him seemed like five months. Hearing his voice on the telephone only convinced me more how much I loved him. Although I had no plan in place for my future career, one thing I was certain of was that I wanted to be with Mark. When I asked him if he had accepted the position with the NSC he answered yes, but said we had a lot to discuss. I realized I was glad he was embarking on a new career and was happy for him. I knew he had a vast amount of education, combined with experience. He'd be a positive asset to Secretary Close.

Walking off the jetway, our eyes connected immediately. My face broke into a smile as I walked toward him and he enveloped me in his arms. We stood there in a tight embrace that was broken when he pulled away to look deep into my eyes.

"God, Maddie, you have no idea how much I missed you these past five days. I had myself convinced you might not come back to me."

"I missed you even more," I said, feeling my eyes become moist. "Being with you is where I'm supposed to be."

"I love the sound of that. Come on, let's get a taxi back

to the apartment. I thought we'd relax a little and I booked us for seven at Alberto's."

"Alberto's? Did you inherit a windfall while I was away?"

Mark laughed. "Not quite, but a prestigious job comes with a good salary. We can splurge tonight with my clinic paycheck, because very soon there'll be a significant increase."

* * *

My body luxuriated in the afterglow of making love. I felt suspended between being awake and being pulled toward sleep. Mark's arms tightened around my shoulder as I nestled deeper into his chest. At that moment, all was right in the world. His thoughtfulness had been apparent the moment I stepped into our apartment. The coffee table held a vase of beautiful yellow roses. Beside them was an ice bucket chilling a bottle of champagne.

Mark's soft and steady breathing told me he had dozed off as I recalled our conversation about the NSC. After he explained his discussion with Secretary Close, he astonished me with the disclosure that I was also being offered a position as Mark's assistant. I knew part of the reason was due to the level of information I had been privy to, but I was confident enough to realize with my experience I could be a valuable asset to Mark.

"So we'll be a team?" I asked him and he nodded. "Hmm, kinda like James Bond and Moneypenny?"

Mark threw his head back laughing. "I guess you could say that. Although she was the enemy, I'd much prefer Pussy Galore."

"You naughty man, you," I said, joining his laughter. Glancing up at Mark's sleeping face, I smiled. We had discussed our ability to work well together in the clinic. Both of us were motivated and willing to put forth that bit of extra, if required. He was right . . . we did make one hell of a team. He seemed both relieved and happy when I agreed to interview for the position. Then he surprised me by hinting that possibly we should consider upgrading our living arrangements. "You mean move? Leave here?" I asked.

"Maddie, we'll both be getting a substantial increase in salary.

Wouldn't it be nice to have a brownstone in Georgetown? A bit of a back garden for Emma? Look at everything you gave up when you left Boston. Now you have a chance to have that lifestyle back. Only this time, you'll be sharing it with me."

As much as I loved the Kaminskis and our small apartment, I knew he was right. We both deserved to have more spacious accommodations. Somewhere we could entertain and be proud of what we built together. When I agreed, Mark said we'd contact a real estate agent to see what was available.

My entire life suddenly seemed to be shifting in the right direction. I was deeply in love with Mark and felt his love in return. I'd soon be employed again with a position that offered status and prestige. Possibly within the next few months, I'd even have a Georgetown address. Yes . . . life was definitely good.

I heard Emma whining and reached my hand over the side of the bed to stroke between her ears. She had been ecstatic when I walked into the apartment. For the first time in my life, because of her and Mark, I felt like I was part of a family.

Mark stirred and kissed my cheek. "What time is it? We have that reservation at Alberto's."

"Five," I said, moving closer to him.

"Plenty of time for an encore," he whispered, as I felt his hands slide down my body.

* * *

The following week was filled with activity. First on the agenda was to interview with Secretary Close. Although he hadn't been specific about my job description, being with Mark on a daily basis was my main criteria for accepting the position. Next, we agreed to give Dr. Stein a two-week notice before leaving the clinic. Mark had hoped we'd be able to have a short holiday together before starting with the NSC, but it didn't look possible. As an alternative, he promised when we could arrange some time off, we'd take a two-week holiday in Italy. With his assumed Italian ancestry, he had always felt a pull to visit there. Now he'd be able to share it with me. We told the Kaminskis that we'd be moving in the next few months. They were sad to lose us as tenants, but they understood and were happy we'd be able to upgrade our residence. With Christmas only two months away, we promised not to move until after the first of the year, which would allow us to spend a final holiday with them.

* * *

True to his word, Jake had contacted me to have lunch with him. When he arrived at the clinic, Mark and I were standing together talking and I introduced them. He insisted that Mark join us. I had been concerned it might be uncomfortable for Mark, but he seemed to like Jake. I'm sure part of it was the fact he knew Jake had been good to me at a time when I desperately needed some good in my life. After we shared news with Jake about our new positions and moving, he surprised me by relating he had met a very special person. Doreen worked in Washington at one of the offices where Jake delivered furniture. They had been seeing each other for the past few months and it sounded serious. He gave me the ultimate compliment when he said, "She reminds me a lot of you, Maddie." The three of us parted with promises to keep in touch.

Sylvia telephoned me that week bubbling over with news. At almost three months old, Marlene was now giggling out loud and appeared to be cutting an early first tooth. Sylvia had been accepted to begin college in January. She had decided to obtain her degree as a social worker. I had no doubt she felt compelled to give back what she had been given. Ben was her constant companion, becoming more attached to Marlene each time he saw her. I laughed at Sylvia's concern that we were moving to Georgetown. She kidded me, saying, "Don't you dare think just because you're moving up in the world with a posh address that you'll forget about us little people." I assured her there was no chance of that. Sylvia and Marlene were family to Mark and me.

All the recent events in my life made me feel loved and secure.

But one nagging anxiety still remained. We were waiting on word about the surgical removal of Mark's implanted device. Once his immoral symphony ceased to exist, my mind would be at ease.

CHAPTER 42

The air was crisp and the sun bright. Frost edged around the perimeter of the thick windows of the old Stockholm building. The offices were the finest in the city and nestled among the most trusted corporations in Europe. International Holding Company continued its operations with barely a step missed. Owens, Witton and Lester had simply changed their operating location and joined other associates in Europe.

Although Owens had signed a treaty with the United States, which represented the world, or at least those who knew about such treaties, he had no intention of living up to it. The European Union offered opportunities until the situation cooled in America. Owens also had some old scores to settle.

Witton was directed to launch a robust program to condition and train young operatives. The presence of more orphanages in Europe than America allowed easy pickings. The technology of direct control improved significantly in the past five years, and devices implanted in young heads were virtually undetectable and very versatile.

President Webb became a villain to the cause when he ordered the removal of leading Visitors from the United States. He would have to pay the price, but later when it made political sense. Secretary Close seemed like the best candidate to follow Webb into the White House, but Owens was becoming wary of too many assassinations in America, more than any other country. The rest of the world simply considered America to be a violent place, but there was a point where too much focus on Visitor activities would be harmful and risked exposure.

On a more personal note, Witton harbored a painful revenge toward one man. He needed approval to proceed with his plan and arranged a meeting with Owens, who had taken another U.N. job in charge of disaster relief.

"Of all the disciples we have recruited, trained and controlled, only one has failed us—Mark Puccini," Witton said. "He also played a role in Mozart's downfall. Puccini cannot be permitted to escape punishment."

"Is it personal? Why should it be? He's under the watchful eye of some of our best men. In his new job, we'll know everything. How can he be a threat?" Owens asked.

"It's for what he's done, not what he will do."

"Puccini's work isn't a reflection on you, Richard. Why can't you leave this alone?"

"He represents my only failure, sir."

"This is very personal, I can see that. You've been faithful. I owe you some flexibility. Do what you feel you must, but don't interfere with the second controlling device. No one would suspect a second implanted device and we must not lose our advantage. It must be saved for a critical situation, not for personal revenge. However you decide to hurt him, remember he must be available for future work when he's trusted and beyond reproach. Close's success placing him in the administration must not be wasted."

"His life will be spared until then, but it may be a life with much less joy," Witton said, smiling.

* * *

The rooms of the Old Executive Office Building were expansive and distinguished, with the best offices reserved for key positions held by the Senior Executive Service–6 elite. I was incredulous when Secretary Close announced my SES-6 rank and presented me with the documentation that made my pay legal. My office was large enough to hold three sofas and numerous occasional chairs, all which fit the stately décor of the building. The desk was solid mahogany and almost larger than the first room Maddie and I had occupied behind the clinic. The balcony overlooked much of historic Washington including the White House and glorious monuments.

The best news for me was Maddie's acceptance of the position as my assistant. Working together, I was sure we could make a difference protecting innocent people from the ravages of uncontrolled power. High-minded, yes, but I believed it. After all, everything had gone so well, especially since the operation to remove the devil's device from my head. The freedom made me feel like a new man.

The day that we were briefed into the compartmented special clearance opened a new world for us. Studying past successes and failures of the Visitors and various administrations was thrilling. News items read in my youth fell into place in a pattern that would never have crossed my mind. The world of impossible coincidences became a regulated pattern of control. People who interrupted the flow of events dictated by the unseen enemy were eliminated with abandon. Not position, money, nor status deterred the crushing impact of the movement. Everything seemed so clear to me now.

President Webb gave us confidence when he said that the treaty would last a generation, but my new knowledge allowed me to see the true situation. Nothing had changed due to that treaty or any past treaties. The entire negotiation rationalized the position we found ourselves in. Negotiating was better than accepting defeat. Treaties provided time to better cope with the Visitors. Could we make the correct decisions and gain back our independence?

That was part of the task that we took on in the stately and historic style of the famous old building. Our lives had taken a turn that I hoped we'd never regret.

CHAPTER 43

Tons of reports I was privy to opened my mental horizon beyond the artificial limits of my education and customs, but medical experience allowed me to do my work with a thoroughness laymen lacked. A tragedy that turned out to be a bit of luck also took me down a path of investigation previously unavailable.

Maddie and I remained close friends with Glen and he often came to dinner alone or with a current girlfriend. The closeness we shared allowed us to see that he had certain habits registering as strange in our minds. One evening after he and Gloria shared dinner, drinks, and a lot of laughs with us, Maddie and I compared notes. Glen had dropped two tiny tablets into his cognac when he thought Maddie wasn't looking. Explaining to her that Secretary Close did the same thing, she asked what it was that he was using. I had to find out, because Glen had a connection with Close that had no obvious explanation.

The plan was to watch Glen every time we were with him to observe any other similarities to Close or co-workers. Our vigil was short lived, because Glen was killed in a gruesome automobile accident a block away from the Old Executive Office Building. His body was taken to a funeral home, but I was able to order an autopsy based on his security clearance, in addition to lack of a family to object to the procedure. I wanted a chart of his DNA, among other data, remembering a study I had read about the similarities found in genetic signatures of severe alcoholics.

Dr. Cleaving, the author of the study, was short on firm evidence. His report was branded as inconclusive at best and contrived in the worst case. He was left with a ruined medical reputation with his tenured position being the sole reason he remained at the university.

Dr. Cleaving told me he had re-evaluated his findings, believing there was a segment of the population with remarkably different DNA patterns on the one percent of the helix which wasn't shared with our ape precursors. Glen had that set of peculiarities; I was certain Close had them as well.

Since the accident had done terrible damage to Glen's body, the casket had to be closed, so the autopsy evidence seemed a minimal risk to my position. However, I failed to consider that my telephone conversations might be monitored. A few days after the funeral, Secretary Close entered my office with a stranger. He introduced him as Dr. Logican, explaining that a terrorist threat required NSC staff members to be immunized against a range of biological and viral agents. The doctor was there to administer the injections.

My trouble antenna went up as I backed away from my desk into the maze of chairs in the office. I asked Close if he knew about the Pageant autopsy. He did, questioning why I'd taken matters into my inexperienced hands, then ordered me to submit to the shots. I refused. Dr. Logican took a needle from his black bag and pushed a few drops of liquid into the air. He walked toward me as Close issued dire warnings about gross misconduct and failure to follow orders. The secretary intended to stay removed from what seemed to be developing as a circus act with me as the pursued animal and Logican as the animal trainer. He watched as I slowly walked around the chairs.

At that instant, my secretary opened the door. I stood leaning on a chair as if I might be talking to Logican, waiting for her to speak. She was sorry to interrupt, but Dr. Logican had an emergency call at her desk. He ought to take it, there had been an accident. Logican turned and I rushed to his side pulling the needle from his grasp. He looked from the secretary to Close and hurried from the room. I thanked her as she closed the door.

I walked toward my boss asking if he had taken his shots yet.

As a doctor, I was qualified to administer them. What was in that needle? Close's eyes flashed recognition of my intentions. He was a big man, but perhaps one who had never had to defend himself from physical harm, except perhaps hazing at Yale. He stepped backward and my confidence rose. Whatever was in the needle represented what Close intended to do to me. Turnabout was fair play.

I held the delicate, but fairly large tube containing the needle in my hand close to my side. Close backed away more. I blocked the exit to the doorway, moving closer.

"Don't do this," he said in less than authoritative words.

When I was three feet from him, I swung my right hand toward his face; he blocked my blow, but my left hand drove the needle into his heavy arm and rammed the plunger home. I backed away, watching him for a few seconds. He sat down and his face became tense, like pain was invading him. He grasped his chest with both hands, leaning forward and driving himself backward. I took the needle, dropping it into the medical bag that I kept behind my desk. Running to the door, I shouted to my secretary to call 911. By the time I returned to Secretary Close, he was dead of massive cardiac arrest.

Logican was gone, but couldn't accuse me of what he intended to do. Both of us would keep silent.

★ ★ ★

The afternoon drive home was worse than usual. While I sat in the noisy, sooty traffic, I relived the scene following the removal of Close's body. On the radio, the administration and country mourned the death of a great man, destined to lead the nation via honorable means to a just world. Making pronouncements of grief and friendship for the man were Washington's top actors and arbiters. No one can ever say he deserved to die, even if he did. The media blitz continued as I shut my engine off, longing to see Maddie, who had taken the day off for a routine doctor's appointment.

After a few steps into the house, it hit me. Pain surged through my body, up my torso and down my legs. From a spot near my groin, what seemed like an electrical charge drove me to the floor. Unable to stand or right myself, I collapsed. Then my head felt like it would burst. I cried out for Maddie, moaning with intense distress, calling her again. Raising my head, I saw Dr. Logican standing over me with a long needle in his hand. His smile told me it was over. Pain surged again and my body stiffened. Logican bent over, intending to stick me with the syringe. My hands were paralyzed as another surge of internal electricity slammed through my system. I closed my eyes, not wanting to witness my murder.

A great weight landed on top of me. His body held me down, but there was no sharp prick from a needle. I opened my eyes. Logican was spread out over my body, the needle full of fluid still in his hand. Realizing that my pain had ceased, I pushed him over to my left side and saw Maddie standing over us with an iron skillet in her hand. She was sobbing.

His head was bleeding profusely, but he was alive. I could see the pulse in his neck throbbing. Getting up slowly, I took the pan from her, dropped it on the floor, and held her in my arms.

There was a noise at our door. John Jones pushed his way into the house, directing another man to examine Logican. They picked him up without a word and started to leave. I shouted at him as Jones turned toward me. He said that Maddie and I were with the good guys now, don't worry about Logican, he'll disappear.

We never heard from the doctor again. His disappearance captured headlines until an announcement by a federal prosecutor stated that Logican was suffering from an overwhelming drug habit and was believed to have fled to Mexico to avoid being exposed.

* * *

A month later, Richard Witton sat in his office grinning like a child at play. An electrical device in his hand flashed red and he called for Lester.

"This damned thing keeps flashing. What the hell's wrong with it?"

"Sir, it's working. If you continue to exercise him, his heart will give out. Mr. Owens said . . ."

"I know what Owens said, Charles. Do you think Puccini's life is worth living?" Witton's laughter echoed through the cold, shiny chrome Swedish office.

"You're enjoying the process, aren't you, sir," Lester said, "thanks to your father."

Witton leaned back in the judge's chair reflecting on his father. "He was a genius of control. Frankly, his success allowed my assignment to operations. It was his idea to implant a second device in the boys. He used to tell me about control of these people when I was just a lad. My father never fully trusted devices implanted in the skull because of the dependence on hypnosis. He distrusted the whole process because control couldn't be absolutely guaranteed. But his device, LCM, was a masterstroke. Remember what it stands for—LCM?"

Lester nodded, but didn't interrupt his boss.

"It's life control module. He determined where it should be implanted. Pure genius. Hard to realize that Beethoven and Mozart were guinea pigs. Did you know they were the first boys to have the LCM implanted in their groin?"

Lester knew, but he tried to look surprised, letting his mouth open slightly.

"The vasectomies simply covered the scar for the implantation. Entering the scrotum ensured secrecy. Because the LCM contained no metal, it was undetectable. It's a good thing the device wasn't left in the scrotum, these human females would find it in their man. Such uncontrolled creatures. But the application of pain topped every idea my father had. He designed a battery powered by heat generated in the body. Ingenious, isn't it?" Witton paused to hear a *yes sir* from Lester before continuing. "I can drive Beethoven mad with pain or simply play with his nerves. That is control and punishment for lack of discipline."

"With your permission, sir."

Witton nodded. "Speak your mind."

"Mr. Owens warned you that Beethoven was too important to lose as we lost Mozart."

"There was something wrong with the switch that time. I intended to turn it off sooner, but Mozart, the undisciplined wretch, couldn't bear the pain. But to shoot oneself in the face. No discipline at all."

"Take care, sir," Lester said looking at the electronic device still in Witton's hand.

"I've shut it off. Enough pain for today." Witton's laughter echoed in the large office. "If it wasn't for Owens, I'd fry Dr. Puccini."

* * *

After the horror of Close and Logican's deaths, Maddie and I seemed to be on our way to a normal life. As near normal as one can be living and working in Washington. Filled with hope for our future, first on my agenda would be a doctor's appointment to assess the cause of those pains.

About the Authors

Bill Bonner

Bill Bonner is a full time writer, after serving over twenty-nine years in the Air Force and CIA, and twelve years in the Systems Integration industry. He earned a B.S. in History and Political Science from Troy State University and an M.P.A. from Auburn University. He was awarded Second Place for the Most Publishable Novel at the University of North Texas in 2000 for his novel *Impure Fire* and Second Place in Gardenia's Press's National Writer's Competition in 2002 for his novel *Goodbye Maple Street*. Bill wrote three technical articles that were published in Marine Corps Magazine and Defense Intelligence Digest. In addition, he wrote hundreds of articles that were disseminated to the U.S. Intelligence Community.

Bill was born in Paterson, New Jersey and spent much time

recreating in New York City during the golden age of New York jazz. In the Air Force, he flew as a navigator in B-52 bombers, RF-4C reconnaissance fighters, as well as cargo type aircraft. The latter part of his career was spent in the Intelligence field, ending in a position on the National Intelligence Council in the CIA, where he was responsible to the Director, CIA and the President of the United States on matters of national warning.

Working in industry, Bill Bonner was an Engineering Manager and then a Program Director, managing multi-million dollar systems integration projects for the Internal Revenue Service, Army, Navy, Air Force and Marine Corps.

His goal is to contribute to the awareness of social conditions and issues by writing mainstream commercial novels illuminating the circumstances of ordinary people.

Terri DuLong

Terri DuLong is a native of the Boston area and now resides on the west coast of Florida where she is a practicing Registered Nurse.

Terri spent her elementary school years outside of Cincinnati. Her family returned to the Boston area in 1960 and she is a graduate of Salem High School and North Shore Community College.

Ms. DuLong has been a contributing writer for the Internet publication, Bonjour Paris, for the past three years. Two fiction short stories have been published in anthologies and her first novel, Lost Souls of the Witches' Castle, was published by Gardenia Press in July 2002.

Terri writes mainstream fiction with an emphasis on human values and emotions, and draws much of her inspiration from the people she encounters in her nursing career.

JUN 0 7 2011

DISCARD